STAKE SAUCE

STAKE SAUCE, ARC 2: Everybody's Missing (Somebody)
Copyright © 2020 by RoAnna Sylver.

Published by The Kraken Collective.
www.krakencollectivebooks.com

Cover art by RoAnna Sylver.
Interior design by Key of Heart Designs.
Typefaces by Misprinted Type.

This is a work of fiction. Names, characters, places, and incidents either are the product of the author's imagination or are used fictitiously. Any resemblance to actual events, locales, organizations, or persons, living or dead, is entirely coincidental and beyond the intent of the author.

All rights reserved, which includes the right to reproduce this book or portions thereof in any form whatsoever except as provided by the U.S. Copyright Law.

for Corey

who gave me armor, and showed me how to write my deepest truths with honesty, bravery, and joy. My gifts are my words, and I don't always have them, but these are for you.

STAKE SAUCE

A MODULATING FREQUENCIES SERIES

Arc 2: Everybody's misSing (somebodY)

ROANNA SYLVER

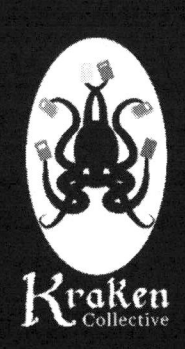

Kraken Collective

Content Notes

- Vampire violence/blood-drinking.
- Missing persons.
- Memory loss
- Stress-related (unintentional and non-romanticized) weight loss.
- On-page murder; light on gore, big on dramatic horror imagery.
- Textbook, recognized deliberate abuser behavior from the villain on-page, both physical and emotional/mental.
- Unhealthy (non-romanticized) vampire/human familiar dynamics.
- References to past and current/ongoing abuse, including sexual.
- Assault, kidnapping, attempted human sacrifice.
- Reference to a near-death experience.
- Family dysfunction.
- PTSD, grief and abuse processing, neurodivergent brains dealing with trauma.
- Depression, brief suicidal ideation. Sustained injury (concussion).
- One sexually charged scene—not non-con or threatening, but does have (addressed) boundary/mental health problems.

Dramatis Personae

JUDE, who is doing his best to figure his life, brain, and self out, and could use a nap.

PIXIE, who was lost, then found, and now belongs. Could also use a nap in Jude's pocket.

EVA, who is done playing games, and strongly feels that communication is the foundation of any relationship.

LETIZIA, doing her best to do right by her friends. All of them. Even when her best isn't the best.

JASPER, whose presence is a gift even if he doesn't do anything.

FELIX, who hasn't given up yet. So don't give up on him.

NAILS and **MAESTRA**, forever a pair, and finally free.

MILO, whose reflection is theirs alone.

OWEN, the picture of devotion, but seen through a mirror darkly.

SANGUINE, who wasn't always like this.

And the incomparable, inimitable, despicable **WICKED GOLD**.

STAKE SAUCE

EVERYBODY'S MISSING

(SOMEBODY)

ACT ONE: But if You Try, Sometimes...

"KNEEL."

The large man dropped to his knees without question, but not without protest.

"Wicked Gold," he said in a harsh, grating voice with an edge of panic. He'd always been imposing, tall and muscular and eager to bare his fangs, which he did now, but his mouth was twisted in despair instead of fury. His head hung down low, hiding his exhausted, defeated face with stringy gray hair, wrists tightly tied behind his back. "You don't want to do this."

"You're right, I really don't," said his captor, hands in the pockets of his expensive, muted violet suit, and far too relaxed.

The vampire, who'd been known by many names, but most recently Wicked Gold, was hundreds of years old and still kicking. Old enough to hide the most obvious signs of his nature, at least outwardly, behind the face of a middle-aged white man with an average build, average looks, and above-average tastes. He was many things—including discerning enough to know when someone had failed him, and more than ready to exact punishment for that failure.

"Unfortunately, in your case, the cost of your mistakes is much too high to justify keeping you around. Too rich, even for my blood."

Wicked Gold let out a short, wholesome-sounding chuckle, as if they were friends shooting the breeze over a beer. Then, without warning, he reached out and shoved at the larger man's back with much more strength than a human his size should reasonably have, sending him sprawling across the ground.

"Cruce, old friend, do you have the first idea why you deserve this?"

Tonight was a strange night, in a strange place. Nobody happened upon this stone circle unless they already knew it was there. The ring of black crystals, like irregular and jagged obelisks, remained unnaturally silent, off the beaten path literally and figuratively; no trails led to it, and no joggers or dog-walkers happened upon it. At all hours, the air seemed charged, stinging static making hair stand on end like every moment was the one just before a lightning strike.

But tonight went beyond otherworldly, into the flat-out sinister. In the center of the stones burned a fire, unwisely large for the flammable surroundings. Eerie orange light illuminated the otherwise pitch-black, overcast night, and cast strange, flickering shadows over the scene and all its players.

"I *don't* deserve this," the bound vampire—Cruce, named after a grisly method of execution and now facing his own—snarled, struggling up onto his knees again. "I did nothing wrong. I've been your faithful servant for a century and a half—your *servant*, when you promised we'd be equals!"

"I did, didn't I?" Wicked Gold raised one foot off the ground and placed it on Cruce's shoulder. Then he rested his elbow on his knee and leaned on his bound thrall like he was nothing more than a rock or piece of sturdy furniture. "But I seem to recall you promising that nothing like exactly this would ever happen on your watch. That I could leave you in charge of my other servants and my pets, focus on my responsibilities overseas and rest easy, no need to worry about anything back here. Seems like we've both broken promises, haven't we?"

He paused, waiting expectantly for the apology, and his eyes drifted to the edge of the circle. Wicked Gold's drama had an audience in the form of two young men watching from the edge of the light.

One, dressed in another suit much too expensive and shoes too shiny to be taken for a night hiker, leaned casually against one of the stones. The other, slight and painfully thin in a black hoodie that covered most of his face, stood with his hands jammed into his pockets, head hanging low and everything about his posture screaming deep unrest, as if it were him kneeling, impudently silent, at Wicked Gold's feet.

Wicked Gold gave Cruce a kick with one shining, gold-tinted shoe that sent him tipping over and sprawling again onto his side, rolling out a bit into the center of the stone circle.

"Fine, if you won't admit when you're wrong, I'll do it for you," he said, stepping forward and turning to circle Cruce again as he struggled on the ground. "I come home after a hard week's work, and what do I find? You let not one, not two or even three, but *four* of my thralls escape—"

"The girls were mine!" Cruce yelled, struggling fruitlessly against his bonds and failing to rise to his knees again without the aid of his hands. There was a definite edge of desperation in his voice now, a panic unbecoming a predator. "And I lost just as much as—"

"You'll lose a lot more than that!" Wicked Gold's gleaming foot shot out and slammed into Cruce's broad chest. "They were yours, yes, and you were mine! And that meant they were mine too, and you lost them! But that's not all, you didn't just lose your own thralls, you lost both of the ones I hand-picked, I sniffed them out and hunted them down and made them mine, just like I did you, and then in a single night, you lost them both! And that's after you let my new favorite escape in the first place!"

"Your favorite," Cruce sneered, spitting out a gob of thick black blood. "After everything I've done—and helped you do? All the plans, all the sacrifices, all the unquestioning obedience—"

Wicked Gold let out a derisive snort, but Cruce kept going.

"All the talk of us being equals! All the promised rewards, all the assurances that *it'll just be a little longer,* and I'd be living like half the king you've called yourself—the centuries by your side! And what do you do? Forget all about that as soon as you lay eyes on a tasty little treat—"

Cruce wasn't even trying to stand up anymore, but Wicked Gold gave him another kick for good measure, closer to his head this time.

"You let my tasty, pretty, ripe-and-ready favorite escape," Wicked Gold continued as if Cruce hadn't spoken, pacing around him with more purpose now. "And you never got him back. Promised that too, didn't you? Broke it, didn't you? And then when Felix got it into his head to fight back when I wasn't looking, you let him go too! And end up running away while they chase you down, your own thralls! You ran, and from what? Some little girls, some soft, breakable humans, and that—that *woman!* That *witch!*"

Cruce wasn't struggling anymore at all. He wasn't protesting either. He just lay there, conscious and aware but silent, and very still, like an animal freezing to escape a predator's notice. It wasn't working.

"You were too busy having fun to use your head," Wicked Gold said with a scornful shake of his own. "Or at least the right one. And look where it got you. Not having much fun anymore, are you?"

"I made a mistake," Cruce said in a low voice, just above a whisper. He'd begun to curl in on himself, nearly into a fetal position, and didn't look up. "Just one. One, in all these years. I was so sure... that counted for something."

"Four," Wicked Gold corrected, crouching to clamp one hand around Cruce's throat.

Each finger was tipped with a long, viciously pointed silver claw, digging into Cruce's skin with the audible hiss and wisp of smoke that carried the smell of burned undead flesh. His hand didn't begin to make it around the larger vampire's thick neck, but Wicked Gold stood and raised him easily, until Cruce knelt before him once more. When he spoke again his voice wasn't furious, not sharp, instead something close to gentle, but even more menacing in its savage contrast.

"You lost me *four* prizes, which is four mistakes too many. I expected better from you. Much better. But I suppose that was *my* mistake. Now, anything to say? Besides 'goodbye?'"

Cruce stared back at him, face now free of panic or desperation. Instead his dark eyes were cold and resigned, and now, very tired. He let the silence stretch between them for a few long and tense seconds and stared back into his sire's eyes, finding no mercy there, no hope for a reprieve, and no question. "What else is left to say?"

Wicked Gold considered this, and him, for a moment, head tilted to one side and eyebrows raised. Then, instead of answering, he gave a one-shouldered shrug and raised his free hand, admiring his deadly silver claws that gleamed in the firelight as brightly as his gold-tipped shoes.

Without a word, he plunged his hand, fingers together, straight and flat like a blade, into Cruce's chest.

"This isn't what I wanted either," he said in a low tone, as thick, black liquid gushed from the gaping hole he'd ripped into Cruce's chest. It covered his hand as well, but he made no movement to pull it out or wipe it off, not yet. Wicked Gold watched the look of unadulterated agony replace the resignation on Cruce's face. His own expression until now had alternated between boredom and fury, but now his face twisted into real and pained disappointment.

"God damn you, Cruce," he said, almost fondly, almost smiling. "You're right about one thing. We really could have had it all."

With an ease that bordered on gentleness, Wicked Gold lowered Cruce down until his back hit the ground. The motion almost seemed intimate, like laying down a lover, but it would soon prove lethal. Wicked Gold's claws had pierced his heart dead-on, each small, pointed tip like a stake from the stories. And, just like in the stories, the silver did its burning work. But that wasn't the only thing searing Cruce's undead body from the inside out. Wicked Gold curled his hand into a fist around what remained of Cruce's heart—it had been said he didn't have one, but some stories really were just stories—and his hold became a crushing grip.

Then, at last, Cruce's heart ignited in his palm. Fire licked its way up Wicked Gold's thin fingers and wrist, forearm up to his elbow, but didn't seem to burn him in the slightest. The fire also radiated outwards, radiating from the hole in Cruce's chest like flames across an oil slick. Soon his entire torso was ablaze, and as his tortured eyes and mouth widened, light spilled from them as well.

Wicked Gold held Cruce down for a while longer, watching the flames overtake him and the second, undead life leave his eyes. Then, slowly, he withdrew his hand and stood as the larger vampire shook and spasmed on the ground, letting out helpless and incoherent gasps.

He waited patiently for the wreckage that had once been his thrall to stop its agonized squirms and soft, dying sounds. Even as Cruce burned, his black blood continued to run out onto the ground of the stone circle, which soaked it up unnaturally fast, as if it was dry from a year-long drought instead of regularly dampened by frequent Oregon rain.

Dirty deed done well but not cheaply, Wicked Gold leaned back on his heels, clean hand in his pocket, and waited. For almost a full minute, he stood there, looking expectant but increasingly confused, a thin line appearing between his eyebrows. At one point he checked his shining gold wristwatch—which remained clean. The other hand, the cause of Cruce's demise, was still covered in the bloody evidence.

"Hm!" the last vampire standing said in an interested but disappointed tone. Heedless of the flames, he leaned forward and gingerly nudged his thrall's unmoving body with one gold toe. Then, finally, he wiped his dripping hand on one of the last remaining clean sections of Cruce's jacket. "Well, that didn't work. I was hoping for some fireworks. Ah well. Still can't always get what we want. But then, sometimes…"

He straightened up and turned his attention to the pair of figures still standing on the edge of the firelight. The thin young man in the hoodie visibly tensed as Wicked Gold raised one manicured hand to point at him, then beckon him closer with a deliberately curled finger. Black blood didn't quite drip from it anymore, but it clung beneath his silver nails. It would take quite a while to get it out entirely.

"Sanguine!" Wicked Gold called, sounding much more upbeat than he had a moment ago, as if he hadn't just killed his longtime partner in vampiric crime and left his remains on the ground. "Come over here."

At the Latin word and the beckoning hand, the uncomfortable-looking young man stepped forward. He moved slowly and reluctantly, taking his bony hands out of his pockets and quickening his step when Wicked Gold's summoning gesture became an impatient wave.

"Yes?" His voice was a faint rasp, like he had a bad cold and sorely needed to clear his throat and have a warm drink, or at least get out of the wet Portland-in-winter night that chilled anyone with a pulse to the bone.

"Yes what?" Wicked Gold asked immediately, like an automatic reflex. His cold eyes fell on a long scar stretching from forehead to jaw on the left side of his servant's face, and he frowned.

"Yes, Lord," Sanguine said just as quickly, but with an edge of anxiety instead of boredom. Now he dropped to his knees before the vampire, who stood casually over him. He brushed stray bits of matted, ginger red hair over his face, hiding the scar and earning himself a very slight nod. "What can I do for you?"

Wicked Gold didn't answer, instead just waited for him to figure it out on his own. Sanguine's eyes, blue and feverishly bright, underlined with dark circles, flicked over to Cruce's remains, and just for a moment, the wary tension in his face was replaced by grim satisfaction. His chapped lips didn't quite turn up into a smile, instead set in a hard line as he gave an almost imperceptible nod. A small, quiet victory.

Then his anxious gaze followed Wicked Gold's hand as it reached down toward him, its long fingers and claw-like silver nails. The vampire made as if to stroke his face or play with his untended hair—but at the last second his hand darted forward unnaturally fast to clamp around the young man's throat and drag him to his feet.

"I know what I did wrong," Wicked Gold said, conversationally, like they were discussing a business strategy over coffee instead of rainy midnight in the middle of an ominous stone circle with a dead vampire in the center.

Sanguine hadn't made a sound as the vampire's hand seized his neck, and he didn't protest or struggle as the grip tightened now. His only visible reaction was to close his eyes, looking tired and long resigned.

"The spell asked for blood, and shame on me, I thought *dead* blood might suffice—two birds, one stone, wouldn't that be nice for once?"

Wicked Gold turned, steering Sanguine at arm's length by the neck until he stood beside Cruce's remains, worn and dirty shoes almost stepping in the growing puddle of black, sludgy fluid. He was squeezing too hard for the young man to speak, even if he'd tried to reply. But he didn't. His knees wobbled, and he surely would have fallen if the vampire hadn't been holding him up by the throat. Wicked Gold continued his one-sided conversation in the same disarmingly casual tone.

"But no, nothing can ever be that easy, not even for me. Fortunately, I've got some of the best blood in town right here. Which means it's really a shame to waste it—yours is just so sweet, so deliciously addictive, you know how I feel about you by now, Sanguine. Taking of your blood and body..." He put the gathered fingers of his free hand to his lips and kissed them. "Ah, closest thing to heaven my sinner's soul will ever see. But if I'm right about this circle and its secrets, it'll be more than worth the loss."

He raised one claw, caught it in Sanguine's hoodie collar, and pulled down as if unzipping the thin, worn fabric. It tore easily, exposing his almost translucently pale, freckled skin and jutting collarbone, then sternum, then sunken stomach. All the way down to the sharp angle of his hip and waistband of his torn and filthy jeans that might have at some point been blue. Sanguine let out a long shudder as the claw descended, scraping over his bruised skin but not quite breaking it.

The unfortunate young man still said nothing, and didn't even attempt to break away, but squeezed his eyes more tightly shut and began to shake.

Finished slicing open the rest of the sweatshirt, the vampire lifted his arm until Sanguine's feet dangled a terrifying few inches off the ground. Wicked Gold raised his other hand, fingers together and outstretched into the shape of a knife, and silver claw-tips shining sharp and deadly.

"This isn't how I expected it to end, or even wanted it," he mused, seeming almost regretful, but not enough to release his hold. "But I do always get what I need. Goodbye, Sanguine. It's been—"

"Wait," someone said, and it wasn't the ragged young man in Wicked Gold's grip, who seemed barely present by this point, limp and paralyzed with terror. The other man stepped forward, the one who'd been leaning against the stones and watching the proceedings without comment until now. He was younger than the vampire by centuries and only slightly older than Sanguine's early twenties, but much healthier and cleaner. He almost matched the vampire's lavish ensemble with pale skin, slicked dark hair, immaculate gray suit, and well-shined shoes—just with much less gold.

"What?" Wicked Gold snapped, plainly annoyed at the interruption, but didn't so much as glance over. His eyes stayed on Sanguine, who trembled violently in his grasp, feet still not touching the ground. His face was starting to regain a bit of color under the dirt, but the redness wasn't a healthy change; he obviously couldn't breathe, and tears spilled from his tightly closed eyes.

"That won't work," said the observer, striding toward the vampire and his terrified hostage in the middle of the circle.

"What, does it need to be a virgin sacrifice?" Wicked Gold grinned at Sanguine's flushed and sweating face, and did not loosen his grip in the slightest. "Not much luck there."

"No virginity necessary," said the other young man smoothly. "But the sacrifice does need to be willing."

"A willing sacrifice, for this kind of ritual?" Wicked Gold snorted and tossed his head, rolling his eyes as if the very concept was ridiculous. "You're pulling my leg, aren't you... aren't you...?" He trailed off, snapping his fingers demandingly.

"Owen."

"Yes, of course, tip of my tongue," the vampire said with a vague wave that suggested he'd forgotten the name as soon as he'd heard it. "So we're looking for some sad soul with nothing left to live for, is that it?"

"There are many reasons to volunteer for a sacrifice," Owen said, keeping his voice and face an impressive neutral. "Despair is only one of them."

"Mm," Wicked Gold said, eyes on Sanguine, who still clung stubbornly to consciousness, and now his wrist. "And I suppose you wouldn't have any of them?"

Instead of waiting for an answer, Wicked Gold opened his hand and let Sanguine fall, legs giving out under him immediately as he crumpled to the ground. The filthy and emaciated young man gasped in desperate lungfuls of air and coughed, lying half-curled into a fetal position.

"I asked you a question," Wicked Gold said after a few seconds went by, while Sanguine wheezed and sobbed for breath. Aside from his moments of singular and terrifying focus, he'd never had much patience or a very long attention span. "You wouldn't give up your life willingly, would you, even now? You honestly wouldn't prefer sweet oblivion?"

He still couldn't speak, but as violent coughs continued to wrack his frail body, Sanguine gave his head a clear, jerking shake. *No.*

Wicked Gold scoffed, then reached out with one foot and gave Sanguine a lazy but not overly gentle poke in his sharp-angled ribs. "Amazing. Truly incredible. And what do you have to live for?"

Sanguine tried to form words several times and failed, then finally got one out in a faint, pained whisper. *"Summer."*

Wicked Gold gazed down at him for another moment as he shivered in the cold night air, then slowly crouched down. As if sensing his proximity, his captive's eyes—now red and watery—opened and fixed on his face. As the vampire reached out to cup his chin, Sanguine immediately stopped his gasping and coughing, holding his breath and going perfectly still, like a rabbit freezing inches away from a fox. Wicked Gold looked smug at the obvious terror his presence instilled, but there was a cold fury beneath his relaxed and affable exterior, and his lowered voice held a deadly promise. "I'm afraid you have the wrong priorities."

"If we're done here," Owen interjected from behind him with a slight sigh, the only indication of any frustration or weariness in his placid facade so far. "I do have other things to attend to this evening."

Wicked Gold stood up straight again and ignored Sanguine, who still lay on his side on the ground, curling around himself. He was now trying to pull the torn shreds of his hoodie closed against the bone-soaking cold, sobbing again, but this time not to catch his breath.

"I suppose sacrificing *you* is out of the question," he said to Owen with an appropriately wicked grin.

If the vampire expected the human to react with fear, he was surely disappointed. Owen simply removed his rectangular, silver-rimmed glasses and pulled a spotless cloth from his pocket, cleaning them of some microscopic or nonexistent speck of dust. "Entirely. By the way, it's the wrong night for such a ritual. The most auspicious one would be in two days."

Wicked Gold fixed him with a dangerously shrewd gaze, evaluating for any weakness as well as strength. "You're more daring than the average human, that's for sure. If not as clever."

"I work for the Lady," Owen said simply, like that explained and justified everything. Then he finished cleaning his glasses and replaced them on his face, never breaking his steady stare. "I make it my business to know what's in her best interests."

"Both of our interests," Wicked Gold corrected with a congenial smile. "Since we're such great friends. Surely what benefits one of us benefits both."

Owen didn't reply, or so much as blink. When it was clear he wouldn't get any kind of response, Wicked Gold shrugged and turned his attention back to the twice-deceased Cruce.

"So, wrong sacrifice, wrong date, that was a waste of a perfectly good evening," he said, sounding regretful of the time lost at least, if not the deed itself. "You couldn't have told me it wouldn't work a minute earlier?"

"He needed to die. I saw no reason to stand in the way," Owen deadpanned, only giving Cruce's body the briefest of glances. "So you were right about one thing after all."

"Oh," Wicked Gold chuckled, sounding surprised and tickled by the novelty. Still lying on the ground, Sanguine let out a harsh noise that might have been a laugh as well. "How delightfully pragmatic. I may like you after all."

Owen simply stared at him with a perfectly blank expression, clearly not deigning to dignify that with a response either. "Now, if you'll excuse me. I've wasted too much time here as it is."

With that, he turned and walked away, neatly stepping over Cruce's remains and keeping his still-gleaming shoes clean.

Wicked Gold watched Owen disappear outside the fire's light, benign smile quickly turning into a calculating stare sharp enough to bore holes in his retreating back.

"There's something he's not saying," he muttered. "Don't you think?"

"I... don't know," said Sanguine, finally finding his weak and rasping voice. He shakily climbed to his feet, every movement pained and hesitant. His hoodie was little more than rags, and tear tracks left clean streaks down his filthy face. He didn't move away, but he kept his wary eyes on the vampire, clearly scared of being choked again, or sacrificed after all.

"There is," Wicked Gold concluded, and if he'd expressed any fondness for Owen earlier, any hint of that appreciation was gone now. "He's holding out on us. Probably has to do with Our Lady, still walking around thinking she's the queen. If I was really lucky, the conniving little bore would get struck by lightning in a minute."

Sanguine did not answer or look up, as if unable to move until his next instruction. But he'd definitely heard the dark intent under the flippant words; his shiver might have been blamed on his lack of defense against the cold night, but the way he shied away just a bit could not.

"Oh, don't worry," Wicked Gold said with a good-natured-sounding chuckle. "I've never gained anything by being hasty. Besides, you remember what happened the last time I asked you to clean up a mess. Disaster. No, I want your focus on the *other* fly in my soup: the Witch. She's up to something, and I want to know what. I'm sure she feels the same about me. Always nice to be thought of. If all else fails, just ask her, and she might actually tell you. She always did love to hear herself talk." He gave Sanguine the same deceptively wholesome and self-deprecating smile he'd given Cruce. "Can't possibly relate."

"Yes, Lord," Sanguine said, but he looked sick at the thought. He hesitated again, then spoke in a rush, getting it over with before he lost his nerve. "But are you sure that's necessary? She could just be—oh."

By the time he looked back over, Wicked Gold was gone, disappeared without sound or ceremony as he was prone to doing, particularly when he considered a matter closed.

Then the light was gone too. The bonfire hissed completely out once the vampire was gone, like it had been doused with bucketfuls of water. The circle plunged into darkness, leaving Sanguine alone with Cruce's body, which still hemorrhaged black fluid. Aside from a startled jump he didn't move, instead just standing there shivering, as if frozen with indecision as well as freezing cold.

When he finally moved, it was to give Cruce's body one last, swift kick, then another, and another, until his strength gave out and he panted with exertion. Unlike Wicked Gold's blows, it didn't shift the huge man's remains at all, but a grim, satisfied smile still spread across Sanguine's thin face.

"Outlived you after all, fucker," he whispered to the body. "I'm still here."

Then the first raindrop smacked squarely on his forehead, making him jump again, and seem to remember where he was. As he scrambled to leave the macabre scene, he flipped up his hood, taking refuge beneath the single undamaged piece of his sweatshirt. A misty and slow-soaking Oregon rain began to fall, white noise filling the unnatural silence. Vampire corpses tended to be quick to decay, and if the rain held, the murder site would be washed clean of most evidence.

The stone circle, however, would still be here, filled with strange and ominous power, and waiting for its requirement to be fulfilled.

Far away, at the moment Cruce expired, two befanged girls woke up with simultaneous starts and yelps. With the night almost over and the sun close to rising, they'd just barely settled down into a peaceful daytime sleep, physically-teenage human forms curled up around each other.

But now they both sat bolt upright and clutched at one another, wide-eyed and startled thoroughly awake. As they exchanged a frantic stare, words began spilling out of both their mouths, all jumbled together. Still, they understood each other perfectly, in fact better than ever in the past century and a half.

"Did you—"

"Yeah, what was—"

"It felt like—"

"*Him!*"

They both went silent and still for a couple stunned seconds. Then Nails, spiked blonde hair even spikier from sleep, started to laugh. More like giggle, the kind of sound that was perfectly natural coming from a teenage girl, but not this one in particular. Her shoulders shook as she tried to keep quiet, raising a hand to her mouth, fingers tipped with appropriately pointed fingernails, but she couldn't, laughter overwhelming her. As Maestra pulled Nails closer and buried her face in her neck, she was laughing too, eyes squeezed shut and tearing. They held each other and shook, until neither of them could tell if they were laughing or crying anymore.

Finally, they fell silent, still clinging together and holding perfectly still, as if trying to elude detection by some stalking hunter. The quiet in the Sunset Towers apartment they shared with their friend and rescuer Letizia was near-complete. Only faint birdsong broke it, preceding a burning sunrise that wouldn't come close to reaching them in their dark, safe room with its blacked-out windows and nearby friends. Nothing bad or dangerous could. They were safe, a condition with which they were both sadly unfamiliar.

And now, perhaps, they were even safer.

"Raphael?" Nails asked after a while in a shaking voice, using the name nobody else used, that no one but the two of them had said in one hundred fifty years. Wicked Gold and Cruce didn't tend to look on their thralls as individuals with names, which was just as well. It meant Raphael had never heard her precious, second, self-chosen name in either of their foul voices, only the one she loved to hear most. It was clean and free, just like her. "Do you really think he's…?"

"I don't know," Maestra—this was her third name, the most casual, most everyday, still self-chosen but not as secret as '*Raphael*,' not as sacred—replied, fiddling nervously with the end of one of her many neat, dark braids.

"Me neither," Nails said—that wasn't her original name either, nor the deepest and most personal. She wiped off her wet face with one forearm. Vampires might not bleed like humans, but they still cried like them. "But I don't really remember what it's like to not have him… here. Do you?"

Raphael didn't answer. They stayed silent for almost another full minute, listening and reaching out with their minds into the dark, nearly unconscious mental realms where until now had lurked only monsters.

"Aletta," she said softly after a while of unbroken, unprecedented silence, both inside and out of their heads. Raphael said the name like a prayer, and Aletta answered it, eyes flicking immediately up to her face. Some people had public and private pronouns, some had names. Like 'Maestra,' she wore the name 'Nails' like a favorite jacket, familiar and comfortable and warm. Just one that she sometimes took off when they were alone. And now, for the first time in several lifetimes, they were finally, truly alone. *"I think he's gone."*

"Like *gone*-gone? Dead gone?"

"Dead gone," Raphael said in a marveling tone. "Dead for good this time. Let's be real, if he was alive at all, he'd still be haunting us, but it's so quiet. It's just... so *quiet*."

"Wow," Aletta said, more an awed sigh than a word. "We're really free."

They lapsed into silence once more, neither quite knowing what to do with this information. Soon they'd probably explode into joyous energy, yelling and dancing and somersaulting through the air the way only Olympic gymnasts and average vampires could do—but for now, just sitting with it felt like the right thing.

"My head feels weird," Raphael said eventually, hesitation creeping back into her voice. Always a little more reserved than her girlfriend and fang-sister, a little less impulsive, less outspoken, more pensive. "It's like, everything's louder and clearer, except when I try to remember things, does that make sense?"

She trailed off, but Aletta was already nodding, looking around at their safe, small room as if it were the first time she'd seen it. "Yeah. This"—she patted Raphael's leg—"is real. I can see and feel everything really clearly, like, better than before. But everything else, like literally everything before right now, it's like—"

"A dream," Raphael finished slowly. "We live here now, with... Letizia. That's our friend. She saved us. She's a witch, and we have other friends too. We were supposed to get up to work at the Pit tomorrow. But I don't..."

"Shit," Aletta whispered. "I can kind of see their faces, but it's like nothing's attached. Why did we forget? I know we forgot things, just not what!"

"I don't know. Maybe it's because he—what do you think killed him?" Raphael asked. "Do you think it was...?"

"I don't know," Aletta repeated, clearly not daring to voice the possibility or the name—even if the vampire in question had gone by many—on both their minds, but sounding apprehensive as well. Whatever had killed Cruce, their sire and a very powerful vampire in his own right, would surely mean nothing good for the two of them. "Can you go back to sleep?"

"No. You?"

"No," Aletta said, starting to wiggle out from under the covers. "Let's tell Letizia right now. Maybe she can help with whatever's going on in our heads too."

"Wait," Raphael stopped her, pulling Aletta back into their messy bed-nest. "Not yet."

"Why not? She'll believe us. She's always believed us."

"I know, just..." Raphael paused, looking down and clearly troubled. Aletta settled back in beside her, curling up like a cat against her side, content for once to lie still and wait until she found the words. "Once we tell her, she'll want to research it and check it all out, and tell everyone else, and it'll start a whole big thing. I just kind of want to enjoy it for a while. I want it to be just our thing for a little bit."

Aletta nodded so Raphael could feel it. "Yeah. That sounds good. Hey," she said, sitting half-upright and propping herself up on her elbow, looking down at the other newly freed vampire girl with a smile on her face that would have been sharp even without the fangs. "I think I know the first thing we should do."

Raphael was already rising to kiss her before she finished talking. They connected almost too fast, fangs clicking together, but quickly melted into something softer, slower, and utterly relaxed with the automatic knowledge that they fit together perfectly—the way they had longer than any human had been alive.

"You guessed right," Aletta sighed when they finally broke apart.

"This was the first one," Raphael murmured as their foreheads rested together. She'd had her eyes closed until now, but now she opened them like waking up to a new night. Aletta's bright grin was the first thing she saw, like it always should be. "First free kiss in forever. The first one that's just ours, just the two of us, he's not here in our heads. *He's not here, it's just us.*"

"Yeah it is." Aletta giggled again, and again the wave of joy and relief threatened to overflow, too big for a small vampire, so big she might burst. "I can't wait to tell everyone!"

"Me neither," Raphael replied, knowing that some things would remain secret, private, no matter what else they shared with others. Like their names. When they went out into the world again, they would be Nails and Maestra once more. Aletta and Raphael lived here, for the two of them alone—but in those hours, they lived lifetimes. "Wow, there's just so much we have to do—we've got so much time to make up for, I don't even know what to think about first!"

"I've got an idea." Aletta pulled her into another kiss, and a thousand bright futures melted away in favor of a sweet, perfect here and now.

It would take a long time to make up for one hundred fifty years, but by the time the sun came up in earnest—though hidden behind a merciful overcast sky—they were off to a good start.

A lot had changed in Jude's apartment, and his life, since *someone* had crashed through his window and into his orderly world a few months ago.

The window had long since been repaired, now covered with a black shade that managed to shut out today's early morning rays, bright and rare after a common, rainy night. Where the fridge had once been neglected and largely empty except for condiment afterthoughts, it now held not only actual food, but an abundance of red bottles of The Pit's local specialty sauce, and although there were just as many locks on the door, no stake or holy water waited in any drawer.

No loud music came from the apartment above, either. Jude no longer needed to bang on the ceiling to get *someone* to turn it down, though it had rarely worked anyway. It was quiet overhead—Pixie had been on the edge of eviction as it was, he'd learned. Now, the place had been taken back and given to quieter tenants, and almost all of Pixie's things were gone. Except for the treasured old guitar and small amp that leaned against the far wall.

Most nights and early mornings were quiet now—aside from lingering nightmares. The sound of ocean waves and memory of stones jutting toward the sky stayed in his head as he got out of bed, remaining a vaguely unsettling white-noise soundtrack to the rest of his life.

Jude secured his prosthetic leg with practiced ease and finished putting on his uniform for the last time. Today was a very special day for him as a mall security officer—his last day. The one he'd been looking forward to since his first day. He'd taken off more and more time to help Pixie adjust, and finally decided to just make it official, so he'd done it. He'd turned in his notice, and now he was free. Or would be, after just a few hours. And first he had to leave without disturbing his new roommate.

Jude stepped as quietly as possible to his bedroom door. Pixie hadn't had the easiest time sleeping lately, and Jude would have sooner crashed back out his own window than risk waking him up. With adorable, sensitive ears like Pixie's, even a small noise meant he wouldn't be asleep for long. He was almost always up before Jude, always said goodbye when he went to work, at least when Jude actually went to work.

There was something nice about telling someone he'd be home soon, and knowing they'd be there waiting for him. Home wasn't just his anymore; it was both of theirs. It felt right in a way little else did.

He didn't make it out the door before the screams started.

Jude almost jumped right into the air, only keeping still through the power of *freeze* over *fight or flight.* Yells—more like cries—rang through the small apartment, high-pitched and terrified. The noise was muffled, but definitely coming from inside this room, and the only possible place within it.

In searching online for suitably coffin-like containers that would make a vampire feel safe and protected from any rogue sunbeams, Jude had come across the idea of a captain's bed, with drawers for extra storage space underneath. Finding one big enough to fit a human could have been a major expense, but local message boards came to the rescue, as did Pixie's enhanced vampire strength when it came to getting the thing up to the third floor.

Now Jude rushed up to it, falling to his knees and knocking urgently on the oak-paneled drawer under his bed. "Pixie? Are you okay?"

No answer came from inside, except for more scuffling noises and soft, muffled cries.

Jude only hesitated for a heart-pounding second—he'd never invaded Pixie's sleep like this before, didn't like the idea at all—before pulling open the drawer, revealing one smallish, chubby, pink-haired vampire, thrashing like he'd been struggling to get out but had forgotten how, eyes squeezed shut and forearms raised to protect his head. It gave Jude an uncomfortably clear view of the vaguely star-shaped, silver-burn scars still visible on both the palms and backs of Pixie's hands.

"Pixie?" Jude slowly reached out to touch one of his hands, but it didn't seem to make a difference. Even more tentatively, he laid a hand on Pixie's chest, hoping the slight pressure would be enough.

"What? J—" Pixie gasped, then cut himself off. Even though vampires didn't need to breathe—and sometimes forgot to, which Jude would never get used to—his chest rose and fell sporadically as he sucked in automatic, near-panicked breaths. Slowly, he brought his arms down and lay still. "Jude. Hey. Hi. What's, uh. What's up?"

"You were having a nightmare," Jude said as gently as he could. He started to take his hand back from Pixie's chest, but Pixie reached out, caught it, and held on. Jude felt warm inside. "At least it sounded like one."

"Yeah. Yeah, it was. Thanks for waking me up. That was... not fun." Pixie's exhaustion and lingering adrenaline was as obvious as the understatement.

"Didn't sound like it," Jude said. Now he wanted nothing more than to spend the day right here, until Pixie stopped shaking and either slept peacefully again or smiled. There were too many things that could invade his dreams, and too many of them were real. Unfortunately, he didn't know the right way to ask Pixie about them, or if there even was a right way. Or a way for him to help. "Listen, I don't even really have to go in today…"

"What?" Pixie blinked up at him, looking confused—then embarrassed.

Letting out a mortified little whine, he covered his face with his hands, hiding in the bandana he always wore around his neck to cover the worst of his visible scars.

Jude had to smile a little; years ago, Jasper and Felix had once made the mistake of teaching him poker, and the ease with which he'd cleaned them out surprised all three. Jude had resting poker face, Felix had said, and he'd decided to take it as a compliment. Pixie would never have such a chance— Jude doubted he had ever been able to successfully hide an emotion. There were things Pixie kept to himself, Jude knew, but not the way he felt about them.

"Nooo, no!" Pixie said. "I don't want to get you in trouble!"

"What are they going to do, fire me?" Jude asked with a rare smirk. "I'm quitting, remember? And even if I weren't, it still wouldn't be a big deal. I have… quite a few paid vacation days piled up."

"A few? You've never taken a day off in your life, have you?" Pixie asked, smiling a little. "Until recently, I mean. And now you're quitting your job. You shouldn't have to do all this just to take care of me and all my crap."

"It's no trouble," Jude said, smirk turning into an actual smile. "If anything, you're giving me the excuse I needed to actually walk away for good. I never wanted to be a cop—"

"You never were a cop. You think I'd be into you if you were? You tried to keep kids from skateboarding inside. Badly."

"Or anything like one—"

"A-C-A-B," Pixie sang, giving him a finger-gun with every letter. "We'll make a punk out of you yet!"

"Don't push it. But seriously, I'm not broken up about quitting, it was just an easy paycheck while I tried to prove vampires were real."

"Well, I guess you've done that," Pixie said, picking at a spot on the back of one gray hand.

"Right. And now I can spend my time on the important things—like protecting this city from actual evil, whether that's vampires or witches or whatever else. You have no idea how glad I am to turn in this badge and start to do some good!"

Pixie tilted his head. "You don't have a badge."

"It's a figure of speech."

"Sure," Pixie said with a good-natured roll of his eyes. "But you really don't have to worry about me—I'm fine. Really."

"Okay," Jude said, reluctantly getting up. "If you're sure. Try to get some more sleep."

"Um, wait, actually—can I go with you instead?" Pixie asked, a little hesitantly, as if expecting Jude to say no, with a sharp bite of irritation for good measure. A few months ago, he might have. Now, he couldn't imagine rewarding such a shy request with anything but *yes*. "I just kind of... don't want to be alone right now."

Pixie did tend to spend most of his time in the apartment—Jude and his friends had saved him from one immediate threat, but that didn't mean there weren't others lying in wait, even if Pixie wasn't ready to talk about them. Or that the memories had yet faded. The scars on Pixie's hands hadn't yet either, even if they were mostly healed by now. Thanks to the silver damage, they might never.

"Sure, I don't think Eva would mind you tagging along while I make my final rounds," Jude said, simultaneously heart-warmed and worried. Jude had never gotten the sense that he was missed, or had anyone waiting for him to get home, until now. Pixie wanting to spend the day with him was... nice. Even if the reason for it wasn't. "Though you might want to put on some longer sleeves. Where's your going-out hat?"

"Not like that. Pocket?" Pixie asked hopefully, visibly brightening at the thought. Even his large, pointed ears seemed a little perkier. "Kinda feel like an all-day cuddle might make a nice nap."

"Sure." Jude didn't try to hide his Pixie-related smiles anymore. Even sleep-deprived and shaky, the uncommonly sweet and squishy vampire was ridiculously cute in a way Jude would probably always have trouble articulating, and once would have found embarrassing. Now he couldn't imagine living without it.

Now he held out his hand, which Pixie took—and Jude's eyes slipped again over to the clear white scar on the back of Pixie's gray hand. He felt a pang at the memory of the wound, and an urge to soothe it. He wanted to pull Pixie into his arms, hold him tight until he smiled again, but held back. He'd been doing that a lot lately.

They hadn't kissed, or even held each other that closely since their first adventure had ended and they'd decided Pixie would stay here. It had been wonderful, one of the best feelings Jude could remember, but there seemed to be no place for it now. Pixie was troubled and seemed to be waiting for him to make the first move. But something about initiating a touch like that—and being misunderstood, overstepping, scaring or hurting Pixie, after everything he'd been through—was unimaginable. So they stayed where they were, which right now seemed to be nowhere.

But before he could say or do anything, or the silence become awkward, Pixie disappeared. In an instant, there was a fuzzy bat with oversized ears nestled in the palm of Jude's hand. Still pink, still chubby, and still adorable. He gave the ridiculously-cute creature a gentle head rub with one finger, before carefully placing it in his jacket's inside pocket.

Hoping the day would bring Pixie a better rest than the night had, Jude headed out the door. He'd never imagined the small, warm weight in his pocket, slightly squirmy as the bat got comfortable, would be so reassuring. Or that he would feel so solid and confident in his own skin, despite his confusion about what exactly lay between the two of them.

When he'd told Pixie it was okay, he meant it, and believed it, something he hadn't been able to do for five years. Even if both of their dreams were still troubled, for the first time in those five years, he was tentatively, genuinely happy.

But he'd be even happier when his last shift was done.

Despite his apathy and general disdain for his job, Jude was enough of a perfectionist that he'd never actually been late for work before, but he probably would be now—and he didn't care. In fact, instead of heading right down the stairwell, he stopped a couple doors down from his apartment, knocking even though he knew it probably wasn't necessary. Not with heightened vampire senses. He also didn't really expect the door to actually open, but that wouldn't stop him from trying.

"Jasper?" he called tentatively, keenly aware of how loud his voice was in the quiet, early morning corridor.

He only called the one name, though Felix's sat just on the tip of his tongue too. Even if there was nobody else in the hall, he still didn't want to yell anything incriminating, or indicative that there might be not-quite-dead people sharing the space with their living counterparts.

"I'm on my way to work. Last day. So I just thought I'd say hello to... uh, you. See if you were okay, and... everything."

Jude slapped his forehead with his palm and dragged it down his face. Of course he wasn't okay. And now, for the first time since he could remember when talking to Jasper, Jude felt incredibly self-conscious, standing out here in an empty hall. Like he was imposing. Never something he wanted to do to his friends, especially after they'd gone through everything Jasper and Felix had.

"I'll see you later," he said with a chagrined shake of his head, and started to walk away when he heard the unexpected sound of locks clicking open from inside. Jude stopped mid-step and turned back around. Despite himself, he felt an excited flutter in his chest, a foolish but irresistible hope, as the door opened wide enough to show Jasper's face.

"Jude," Jasper said, a tired smile spreading across his face at the sight of him. "It's been too long."

"Hi," Jude said, keeping his voice down despite the empty hallway. Old paranoia died hard, and besides, it looked like Jasper could use as much quiet as he could get. "Just thought I'd drop by, check on… everything."

Like Pixie, his old friend looked drawn, as if he hadn't slept well. Jasper really hadn't slept well in years, Jude knew, but this seemed like a different, less-despairing kind of tired, a mild improvement over the bone-weary grief and exhaustion than had dogged his every step before their lives had been turned upside-down for the second time. They all kept different hours now, living with vampires. Jude often felt the same jetlag-like sleepiness, since the rest of the world didn't function according to their timetable anymore. But even if his monthly coffee expenses increased, it was a small price to pay.

"Is he, uh…?" Jude asked, raising his eyebrows in lieu of voicing any unwise specifics.

"He heard you," Jasper said, not altogether happily, sounding a bit disappointed but a lot more resigned.

"Good, that's good."

"He's just not…"

"No, no, I understand. No pressure. On him or you."

Jude fidgeted a little. He felt awkward in a way he wasn't used to, not around Jasper. And at one time, not around his fiancé—was 'fiancé' even the right word anymore? So many things had been put on hold or dropped entirely, and it was more than a little unsettling to realize that Jude didn't know if this was one of them. That was another change, the distance between the three of them, but at least it was far preferable to the pangs of grief and regret he'd felt whenever he thought of Felix until recently.

They'd almost been something, back then, the three of them. Just barely been on the cusp of defining what.

They'd kissed, once. Him, Jasper, and Felix. The night they'd asked him to be their best man. A sense memory of warmth and touch and taste he didn't let himself think about very often; it was painful and confusing as much as pleasant. He'd melted into both of them, felt overcome by belonging and rightness for one wild minute—and then overthought it. As he did everything.

Jude had made stammered excuses and run away, and they'd never had a chance to actually talk any of this through.

Because the very next night, it was a full moon and Felix was dead.

Now, what felt like a lifetime later, Jude felt like he'd been dropped right back into that "almost" state, questioning and between and uncertain.

He'd loved both of them. Still did. And they still loved him, in a way that made his head spin, impossible to make sense of.

And now here was Pixie, in his pocket and close to his heart, wonderful and good and making everything so, so much harder to figure out.

Figuring out attractions and connections between three people was hard enough even if you weren't an autistic, gray-ace-and-aro-spec—*demisexual, demiromantic,* he thought; sex and romance were non-considerations with everyone but three people in the world, but oh, he was starting to consider them now—trans guy who forgot how words worked and froze up when he got overwhelmed... which was unfortunately often.

"We always want you around, Jude, it's just..." Jasper trailed off again, as if he didn't have the energy for things like complete sentences.

"No, I get it, don't worry. I've got, uh, company too." Jude gently patted his pocket and felt an answering wiggle.

"Try again later," Jasper said, not unkindly, and he sounded optimistic at least. Still, Jude could practically feel the worry coming off him along with the fatigue. "He's sleeping right now—finally. He didn't get much yesterday."

"Seems like nobody's getting much sleep right now." Jude's brow furrowed a bit. He couldn't see the rest of Jasper, but he began to suspect it wasn't just fatigue making his old friend look especially drawn; he looked like he'd lost weight around his face and worry began to coil in the pit of Jude's stomach.

"Indeed." Jasper was deadpan—a good sign for him—but Jude could only imagine what Felix's sleepless days were like, for either of them. He didn't ask, and he had the feeling Jasper appreciated it. After all this time there just wasn't much they could hide from one another, but sometimes they still had to make an attempt.

"Nightmares?" Jude did have to ask that part, feeling his ever-present twinge of worry intensify a little. This wouldn't be out of the ordinary, even if everything else was, he told himself. Of course Felix and Pixie would both have nightmares; it would be more unusual if they didn't. Still, he was hard-wired to pay attention to coincidences, and not to trust them.

"Bad ones," Jasper said. "But I mean it, please do try again later. And try not to take it too personally. It isn't just you, Jude, Eva was by earlier and he wouldn't see her either. I know he misses you, and I think he's getting closer to surfacing again. He just needs..."

"Some time, yeah," Jude nodded and picked up where Jasper trailed regretfully off.

It was almost a script by now. They'd had that same interaction almost every day ever since they'd gotten Felix home, so this hardly came as a surprise by now. He also understood Felix's urge to withdraw, but he couldn't say it didn't hurt, knowing Felix was alive and right here, but still too far away to touch, still buried too deep for Jude to speak to him and start to make up for all their lost time. They'd all lost time, even if they hadn't lost each other in the end.

"I'll talk to you after work," Jude said, trying to inject some positivity into his tone. He never could tell if he really succeeded. "Tell him... I'm thinking about him."

"I definitely will." Jasper smiled gently, and for just a moment, he looked like himself again. Jude hoped he also got the sleep he obviously needed, and that Felix found some peace of mind. Maybe Jude would be able to tell Felix himself soon. It didn't hurt to hope, at least, another lesson he'd learned hard and well.

"Just... don't give up on him," Jasper said. "Or us. Please."

"Never," Jude said without hesitation. "I'll be right here when he's ready. When both of you are."

"That's all I can ever ask," Jasper said as Jude started to go. "And Jude, wait—"

"Yes?" He stopped, turning around quickly, and surprising himself with a wave of anticipation and hope. He missed Jasper, and Felix, more than he was comfortable letting himself acknowledge; something about pining after them when they were dealing with so much uncertainty and pain felt intrusive. But he did, and he hung on Jasper's every word.

"Did I hear it was your last day?"

"You did, yeah."

Jasper grinned, and he looked even more like himself now, bright-eyed and mischievous. "Make it a good one. If you've ever dreamed about keying a deserving colleague's car, now would be the time."

"I'm deciding that I didn't hear that suggestion of malicious vandalism," Jude said, looking pointedly up toward the ceiling. "Because I'm not done yet."

"No, you're not—and neither are we. I'll see you soon."

As Jasper quietly closed the door, Jude gave a parting wave and headed down the hall toward the stairwell, forcing himself to leave his worries behind him. Some, at least.

ACT TWO: Witches Gotta Stick Together

IT WAS NOT Eva's last day, and even if were, she'd most likely still dress like it was her first. Heels at the very least. Never higher than an inch or two—she liked the power click, but she also liked to be able to move. Old firefighting habits died hard, and particularly now, after everything she'd learned about vampires, witches, and general peril, she was extremely aware of the importance of being able to duck and run with no warning, even during the daytime.

Her shoes did indeed have a satisfying *click-click-click*, though, so nice that they almost created the illusion of productivity and purpose. But she was really just wandering the length of the mall, like Jude on his rounds (or whatever he was actually doing). And her mind was elsewhere. Specifically, back in the apartment complex she shared with Jude, Jasper, Letizia, Nails, Maestra, and now, once again, Felix.

That place was getting crowded, with friends and secrets.

Felix. She'd taken a rare day off yesterday, spent it resting, relaxing, exfoliating, wallowing in her jealousy that Jude was really leaving all the nonsense behind—doing all the things she felt so guilty about indulging in ordinarily. And talking to her once-lost friend, but not face-to-face.

She'd stood outside the door. Then sat on the floor. She knew he was there, the same way he had to know she was there. She just started talking. About her day, her week, how it had been before they'd gotten him back. How boring, compared to their old lives. How she'd actually liked the boredom sometimes, found it restful, but how it could never compare to having Felix home. How much they'd all missed him. How much she still missed him.

He never opened the door, but when she finally got up to leave, she heard something, a reply from inside for the first time.

"Don't give up on me."

His voice was so much rougher now, distorted, like his half-transformed features. Nobody who didn't know him would say he looked or sounded remotely like he used to—but Eva did know him. Too well for a thing like a permanent vampire morph to keep her from recognizing her friend. Felix was Felix, no matter what else changed.

"I won't. I didn't," she said immediately, maybe a little too quickly. The first part might be true, but the second one sounded fake even to herself. There was only one of them who hadn't given up on Felix, and she couldn't escape the thought that she and Jasper had almost given up on Jude too.

As Jasper's name crossed her mind, his shop crossed her path. She hesitated. The storefront was closed, metal grate pulled down to the floor, but she caught a glimpse of someone moving around inside. Which wouldn't have been unusual, except that Jasper was home, last she'd heard. He definitely wasn't in today.

But someone evidently was.

"Jude?" she said into her walkie. It would be so hard to break that habit. "Jasper never came in today, did he?"

"No," came his reply after a second. "I just talked to him, he's at home. Why?"

"His store's closed but there's movement inside. Probably just maintenance or something, but… you know, with everything new…"

"On my way," he said without hesitation.

"No, I'm on it. But if I don't call back in ten minutes…"

"Got it. I'll be here—for a little while longer."

"Thanks. Have a great last day, by the way. Over and out."

And that was that. Eva didn't have to say what was on both of their minds, and he didn't have to ask. He had her back, and always would even if he didn't work here anymore. Some things would never change. The knowledge was comforting as she dug out her keys and unlocked the grate as quietly as possible.

"Jasper?" Eva called as she slipped inside, on the off-chance they'd been wrong, and he had come in today without saying anything. Maybe it was him. And if it wasn't, it probably wasn't human, which meant it would know she was here already.

She moved as silently as possible through the maze of packed shelves and tight turns, painfully aware that she was armed only with slightly pointy keys, tension building in her stomach with every step. Slowly, she peered around the last shelf at the back counter, and at who stood behind it.

It wasn't Jasper. It wasn't even human.

But Eva still relaxed all at once, letting her breath out in a rush. "Oh, it's you. You scared me!"

"Yes, it's me. Sorry to frighten, but I had urgent business here." Letizia stood behind the counter, poring over a heavy, leather-bound book, as Eva had seen Jasper do several times before. The witch turned a page too quickly, almost tearing the aged, thin paper. She didn't look up as Eva came near, just kept turning through the book with a fervor that bordered on the frantic.

"What are you doing in here?" Eva asked. Letizia was a frequent visitor for the shop's under-the-table magic trade and loose regulations about smoking joints on the premises, but Eva had only known her to drop by when the owner was actually present.

"Looking for something," said Letizia, who stayed absorbed in the book.

"What kind of something?" Eva moved up to the counter and putting her hands on it as well. "Is there some… problem?"

"There's always some problem," Letizia said, and her voice was unexpectedly tight, anxious. When she looked up, her face was equally disturbed.

"Well, what are we dealing with?" Familiar adrenaline made Eva's heart beat faster, making her stand more solidly. "Is that big bad vampire back, what's his name—Cruce?"

"No, he's dead."

"Dead?" Eva's eyebrows shot up. "Dead how? When? Wait." She pressed her lips together, spine straightening as tension spread throughout her whole body. "And how would you know?"

"Relax," Letizia said, and her slight, tired-looking smile actually made it possible. Just a bit. "I didn't kill him. Though often's the time I wish I had. No, I hear things, and when I heard this particular thing, I simply verified. Cruce is indeed dead—I just wish he'd have taken a few more problems with him."

"What kind of problems?" Eva asked.

"Nothing you need to concern yourself with," Letizia said, not unkindly, but with a definite current of tension underneath. Still, Eva had never accepted words like those, no matter the tone.

"It doesn't sound like nothing. If I had to guess, I'd say you were scared—"

"I am not scared!" Letizia snapped, eyes briefly flashing white. Eva had been right; she was definitely tense, worryingly so. Eva didn't move, instead watching carefully as the not-quite-human scowl faded from Letizia's face and her eyes dimmed to normal. She sighed then, shoulders that had bunched up around her ears dropping until she just looked tired instead of annoyed. "I'm sorry. And… you're right. I'm also scared."

"I thought so," Eva said, but her voice and mind were free of any triumph. "And I'm feeling like maybe I should be too."

"Shitless." Letizia's shoulders slumped, and she rested her elbows on the counter and her face in her hands.

"So how about you tell me what's going on?" Eva asked, stepping up to lean against the counter herself. "Cruce is really dead, right?"

"He's dead," Letizia said quickly, still sounding exhausted and frazzled at the same time. Eva felt a wave of empathy. Holding yourself together for other people was draining for vampires too apparently. "Nails and Maestra told me they felt him die, and they wouldn't be wrong. Even with my spell, their connection was weakened but not broken. He's their sire, you can't break that bond entirely without permanent death, and when it's severed, you—you feel it. You feel it hard."

"So what did happen?" Eva probed, readying the substantial logical part of her brain to shut up and accept whatever vampiric plot twists were coming her way. "Some other hunter finally get him? Because if it wasn't you, and I'm pretty sure it wasn't any of us…"

"No, not a hunter," Letizia said with a shake of her head. "There's only one other monster that could take Cruce down."

"Another one," Eva said, and it wasn't quite a question. "Should've known. I take it we'll be meeting him soon?"

"No, if I do everything right, he'll never even know you exist." Letizia let out a frustrated noise. "But, it's not even about him really, there's something else happening, something potentially…"

"Dangerous?" Eva finished, though that wasn't the part she found the most tantalizing. Still, her instincts advised against asking directly about whoever 'he' might be. Letizia had already shut down two attempts at unraveling whatever she was wrestling with, and Eva didn't intend to try a third.

"Not for you," Letizia said firmly. "At least, not if I can help it."

"That's not exactly what I was asking. I don't want you going up against any monsters all by your damn self."

Letizia almost smiled, looking mildly surprised and pleased at the concern. "Probably not dangerous for me either. Thanks. It's really nothing any of you should have to worry about, but it's…"

"...Obviously important to you," Eva finished again, since she seemed to be on the right track so far.

"I wouldn't be here otherwise." Letizia nodded, and looked up now. Eva wasn't sure how much sleep vampires needed, but it definitely looked like she wasn't getting enough. Or maybe it was The Pit's sauce she needed, or more specifically, its signature ingredient. "That's why I'm here. Looking for anything I can find about the magics and artifacts involved. Jasper did say I was welcome, though, whenever I needed... help."

It didn't sound like this was something she was used to asking for. Or like it'd been easy, however indirect the request. So Eva tactfully let it go without comment and asked the other question on her mind. "Magic and artifacts?"

"Yes, extremely powerful ones. It's a long story. It's... personal." Letizia paused for a moment, carefully chewing her lower lip with very sharp teeth.

"Personal how?" Eva asked, point-blank. Usually when people danced around a question, it was about being polite or sensitive. Eva had never enjoyed such social dances, and she enjoyed them even less when it seemed like they were actually about matters of life and death. "I know you've got your business, but this sounds like it might not stay personal forever. If it's going to affect us, then we deserve to know what's going on. Besides, you've got friends now." Letizia's expression seemed to reflect a new and unexpected worry and Eva added, "If you're so worried about keeping us safe, then yeah, I'd call us friends. Sometimes it's not a bad thing if one person's business becomes everyone else's."

"Eva, please understand." Letizia pushed herself off the counter and straightened up. "I know I'm being enigmatic, and that's annoying as every hell, I know. Just give me until tonight, then come to my apartment. I'll tell you everything, you and Jude—and Pixie and Felix, if they want to know. Considering what they've been through, they might not."

"I take it Jasper already knows?"

"Probably more than he should." The witch smiled a bit, obviously fondly. "As usual."

"We'll help however we can," Eva said, and despite the murky specifics, meant it. "But no promises. We're just lowly humans, after all. Most of us, anyway."

"I'm not asking for your help yet. I just want you to be aware." Letizia gave her another faint smile, but this time it was one that lasted. "But thank you. And watch it—some of my best friends are lowly humans."

🔥

Eva and Letizia exited the shop together, walking in a companionable silence. Eva had a mountain of office work waiting for her, but she wasn't in all that big a hurry to get back to it. It'd still be there, and moments of relative calm spent with a friend were much harder to come by. As it turned out, she was right, as this moment was interrupted much too quickly, and loudly.

"Hey!" someone yelled from behind them, the angry shout echoing in the open, tiled space.

Both women stopped, turning to see someone barreling toward them from the other side of the mall thoroughfare. Eva frowned immediately. She didn't know him by name, but she recognized the dirty clothes, wild red hair, and aggressive attitude. Wherever she'd seen him before, it wasn't under good circumstances.

"Hey, you! Not you," he said as Eva spread her hands in a 'yes, what?' gesture. He jabbed a finger toward Letizia, who'd replaced her dark sunglasses now that they were out in public again. "*You!* You've been avoiding me for the past whole week!"

"I can't imagine why that would be."

It wasn't Letizia who answered, but another newcomer heading toward them from the opposite direction: around the same age, but much calmer, cleaner, and more goth. Eva recognized them too, but only by reputation, the heavy eyeliner, and the neon purple hair; Milo, she recalled; they worked at one of those stores punk-ish teens liked that seemed to have a Halloween theme year-round. They moved quickly to intercept the aggravated young man, putting themself smoothly between him and Letizia.

"Get out of here, Milo!" he snapped, looking like he wanted to stomp his foot in frustration, preferably on Milo's own. "This is between me and her, it don't concern you!"

"People don't usually enjoy being stalked," they said as he started trying to edge around them to get at his intended target. Milo moved to block him, not aggressively, but not backing down either.

"I wasn't stalking anyone!" the first near-stranger yelped, indignant. "This is a public place, and I got just as much right to be here as she does!"

"Not if she doesn't want you following her," came Milo's much more level reply. "Which you were. Very obviously. If you have a question why not just ask nicely?"

"Because she won't talk to me," the skinny punk said, turning his complaints to Letizia, who remained impassive and poker-faced. "Right? You don't wanna give me the time of day!"

Letizia said nothing, and took a calm sip out of the thermos Eva could swear she hadn't been holding a second ago. She knew enough to suspect its contents weren't just coffee, and that giving her trouble about it was unlikely to go anywhere.

"Well, that's a mistake!" he shouted, his hands balling into sharp-knuckled fists. "Seems like you've been making a lot of them lately. You'll back the hell off if you know what's good for you! Just don't come crying to me if you end up dead!"

Eva stepped back and grabbed at her walkie. Fortunately, the guy now yelling about ending up dead didn't look armed—he was dressed only in a long-sleeved but thin shirt, even in the cold weather, and wouldn't have had many places to hide a weapon at least. He also wasn't paying attention to her, continuing to rail against God-knew-what, and right now, Eva had no desire to find out more specifics. That was a major escalation, one she didn't feel entirely equipped to handle. At least not without backup.

"Jude?" she said into her walkie as she watched the tension build from a relatively safe distance away. "We might have a problem here. Still near Jasper's shop."

"Almost there," he answered almost immediately. "Is it a—a day problem, or a night problem?"

"Day problem so far," she said, sizing up the interaction that quickly seemed to be turning into a confrontation. "And I'd like to keep it that way." With that, she stepped casually up to the other three in time to hear Milo's tone shift into what sounded like actual concern.

"I haven't seen you around in a while," they said, giving the scruffy young man a searching look, up and down. "Have you eaten anything today? You look like you could use—"

"I'm—no, that's not—*shut up,* Milo!" His face started to turn red under the grime as he went from frustrated to flustered very quickly. "Stop trying to distract me! You know I'm just here for her!"

Milo chuckled; it wasn't an angry sound, more fondly exasperated, which only seemed to annoy the young man further. "You're stubborn as always. But you can't eat stubborn. Seriously, let me—"

"I don't need a damn sandwich, I need *her* to keep her nose out of shit she shouldn't be into!"

"Hey," somebody said from behind her, and she turned to see Jude, standing tense and a little out of breath. Both Milo and the punk kid jumped and turned to stare at him with surprised, anxious expressions, as if they were kids caught with their hands in a forbidden cookie jar. "Everything okay over here?"

"We're fine," both of them said at once as they turned to face him. They simultaneously glanced at each other, then back at Jude, one smiling, one scowling, both clearly lying.

Eva watched as the sour-faced young man's gaze took on a definite shade of panic, flicking quickly from her to Jude and back, then at Milo and Letizia. He must have felt distinctly outnumbered, because he took a step backwards, then another.

"You know what, screw all of you! I'm done! End up dead, see if I care!" With that, he practically sprinted toward the mall exit, stopping only as he passed a cluster of posters on one of the support pillars. He ripped one down in a fast, jerky motion with an accompanied angry grunt, then rushed out the sliding glass doors.

Nobody moved to follow him. Eva considered it, and could see Jude clearly pondering the same thing—and rubbing at his jacket pocket, which was subtly squirming—but since the conflict had apparently self-terminated, there was little point.

"Thank you, little friend. That could have been much more exciting than it was," Letizia said with a nod in Milo's direction. Still, Eva could see the tension on her face and stance even with her dark shades and general inscrutability. She'd been rattled, that much was obvious.

"Oh, of course," Milo said, a smile that looked equal parts cheery and anxious spreading across their face. "Witches gotta stick together."

"Witches?" Eva repeated, turning to them with new interest.

"Figure of speech! You know, for us goth types!" Milo said with a distinctly nervous-sounding laugh. "Now my break's almost over, I have to get back. Sorry!" Before Eva could follow up on that and all it implied, Milo gave an apologetic wave of their black-nailed hand and hurried off, just short of actually running.

"You heard that too, right?" Eva asked, turning to Jude, who was also watching Milo's retreat with a pensive expression.

"Sure did," he said, and gave Letizia a sidelong look. But she said nothing, simply folding her arms and looking lost in her own hidden thoughts. "Any idea what that guy was yelling about? Sounded ominous."

"Sure did. And no, none, but at least this part's over without any mess this time," Eva said. "If only every mall fight could be self-diffusing."

"It'd be nice," Jude said. "But I'm still going to follow up with Milo. If nothing else, they seemed to have some history with the other guy. But that also really didn't seem like a figure of speech, at least not when it's said to an

38

actual—" he said, then stopped. When he and Eva turned to where Letizia had been standing, there was no trace to be found—witch and thermos seemed to have disappeared into thin air. "Of course."

"I love the smell of weirdness in the morning," Eva said dryly. "Aren't you going to miss all this?"

"Oh, yes. I don't know what I'd do without our morning adventures." Jude's tone was only half-sarcastic, and she half-smiled in return. "Did you hear exactly what they were arguing about? Shh, hang on," he added in a low voice directed toward his pocket, which had started to quietly squeak.

"Not much more than you did. That guy followed us for a little, then went off at Letizia, yelling about how everyone's doomed. Then Milo called him out on it, which he didn't seem to appreciate either."

"Maybe he wanted a free tarot reading," Jude said, in a tone that if Eva didn't know any better, she'd call joking.

"Or some of her other secret stash. Boy could probably use some," Eva replied, in a tone that definitely was. Still, she knew neither of them would forget the actual words of warning. "In any case, we can find out for ourselves later. She asked us to come by her place tonight so she can fill us in on the latest fun. Which will hopefully turn out to be nothing, but just in case it doesn't, we should probably have the heads-up."

"About what, exactly?" Jude frowned, reservations immediately apparent, even as Eva felt that much more secure. An uneasy, dubious Jude meant she was back on familiar ground.

"I don't know. I just have a feeling we might have another... complicated situation on our hands."

"Complicated—as in a night problem, then?" Jude's thick black eyebrows came together, telling Eva immediately that, as usual, they were on the same page.

She almost replied with something like 'I hope not,' but stopped herself, instead thinking about the way Letizia had smiled with obvious relief and fondness when Eva let her know she wasn't facing whatever nightmare came next alone. She thought about how wildly, irrepressibly happy Nails and Maestra must be, freed from their last tie to their abusers. The telltale lump in Jude's pockets and the irresistible onslaught of cute that was Pixie's fluffy bat form with its huge ears and beady little eyes looking up at her. The mixed fear and hope in Felix's voice when he begged her, out of sight but now just a room away, *don't give up on me.*

Somehow, Eva found it easier to smile than scowl. "Seems that way."

"Meet you tonight, then," Jude said with a nod that held all the quickness and efficiency of a salute. The high-pitched squeaking from inside his jacket grew more urgent, sounding like a particularly weird ringtone. "I'd just as soon avoid any more surpri—hold on, I uh, have to take this."

His pocket could no longer be ignored. Jude half-opened it to give Pixie some air, and reached inside to pet the top of his fuzzy head.

"Bring your bat to work day?" Eva asked, half-turning away with hands on her hips, looking up to the ceiling. "Which I definitely didn't see. I know nothing about any unregulated animals in here, and even if I did, they'd be emotional support bats. Right, Jude?"

"That's right," he said, then whispered directly into his jacket, apparently past caring if anyone saw him looking strange. It'd be far stranger if anyone saw Pixie appear from nowhere. "Okay, I'll let you out in just a minute, too many people here, try to hang on until—" He looked around, trying to look as casual and unruffled as possible as he fixed his eyes on the nearby bathrooms.

"Go," Eva said, and Jude shot her a grateful look. "Just make it a quick break, all right? Busy day on the job ahead of both of us—and not everyone's lucky enough to call it their last."

🔥

"Okay, here we go," Jude said, closing and locking the single-stall bathroom door and digging the bat out of his pocket as fast as he could while not being rough with the little creature. It wiggled a bit in his hand, then hopped off, turning from bat into boy long before it hit the ground. "Are you okay?"

"What happened?" Pixie asked in a tight voice as he stood up, eyes wide and fixed on Jude's face. He looked disoriented, dizzy, and shaken up, like he had back at the apartment. "Are you okay? I heard yelling! Were you in a fight? Is somebody after us again?"

"No no, everything's fine," Jude reassured him, wanting nothing more than to wipe that fear right off Pixie's sometimes too-expressive face. "I ran into Eva—and Letizia, and that Milo kid—talking with a guy who seemed... upset. Loudly upset. That's probably what you heard. You and the rest of the mall."

"Okay, okay good," Pixie nodded, but didn't look very reassured. "It's just, I thought I heard... never mind."

"What did you think you heard?" Jude felt a twinge of foreboding, seeing how Pixie seemed to shrink down a little at the thought, like it was the cause of all his unrest.

"I don't know. Maybe I was dreaming. The only times I've been able to really sleep lately is in your pocket, as a bat." He tried to smile, but it only succeeded in making Jude's heart ache. "Bats don't have bad dreams."

That didn't really help the worry worming around in Jude's stomach, but when he tried to smile back, he had more success than Pixie had. "You can sleep in there whenever you want."

"Thanks." And Pixie brightened a little bit at that. Not enough, but it was there.

It was never hard for Jude to tell how Pixie was feeling, but vampires didn't seem to show the same kinds of signs of distress as humans did. Their bodies were warm, contrary to popular belief—but no dark circles under their eyes when exhausted, no sweat or shivers, no actual need to breathe fast during a panic attack, and they likely didn't lose or gain weight in the same way as the living.

Jude was actually relieved about that one. Worrying about Jasper was enough; if he ever saw Pixie looking thin and drawn, Jude would find staying calm and level even harder than usual.

"You can talk to me, you know," Jude said after hesitating a moment. When had he become the person anybody talked to about their problems? He'd never been the most stable or responsible. Nobody had ever really needed him to be before. "I want you to feel like you can talk to me."

"I know—it's not that I don't trust you. It's not you at all." Pixie still looked troubled, but a little less so than before. He reached out to touch Jude's wrist, lightly take his hand. "It's just... a lot."

"Yeah." Pixie had been through Hell. The closest to actual-Hell-with-a-capital-H Jude could imagine this side of living, or on the undead side, and that was only the part Jude had personally witnessed. But that alone—the kidnapping, torture, crucifixion, almost dying for a second time—was enough for anybody's life to be forever changed and shaken. "Whatever it is... I'm here."

"I know." Pixie gave his fingers a squeeze as Jude ran his thumb over the smooth skin on the back of his hand, and the rougher scarring.

"Are you going to go home?" Jude asked after a second. "Or pocket again? I meant that, you can stay in there all day if you want to."

"Um, I..." Pixie trailed off. He looked so lost.

Jude's stomach clenched. Again, he wanted quite badly to pull Pixie close and squeeze him until all his worries disappeared. More than that, kiss him, wrap all of Pixie and his wonderful warm softness up in his arms and breathe him in, the way they had the night Pixie had agreed to stay with him. Jude hadn't dared since, though every time he thought about it, the combination of wanting and uncertainty made his chest ache, and rooted him to the floor.

And, as always, no matter how badly he wanted to, Jude couldn't bring himself to move. He never knew what to do at vulnerable moments, especially not when he suspected there was a lot more at work here than he could ever know. Not when he didn't know what would help, or hurt, and Pixie didn't need any more hurting. This was how he'd been for more of his life than he cared to admit, so afraid of making the wrong move and only driving them further apart that he ended up doing nothing at all.

"Who else did you say was there?" Pixie asked, sounding a little more relaxed, tired but calm. "Besides the yelling guy. I heard someone else."

"Letizia, but she took off pretty fast. Eva—oh, and Milo. Purple hair, goth, they work around here somewhere," Jude said, as if he didn't know the exact layout and schedule of every mall employee, or at least the closest anyone could come to omniscience in the wild world of retail.

"The Abyss," Pixie said immediately.

"Yes. The Abyss." Jude said the word like it tasted bad. "The Halloween store that's still open in January for some reason."

"It's called *being goth*, and goth doesn't take a vacation," Pixie said with a tiny upward curl of the corner of his mouth. "I love that place."

"I know," Jude said. After a beat, he sighed in mock despair, and only a little genuine resignation. "You want to go, don't you?"

"Heck yes. You can drop me off, you don't have to go in! I just at least want to make sure Milo's okay—and to let 'em know *I'm* okay. They're cool. We were buds. I mean, we still are, I hope. It's just been kind of hard keeping up with people with, uh, all this." He gestured to his fangs, then down to all of himself, looking self-conscious and uncertain.

"I can imagine," Jude said, trying not to let the alarm bells going off in his head leak out into his voice. "But are you entirely sure it's a good idea to… That is, I take it, they're familiar with…" now it was his turn to gesture to all of Pixie, eyebrows raised.

"Yeah," he said with a nod that was only a little hesitant. "They should be. I mean, I don't know for sure, but they always seemed into witchy type stuff before, so I was hoping… but I dunno, maybe they didn't mean *real* witchy type stuff. Maybe I shouldn't."

"You could at least say hello?" Jude suggested, surprising himself with the daring thought he'd never contemplate for himself. It was well worth it to get that anxious, self-doubting look off Pixie's face. "Seeing a friend might do you some good."

"Yeah, but what if they notice something's wrong with me?"

"Nothing's wrong with…" Jude started, then stopped. Arguing this particular point, however much he believed it, was semantics, and likely not the point Pixie was trying to make. "You don't have to, obviously. But now that I think about it, Milo did say something earlier, to Letizia, something like 'witches have to stick together.' That seemed fairly serious to me. If they're friends, they probably know about the… other side of her, as well."

"Yeah. Yeah, you're right," Pixie said, brightening a little, even if it still seemed like he was trying to convince himself. "I bet they do know. And if they don't…"

"Then they should still hear it from a friend," Jude said. After a pause, he made another decision the old him would have balked at, and said, "And I'll be right there with you. If you want me there."

"You will?" Pixie's eyes were suddenly much bigger, shinier, and that much harder to resist.

"Yes," Jude said with the seriousness of a man swearing to stand beside a comrade in the calm before a harrowing battle. "I'm behind you every step of the way."

"Okay. Okay, yeah." Pixie gave a resolute nod, seeming suitably convinced. "It'll be good to catch up a little." He gave Jude a refreshingly winning smile. "And maybe get some new earrings."

Jude's chest twinged again. That bright, pointed smile just made the desire to pull Pixie close and kiss him surge up again, but for a different reason than before. Then he'd looked so scared and hopeless, now he radiated his usual exuberant energy that sat polar opposite to Jude's, an opposing charge that drew him like a magnet. But Jude still couldn't risk making a move, not when Pixie's smile had just barely come back.

He settled for a mock frown that looked nothing like his real one. "I'm buying, aren't I?"

"Hey, it was your idea!" Pixie said happily, and rushed outside.

Jude sighed and let a moment pass before following. Still, whatever anyone might have to say about two men emerging from a single-stall public restroom, one of them a uniformed security guard, it just wasn't his biggest problem today. If the rest of the day behaved itself, he wouldn't have to add too many more to the list.

🔥

"You're going to be my buffer, all right?" Jude said under his breath as they neared the fanged black arches of The Abyss. "I hate going into this place alone. It's always crowded, loud music, everyone's dressed depressed but acting happy—it's the worst combination of edgy and perky."

"That's a *bad* combo to you?" Pixie raised his pink-dyed eyebrows.

'You're not 'edgy.'"

"Oh, Jude, that's hurtful. I'm hurt," Pixie said, hand on his chest, but he was giggling. He'd pulled his hoodie down to shadow his face, which hid his most obvious vampiric attributes, but Jude still made a point to stay between Pixie and as many mallgoers as possible. "But sure, no problem. I love this place! Especially the way they greet you."

"That's never made sense to me," Jude said with a furrowed brow. "Aren't you always saying that true punk is inherently counterculture, and once it's been absorbed into the mainstream and watered down for corporate profit, it ceases to be the tool of marginalized expression it once was, becoming another dead capitalist gimmick?"

"Aw, you do listen!" Pixie sounded delighted. "And you made 'bite the rich' sound a lot smarter than it does coming from me. If we'd met in high school, you'd be making bank writing my essays."

"You didn't answer the question."

"Yeah, I usually try to buy local," Pixie said, fiddling with one ear piercing. "But Milo's local! And okay, fine, The Abyss has some cute stuff. And cheap. I mean, come on, buying entirely organic homegrown punk, in this economy? Must be nice to be made of money."

Jude let out a snorting laugh. Pixie might still look tired after a poor day's sleep, but at least he seemed much closer to his regular ball of undead sunshine. His smile made the ever-present knot of tension in Jude's stomach unravel a little more every time he saw it.

Fortunately, for once, when they got inside, the place was empty. Almost.

"Hi, welcome to The Abyss," Milo said with a tired smile and little wave, looking up from where they'd been leaning against the counter, resting their head on their arms. "I'd say the rest of the required greeting, but it's you and I'm tired."

"That's okay," Pixie said, looking around the nearly-vacant store and only sounding slightly disappointed. "Just tired, or…?"

"It's about earlier," Jude said in response to Milo's confused look, while Pixie wandered off to peruse a stand of spiked and shiny jewelry. "That guy bothering Letizia, and yelling at you. Anything I should be aware of?"

"What? No," Milo said quickly, and Jude wasn't convinced, but he didn't pursue it either. People didn't tend to open up when badgered, a lesson he'd come to reluctantly learn. "No, he's just noisy. Nothing to worry about there."

"Okay, just making sure," Pixie said, looking up from where he'd found a pair of earrings, cartoon bats with pink, glittering eyes hanging upside-down from his hand. He glanced around the empty store. "Pretty dead in here. In a bad way, I mean. Usually you got a packed house."

"I'd rather it stay dead, present company excepted. You're someone I actually want to see," Milo explained, a tired smile growing across their face as if the odd statement was a joke Jude didn't quite get. "Great to see you again, Pixie. I was starting to get a little worried. It's been a while."

"Sure has," Pixie answered, replacing the bat-earrings and stepping toward Milo, but stopping a moderate distance from the counter. "A lot has happened, good and bad. It's just been… a lot."

"Sounds like more bad than good," Milo said, a concerned-looking wrinkle in their forehead. "Have you talked to Natalie lately? She's been around here a few times looking for you."

"Oh—no, no, I'm just kind of, uh, keeping to myself lately. But it hasn't been all bad," Pixie said with a glance in Jude's direction that made him feel a little warm inside. He gave a little nod back, and this seemed to put both Pixie and Milo a little more at ease. "More like, uh. Transformative."

"Ah," Milo nodded sagely, cast a glance at Jude, who had stepped away to let them speak, and lowered their voice, which still carried in the unusual quiet. They murmured something that sounded like, "New pronouns?"

"Not yet," Pixie laughed, as if he'd been taken by surprise—both by what Milo had said, and at how much he was enjoying being here. "But there are a few other new things." He carefully lowered his hood to reveal more of his telltale gray skin, pointed ears, catlike eyes, and pointed smile.

"Oh," Milo said, eyes widening and mouth becoming a perfect 'O' to match.

"Yeah."

"You're—are you—?"

"In the flesh," Pixie replied with a somewhat sheepish, yet pointed smile. "You know, so to speak."

"That explains a lot," Milo said, letting out a kind of combination laugh and relieved sigh. No horror in their face, or even much surprise, Jude noted. His hunch had been right. This kid must be a lot more familiar with the night's hidden citizens than he'd been when one of them had crashed through his window.

"You don't seem exactly shocked to learn that vampires exist," Jude observed. "Witches aren't the only ones who need to stick together, is that it?"

"Oh, I'm not a vampire," Milo said, giving Jude an appraising but open look. "Though this is a designated safe space. With magic, I mean. That, and common decency."

"I'm afraid I'm one-hundred percent human, mundane and ordinary," Jude said.

"Lying," Pixie said with a snort. "You're kinda norm-core, extremely straight-edge, but way less of a buzzkill than you think."

Jude covered a laugh that would have clashed terribly with his work uniform. "I'm going to pretend I know what those words mean, and take that as a compliment."

"Glad to find another ally. We can always use more," Milo said, with another enigmatic little smile that reminded Jude a little of Letizia. But instead of her cocky assuredness, Milo looked more... sad. But then they brightened, and leaned over the counter in a conspiratorial way. "But Pixie! I'm so glad you came to me, there's so much we need to talk about. You wouldn't believe what happened just last night. Cruce, the monster himself—he's dead." Milo's voice dropped to an intense whisper. "Dead-dead. Actually destroyed. He'll never hurt anyone ever again. I never thought I'd see it."

"I did," Pixie said with a sudden ferocity, eyes hard and haunted-looking. Then he seemed to catch himself, some of the fire in his voice fading, but he didn't look any less shaken. "I mean—somebody had to, eventually. It's about time."

"Yes, it is—are you all right?" Milo asked, clearly a bit surprised at his uncharacteristic demeanor. "This is personal for you, isn't it?"

"You could say that," Pixie said with a halfhearted laugh. "Cruce wasn't my sire, but he, uh... made my life a lot harder. Before-life, and after-life. I guess. So yeah. I'm good with him being deader than dead—better than good."

"Oh," Milo said, and their mouth didn't drop open this time. Instead, their violet eyes clouded with pained empathy. "Oh, I'm so sorry. He's... I've heard what he..."

"It's all true." Pixie's voice went a little flat, and Jude noticed him tracing the scarring on the back of one hand. "Everything you've heard, and a lot worse. I guarantee it. But he's gone now, and everyone he did turn is free, so everything's coming up us, I guess."

"It's a start. I'm just so glad it wasn't him who turned you," Milo said vehemently, and Jude believed them, even if Pixie's smile looked a little strained. "Turning's hard enough even if the one doing it isn't a complete monster. In all sincerity, good riddance. I wouldn't be surprised if someone throws a 'B-I-H Cruce' party."

"B-I...?" Jude asked, frowning.

"Burn In Hell," Pixie supplied with mildly unsettling perkiness.

"Speaking of sires, is yours—no," Milo broke off, pushing themself back a bit from the counter. "You don't have to tell me, not my business. You look great, that's all. Might sound weird to say, but un-death really suits you. It just does for some people."

"You know, I thought so too actually," Pixie said with a nod. "It's a major adjustment, for sure, but I'm making it work. And I do make it look good." He chuckled at himself, then looked more serious, but just as happy. "Seriously, I'm so glad you're up to speed, I'd pretty much given up on talking to anybody but like three people in the world about this. It feels good."

"I'm really glad to hear that," Milo said with a small, sincere-looking smile. "Gives me a bit of hope. I've been hearing some... some concerning things, lately."

"What kind of concerning things?" Jude asked in as level a tone as he could, the familiar tingle of anxiety beginning to sweep through him. "Is there something going on I should know about? Not as, ah, this," he said with a self-conscious gesture at his security guard uniform. "Just as a... concerned friend and ally. This is my last day, anyway."

"Sorry to see you go. And when I say 'concerning,' I mean..." Milo's smile faded, and they didn't continue right away. Some of their scant color began to drain, making their makeup look bolder, and their face younger, less sure, more vulnerable, and that just made Jude even more hyper-aware of the difference in their stations. It felt like an interrogation, but not one that he'd intended.

Jude shifted uncomfortably, his uniform suddenly not seeming to fit right—but then it never really had. He'd never actually liked being looked at as some kind of authority figure; it was too much pressure and too much responsibility—and where some guys might get off on the power and fear afforded even to a mall cop, it just made Jude feel wrong. Besides, the uniform was a barrier, keeping people at arm's length when he was just now trying to open up.

When Milo spoke again, Jude got the impression that they were choosing each word with care. "If I told you that something big and potentially dangerous was coming, and to make yourselves scarce for the next few days, would you listen?"

"I mean, I want to say yes," Pixie said with a wary glance at Jude. "But I don't think I can say that and stay honest."

"Definitely not," Jude confirmed. "And I do appreciate you just coming right out and asking."

"Cutting to the chase does save a lot of time," Milo said levelly. "Then, if you felt bound and determined to involve yourselves in this dangerous event, would you feel confident in your chances?"

"Of what?" Jude asked. "Defeating it, or staying alive? Because those are two different things."

"Both. Either."

Jude slid Pixie a slightly dubious glance and saw him looking warily back. "I mean, so far, we're at a one hundred percent success rate for survival—even if not all of us are exactly, ah, alive to begin with. That's pretty good, right?"

"Yeah," Milo said with a nod, but they didn't look at all comforted. "While we're cutting to the chase—it's a good thing Cruce's dead, but it also raises a lot more questions. Like, do we know who to thank for that... public service?"

"No," Jude said, folding his arms. "I've been wondering who or what could be powerful enough to take him out."

"That's exactly what I'm afraid of too." Milo took a breath, drumming their black nails in an anxious rhythm on the glass counter. "I just have the terrible feeling that something major is building."

"What kind of 'something major?'" Jude pressed.

"I... I think it's the kind of thing where the less you know, the safer you are," Milo said, after a pause in which they pressed their purple-stained lips tightly together. "I'm sorry. I know that's an aggravating non-answer, I swear I'm not trying to be witchy and mysterious, but it's all I feel confident saying. Just please, take my word and lie low for a few days, that's all."

Something occurred to Jude, and he furrowed his brow. "Would this have anything to do with that guy who was stalking Letizia, and yelling at you?"

Milo paused then, as before, spoke very carefully. "He isn't a direct threat. If anything, he's in much more danger than any of us. But interfering would only make it worse, so it's best to stay away from him as well."

"I knew he was involved," Jude muttered, but nothing more. Following one known lead seemed easier than digging unknowns out of someone so obviously scared and likely to clam up if pushed.

"It's not that simple," Milo said with a bit of desperation that told Jude he'd been right to be careful. "You're right, he's involved with some very dangerous vampires, the worst I've ever known, but he's not one of them. Consent doesn't exist with—with the types of people we're dealing with."

"Ain't that the freaking truth," Pixie muttered.

"Please," Milo insisted earnestly, looking Jude directly in the eyes with an intensity that took him by surprise. "I'm asking you as a friend, and a witch, and anything else that gets you to listen. No matter what he says—and he will probably say some unpleasant things if you run into him again—he's not the threat here. Don't hurt him."

"We wouldn't…" Jude stopped. It was true, as long as the noisy punk didn't take the first shot. "We won't hurt him. Unless he tries to hurt us first."

"He won't. Thank you." Milo still seemed relieved, despite the possibilities that seemed all too obvious to Jude. Maybe they were just relieved that Jude would try to keep their complicated friend safe at all. "He's been hurt enough." Their gaze went back to Pixie. "And so have you. Keep yourself safe, Pixie."

"Hey, don't worry," Pixie said with a lightness Jude knew very well he didn't feel. "It'll be fine. Your friend will be fine, and I'll be fine too. Whatever happens, happens, and we'll figure it out when we get there. Remember, we're down one monster. With Cruce gone, I think our lives are gonna get a whole lot easier."

"I really hope you're right," Milo said, but they didn't sound convinced.

"Sure I am," Pixie said, still sounding rattled, but he gave an attempted smile and wave, pushing himself away from the counter and stepping toward the door. He hesitated only to cast the bat earrings a longing glance, then resolutely headed for the exit. "It really was great to see you, buddy. Talk to you later. And it won't be so long this time!"

"Pixie, wait," Milo said, and both he and Jude stopped. In a contrast to their previous care and reticence, Milo's words came out in a rush now. "Listen, I might not have gone through it myself, but I know enough about turning to know that it really is an adjustment. More than that, it's a major trauma, no matter how smoothly it goes. If you ever need someone to talk to… you know where to find me."

"Thank you," Pixie said with a smile Jude knew to be entirely real, genuine, and heartfelt. Now, he meant every word. "I'm totally gonna take you up on that. Really glad you're here."

The relief so clear in Pixie's eyes and the deep gratitude so obvious in his voice made Jude's stomach twist just a bit. All this time, he'd been floundering, hadn't known the first thing to say or ask Pixie about any of this, or had the slightest idea how to help. Now this familiar-but-new face seemed to have gotten him to open up more and better in ten minutes than Jude had in months.

Maybe it was small and petty of him to feel anything like jealousy, but apparently Jude was smaller and pettier than he'd thought.

"It's no problem," Milo said. "Oh, before I forget again, would you like me to let Natalie know you're okay? I won't say anything about—"

"Nah, don't worry about it," Pixie said, and Jude felt more than heard the tension instantly come back into his voice. "I'll handle it. See you!"

"Have a great day!" Milo called as they exited the store, in a blandly pleasant voice with a matching smile. It seemed automatic, a reflex customerservice mask, but Jude had seen both the sharp acuity and the churning worry that lay behind it. Milo would never be just the sweet mall-goth kid to him again—or at least, not only that. "Thanks for staring into the Abyss."

They stepped out into the mall's manufactured light and ambient noise, but Jude only had eyes for Pixie, who still seemed troubled and downcast, and somehow even more worried than he'd been before.

"So, Natalie?" Jude had to ask as they walked, watching carefully for his reaction.

"She's just… you don't have to worry about that either," Pixie said, looking like he was doing enough worrying himself for the three of them. "I got this. Can you, uh?" After a quick look around to ensure there were no potential witnesses to the paranormal, he tugged on Jude's sleeve and held his hand—which suddenly held a small pink bat.

Jude tucked Pixie back into his pocket, thinking how nice it must be to have such an easy way to avoid an obviously unwanted conversation. But he was thinking more about everything he'd just heard, and everything yet to come, both from Letizia later, and from God knew what direction next. Jude sighed as he forced his brain into something resembling work mode, and strode away from the Abyss.

It wasn't even ten o'clock yet.

&

The next time Jude saw Eva, it was in the hall outside Letizia's apartment, two floors up from his own. She was leaning against the wall, head back and eyes closed, as if she were trying to catch up on hours of sleep missed, of which Jude suspected were many. Eva always did try to take everything on herself, he thought. Whatever came next, he resolved to make sure she didn't have to.

"Hey," he said as he and Pixie—in human form, and no longer in Jude's pocket—approached, trying to make enough noise so as not to startle her in case she really was doing more than just resting her eyes. "Is she home?"

"I don't know," Eva said, stretching and rolling her shoulders. Jude thought he heard a joint pop. "I knocked, but there was no answer. She didn't really give me a time, so I figured I'd just wait for you and then see what…"

She trailed off and looked down at the soft click of the lock. The door opened smoothly, but as Jude soon saw, the doorway beyond it was empty. No hand had unlocked or pushed it open, but with this particular occupant, it was fairly certain who was responsible.

"I'll take that as an invitation," Pixie said, stepping over the threshold and turning to them with a confirming nod. "Yep! It's for us. Hi, Letizia!"

Nobody answered at first, and the room past the small entry space was dark, lit only by the flickering light of candles.

"We're in here," someone called then, but it wasn't the Witch. Jude would know Jasper's voice anywhere, and, as he was inclined to do whenever he heard it, he followed.

The place seemed like the same layout as Jude's—kitchen, living area, and a short hallway to a bathroom and two bedrooms. No spatters of blood or visible coffins. It was pretty sparsely furnished, really, and didn't look very used. She must not spend much time in it, or at least not as a human.

The biggest indication that anybody lived in here at all was the piles of books and papers strewn around, as well as the odd piece of polished stone and a few rows of indoor plants. It looked like an extension of Jasper's shop in that way, and Jude thought he actually recognized a few of the books, like the large, leather-bound one that lay open in the middle of a cleared area on the floor. The plants under their tubular lights looked normal enough, aside from the five-leaf shape Jude immediately pretended he hadn't seen.

The very Witch herself sat on the floor, shuffling her usual deck of cards, but with more of a frenetic energy than usual. On the floor in front of her was a round metal frame, and inside it, large shards of jagged, shattered glass. A broken mirror, with several pieces missing. More cards were spread in front of her, like she was halfway through laying them out, but then started to shuffle in a nervous habit.

Letizia didn't look up as Jude, Pixie, and Eva entered, but Jasper gave them all a friendly nod from where he sat in a nearby chair. He said nothing, just held one finger up to his lips. It looked like he had been here a while. Again, Jude frowned slightly as he took in Jasper's face, and now the rest of him—it was hard to tell by the way he was sitting, but he did indeed look thinner than Jude remembered, and generally more ragged. Anxiety ran through Jude again, but he pushed it down. Not the time or place to check in, he thought—but soon.

Jude peered at Letizia's cards. Even if he didn't know much about tarot, Jude thought the spread looked messy, like she'd laid them down hastily. He couldn't read many from this angle, except for one that faced him—the Devil. Letizia scooped up the cards, dropping one, and Jude crouched down to pick it up. The Sun, he noted, its golden rays still brightly shining in the low light.

Now Letizia looked up at him, or rather, at the card in his hand, holding out her own expectantly. She'd removed her usual sunglasses, and now he could clearly see how steadfastly she avoided eye contact.

"Your door was, uh, open" he said as he handed back the Sun card, half greeting, half apology. "Which I'm guessing was for us?"

"Are we waiting for anyone?" Eva asked when Letizia didn't answer. "The girls? Felix?"

The Witch still didn't say anything, and wasn't looking at them anymore, so Jude took another stab. "What is all this?"

"Letizia, dear?" Jasper called when she didn't answer that either, and now her head jerked up and she seemed to see them all for the first time. "Are you all right?"

"Yes," she said shortly, shaking her head as if to clear it. "Yes, I'm fine now. Thank you for coming. The girls are in their room, recovering from being severed, adjusting, and I didn't want to press anything more on them than that. It's getting too complicated already."

She spoke faster than she usually did and tended to blurt out her sentences all at once, a far cry from the cool, laid-back witch he knew. Letizia always seemed to have the situation well in hand, but not right now, clearly. It must have been an effort to keep her hands still, because she folded them, bouncing them a little on her crossed legs.

"Letizia, what's going on?" Eva asked again in a gentle tone.

"There's a center of extremely concentrated magical power not far away," Letizia said, without preamble. "No, you won't have seen it, nobody finds it unless they already know where it is, or they're a witch. That place is very important to me, and to a very powerful vampire named Wicked Gold. He's Cruce's old master. And he wants it—more specifically, he wants the magical power I've stored inside it."

"Did you say…?" Pixie asked in a whisper that made Jude turn to look at him immediately. His voice shook, and while vampires couldn't really pale or blush in the same way humans did, his eyes were wide and clearly frightened, vertical catlike pupils thinning to slits. "It's—it's him? He's here?"

"Yes, little friend," she answered, and Jude remembered her using the same phrase of endearment on Milo. This time, though, her tone was softer, sympathetic, deeply understanding. "Wicked Gold is here. But, remember, so am I."

Jude almost asked more—that name rang inside him like a pounded gong, Wicked Gold, those two words had weight, meaning, an energy all of their own. But Pixie looked like he was going to be sick, and Jude couldn't stand to make that worse. Instead, he put one hand on Pixie's back and asked something else, just as important but not quite as unnerving. "A center of power?"

Letizia nodded. "It's like a battery, a lightning rod, a huge receptacle of magical energy, and whoever manages to unlock it will receive all the power it's absorbed over one hundred and fifty years. I need to stop that from happening."

"What kind of power, exactly?" Eva asked. "What does it do?"

"Whatever the one who holds it wants," Letizia intoned. "Magic in its raw, wild state is neither good nor evil, it is a neutral party, it does what it's told, as long as you're strong enough to command it. It's a tool, a means to an end, not the end itself. Some people simply should not ever lay hands on such means."

"So magic doesn't kill people, people kill people?" Eva said with a shaky smile Letizia did not return, or comment upon.

"And I take it you want this power?" Jude prodded. Maybe one thing here could make some sense.

"No, I want Wicked Gold *not* to have it," she said firmly. "I don't care if the power is mine, but he cannot get his hands on it. I don't think I need to tell you why."

"I mean, I'd appreciate knowing why," Eva said, echoing Jude's thoughts.

"I—it's—" Letizia dropped her cards and made a helpless gesture with her hands. "Hard to explain. It's just a very valuable source of energy that could be very dangerous in the wrong hands."

"You never mentioned anything about this before," Jude said, watching her carefully. "And if it was so important, I'd think it would have come up."

Letizia opened her mouth but paused. A bright, synthesized melody started to play, something familiar that Jude didn't place immediately. She pulled out a cell phone from one pocket, a perfectly ordinary-looking, modern smartphone in a shiny black case, and glared at the screen. She stabbed one black-nailed finger at it, and it went silent.

The Witch looked back up at Jude and hesitated. Once the irritation from the phone call faded from her face, she looked frightened in a way he had never seen before.

"The center has been building power for one hundred and fifty years and is very nearly at its peak—but at the same time now it feels… like it's decaying. That's the best I can describe it. It's weakening, destabilizing. I don't know if something specific is draining it, like malevolent vampires trying to leech it, or if even the most powerful spells break down after a century or so. But it is, and so are the defenses around it. Unless the power is drained at its apex—in two days, at midnight—the entire spell is going to collapse, and Wicked Gold can't have that. And neither can I."

She stopped, looking anxious as if they might all refuse, and Jasper threw her a bone. "It does sound like the sort of thing we should try to prevent. This fellow seems dangerous enough without a surplus of magic."

"There's more to it than that, isn't there?" Eva asked, watching Letizia with a thoughtful expression. "This sounds personal. A lot more so than just some magical power."

Letizia just nodded, but met none of their eyes. She resumed shuffling. "Yes it is. I wish I could tell you everything, but some things—some deals, some bargains—have power even over a witch. All I can do is ask that you help me, even if you don't know the full picture. I promise to keep you as safe as I possibly can. And I'm—"

Letizia stopped as her phone began to ring again. Rolling her eyes, she turned it off completely, but this time Jude recognized the music. Mozart's Requiem in D Minor; the eerie strains of 'Lacrimosa' echoed across his memory. The last time he'd heard it, he'd been a teenager at a particularly somber mass. A funeral? Probably a funeral. Who chose that mournful ode to exquisite pain for their custom ringtone? Despite being both a vampire and a witch, Letizia had never struck him as being quite that... goth, as Pixie would helpfully say, under happier circumstances.

"Ignore that," Letizia said with a fangy sneer. "I certainly wish I could."

"Well, you know I'd help you however I could, but none of us are witches," Eva cut in, throwing a suspicious glance at Letizia's phone, but not pressing further. She half-turned toward Jasper. "Even you, unless you've gotten in a lot deeper than you've ever told me."

"I'm afraid not," he said, with a noticeably strained-sounding laugh. "And I do hope that won't be a problem, Letizia?"

"No, not at all," Letizia said, sounding genuinely relieved that they were even considering it. "The magic is all mine; I only need your help in the preparation. The apex is in two days, and I won't be ready for at least one.

Actually, I doubt I'll ever be truly ready. This is… bigger than I am. It's circles upon circles. History repeating itself. A circle of bones. A circle of friends. Siphoning the magic away before Wicked Gold can take it."

Jude suddenly didn't quite feel entirely present.

His head spun as he tried to decide whether all this was real or a very real-seeming dream. There was something about those words. A center of power, secret and vital and sacred.

The feeling of vibration was back, but instead of a gong this felt like a bell, high and clear, a signal of importance instead of warning.

Jude's entire brain felt filled with the sound of crashing waves, and he could almost smell the wet, salt-tinged scent of the sea.

But he didn't know how to say any of this, didn't know what it meant or why, so he blinked hard and rubbed at his eyes until he felt grounded again. There was enough strangeness afoot without his own brain getting in on the action.

"That all sounds extremely dangerous. Seems a lot to ask of us non-witches," Jude said instead. He gave Pixie another glance and found him just as blank-faced as before. With an uncomfortable pang of worry, Jude realized that ever since she'd mentioned Wicked Gold, he'd hardly said a word. "Risking our lives for some unknown quantity."

"You won't be risking your lives," Letizia said quickly. "You should never have to be near the place. And no fighting necessary, I hope. Do you remember the caves under the mall, where we fought Cruce? That's where I need to cast my spell. That place holds enough power still that if I can tap into it, I won't need to touch the center itself." She hesitated, looking embarrassed. "But I do need your help. I know that I haven't given you many details to work with, so the real question is, do you trust me?"

"I do," Eva said immediately.

"I'm with you," Jasper said as well. Jude noticed that it wasn't a direct answer to the question, but Jasper's presence alone said more than he generally did in words.

When Jude didn't answer right away, Eva gave him an expectant, eyebrow-raised look. Sea birds called out faintly in his head, though the room remained still and silent.

"Fine," he said, after a glance at Pixie, who nodded. He was still silent, which was enough to make Jude worry, but also enough to convince him this was the right decision. Anything that struck a blow against one of Pixie's nightmares was good enough for him.

"Thank you," the Witch said, clearly relieved and maybe a little surprised. "I have some preparation to do in advance, and I may need help in procuring certain ingredients—nothing illegal, and nothing dangerous," she promised before Jude could object. "If all goes well, the spell should be ready soon, and even if all doesn't go well, it must be activated two nights from now. Midnight, exactly."

"What exactly do you need?" Jude asked cautiously.

"*Earth, gathered at high noon,*" Letizia said, voice dropping and sounding suddenly faraway, as if she were reciting a memorized poem, half-asleep. "*Drenched with unbleeding blood spilled at midnight.*"

The witch then turned to Jude and looked him directly in the eyes for the first time, and he felt something like an electric shock. Usually hidden behind her dark glasses, Letizia's eyes were dark, almost black, and Jude had the sudden feeling that she saw much more of him than he did of her.

His stomach turned over and he wavered on his feet, feeling like he was caught in an overpowering ocean wave. Eyes like that. He'd seen eyes like that before, striking and mystifying and unforgettable. He'd never seen the ocean in person, but he had seen it—and when he'd stood on the rocky shore, he hadn't been alone.

"*From you, the hope of a dream seen with eyes wide open.*"

Something about that made Jude shudder. The only 'dream' in his head was the one he felt caught in right now, the things he'd seen when his heart had stopped beating. Had his eyes been open then? Was that such a thing to hope for?

Letizia released Jude from the hold of her stare and, as he reeled, turned to Pixie. She fixed her gaze on him with the same fiery intensity, and continued.

"*From you, a dream of rose-tinted happiness.*"

Then, to Jasper, who met her eyes calmly, as if he'd expected something like this.

"*A sign of a promise kept, a symbol of intention, everlasting and yet reborn.*"

Letizia stopped turning, blinked a few times, and her face became pensive, attention shifting inward instead of out at them. "And from myself... the sign of a promise broken, promised to be mended."

"Nothing for me to do?" Eva asked in a level voice that sounded like it was fighting valiantly to remain so.

"You're doing something right now," Letizia said.

"Okay," Eva acquiesced, but she obviously wasn't completely satisfied. "So then can you give us some... specifics on any of that? Any clues at all?"

Letizia shook her head. "Only that the spell must be performed at midnight, exactly. We have a very small window of success. But other than that, no. There aren't any real rules for this, no matter what you may think. Just do your best to find objects that may work and bring them to me—I'll know if they're right."

"That first one," Jude said, finding his voice surprisingly raspy; his throat had closed a bit with anxiety or whatever it was he'd been overwhelmed with. Recognition? He cleared his throat and tried again. "The thing about earth at noon and midnight and unbleeding blood..."

"Unbleeding blood spilled seems like a cryptic way to say 'a vampire slain,'" Jasper said thoughtfully.

"You're correct," Letizia nodded. "If there's anything vampires like, it's drama—self included. Cruce was indeed slain at midnight."

"And I know where," Jude said, softly, without quite deciding on the words, or to speak them. "I've seen it. I've been there before."

He was suddenly extremely aware of everyone's eyes on him. Again, one pair in particular. "Where have you been?" Letizia asked, just as quietly. It sounded like she may already know the answer.

"This center of power. The place all of this is happening—it's a stone circle, isn't it?" Jude asked, though there was no doubt in his mind. "Huge stones—more like crystals. Black crystals, pointing up at the sky. When I was there... when I saw it, it was by the ocean. But it's not there anymore, is it?"

"Not an ocean... a sea," the Witch said. "And no, it's much closer nearby now. When were you there?"

"It was a dream," he said, brow furrowing as his head began to ache. The ground felt uneven now, like sand shifting under his feet. "Five—over five years ago. The night that..." he patted his thigh with one hand, the leg that ended in a prosthetic. "This happened. And Felix. That night. When I... when I died."

"And when you saw the circle," Letizia continued, words slow and careful, staring at him unblinking once more. "Were you alone?"

"No," Jude said without question. "There was someone there. In the water—but it looked like they'd been burned. I tried to help them. They asked me..." His voice cracked; suddenly his throat felt uncomfortably dry. He licked his lips, but it didn't help much. "They asked me 'is he all right?' I didn't know what that meant. I still don't. But that dream—I remember it like it just happened. Like it's still happening now. It just feels important, that's all."

He looked down at his arms, unsurprised to see every hair standing on end in response to the wave of shivers that had swept through him from the first spark of recognition. He could imagine the concern on Jasper and Eva's face; they'd heard all this before, hadn't known what to say then, and probably wouldn't now. Pixie, he hadn't told yet. But Pixie seemed to have his own problems at the moment, and Jude could only hope his own hadn't made them worse.

"And that is why you are the one to bring me the earth from the circle.

You were there. You saw it. That was no dream. You were in exactly the right place, at the right time—as you are now." Letizia said firmly, as if trying to impress every word into Jude's heart. But then her shoulders sagged, like she was weighed down by crushing fatigue. "And that is all I have today. That is all I can tell you, or do until I have your gifts to work with."

"Well, guess I'll help Jude grab the dirt," Eva said, and the lightness after the tense exchange only sounded slightly forced. "Because I really doubt it's as simple as it sounds."

Letizia actually smiled. "Magic rarely is."

The quiet was almost comfortable, at least between the two of them. Jude still felt half-dreaming, half-awake, and Pixie remained silent and much too still. Jude wondered if he was hearing any of this at all. Then Letiza's phone rang again.

"Wasn't that turned off?" Jude asked, puzzled.

"Yes."

"If it's broken, can't you just magic it quiet?"

"It's not broken," Letizia said shortly. "It's working exactly as intended, and will continue to, as long as the man on the other end wants to get ahold of me. But I can do this."

Letizia set the ringing phone down on the shards of glass and fixed it with a deadly glare, which she then covered with her usual dark sunglasses. Smoke barely had time to rise before the entire thing caught fire.

"Did that break the spell?" Eva asked, holding her nose against the stink of melting plastic.

"No," Letizia said, flames reflected in her shades. "But it makes me feel better. One last thing!" She held out one hand and swept it before her, like she was wiping a window clear, or spreading something over all of them. "Now you'll be able to find the stone circle. Do not bring anyone not in this room, or speak of it to anyone else. Now go. I have too much to do, and not enough time to do it in."

"I'd say that was weird, but it's really not for us anymore, is it?" Jude said as the apartment door closed behind him and Pixie.

Jasper and Eva, bless both of them, had said good night without asking either of them any uncomfortable questions, although they both had a definite air of sympathy. They hadn't missed Pixie's odd state either, and they got the same look whenever Jude talked about his dream. He never knew what to do with that look, and was always glad when the moment passed and they could go back to pretending it hadn't happened. Now, however, there was no way to pretend he hadn't seen Pixie's reaction, or that it didn't worry him.

"Mmm-hmm." Pixie said in noncommittal reply. With his ears, Jude could be sure Pixie had technically heard him, but whether he'd understood the words was another question.

"I don't like it."

"Mm-hmm."

"And I don't think you do either."

"I—what?" Pixie said then, giving his head a little shake and turning to face Jude, looking sheepish. It seemed as if he hadn't absorbed a thing Jude had said. Maybe he hadn't truly heard a thing Letizia or anyone else had said either, after whatever had affected him so much a few minutes ago. "Oh. No, I... really don't."

"Pixie, what happened in there? What's wrong?" Jude asked, unable to keep the concern out of his words

Pixie hesitated, and that was all the confirmation Jude needed. He hadn't been imagining things; Pixie hadn't said one word almost the entire time they'd been in Letizia's apartment, obviously shaken, and now he seemed to crumple further. His eyes were wide and frightened, and Jude shifted a bit closer. He didn't reach out for Pixie's hand, however, having the uncomfortable and too-familiar feeling that even the gentlest touch would do nothing but startle him right now.

"Talk to me. Please?" Jude asked, not at all liking the look on Pixie's face or the shake in his voice.

"Wicked Gold is... my sire," Pixie said, and now more than his voice was shaking. Now Jude did reach out to put a hand on his arm, and Pixie didn't turn, but leaned into the touch. "He's the one who turned me. He's bad—very, very bad. And he's involved in this? We're going to fight him?"

"No," Jude said immediately. "You don't have to. I won't let him hurt you—I won't let him get near you at all."

"Don't make promises you can't keep," Pixie said, looking haunted. "And nobody can keep that one. I... I can't do this. I can't be near him. I can't see him. I—I see him too much already."

"In nightmares?"

"Yeah." Pixie said. He opened his mouth, then shut it, as if he'd been about to say something and then thought better of it.

"Not just in nightmares?" Jude pressed, voice dropping.

"I... I saw him do it," Pixie said, his own voice falling until it was close to a whisper. "Kill Cruce. I saw it happen. It wasn't a dream, it can't have been a dream, because it came true. I mean, a lot of my nightmares have come true, but this—this was different. He's close, I know he's close, and that means he'll come after me. And if he gets whatever power's in that stone circle, he'll be even more dangerous than he already is. He's already ruined enough lives! And not even just him, this place eats everything up, even without magic. It makes people disappear. With nothing left behind, especially not answers!"

"Why didn't you tell me?" Jude asked as gently as possible. "If this Wicked Gold bastard is still in your head, he's still hurting you. That's not okay. You can't keep on like this—we can't keep on like this."

"I know!" Pixie groaned. "But I was hoping I was wrong. I was hoping he'd just stay gone, and we'd never have to worry about him again, and I didn't want you involved in this if he did come back. It'd just be dangerous and... full of stuff you probably don't want in your head."

Jude was painfully aware that Pixie had largely left the pain he'd suffered at Cruce's—and Wicked Gold's—hands up to imagination, and he didn't like anything he imagined at all. "You don't have to tell me anything he did to you, not until you're ready, if you ever are. Just promise me you won't wait the next time you feel him near. I don't care if it's 'just' a nightmare, if he's here and scaring you, I want to know."

Pixie didn't answer for a while. When he did, it was just above a mumble, eyes on the floor. "I'm sorry."

"For what?" Jude asked, completely lost. "You haven't done anything to apologize for."

"Just all of this," Pixie said with a listless shrug. "I come with a lot of baggage. I just hope that it's not more trouble than it's worth."

"Hey," Jude said, putting himself directly in front of Pixie. He didn't make Pixie look up, but he was happy when he did anyway. The words he said next were unexpectedly easy, automatic in a way that surprised himself, and entirely truthful. "You're worth it. You're worth all of this. More."

"Thanks," Pixie said, and now he really was whispering. "I mean it."

"So do I," Jude assured him. "You probably figured out that I'm pretty serious about most things."

"Naw," Pixie said, and now he smiled a little. Good. "Serious? You?"

"That means I'm serious about you. I wouldn't be here if I wasn't sure."

"Really? You mean that?" Pixie's eyes were bright and hopeful again.

"I do," Jude said without hesitation or a shadow of doubt. "I want you here more than anything."

Pixie smiled, and though he didn't answer, he did seem to be watching Jude in an expectant, happily anticipatory kind of way, leaning just a little bit closer and turning his face up. Waiting.

For once, Jude knew exactly what he was expecting. Everything about Pixie—from his excited eyes and sweet, chubby cheeks to the tips of the toenails Jude knew to be painted pink to match his hair—seemed made for affection, or at least begging for it. Like he knew exactly how cute and irresistible he was, and was just waiting for Jude to catch up.

But Jude couldn't bring himself to make that move, kiss that boy, or do anything but stand there paralyzed by indecision and fear of making everything worse.

"So do you have any idea what you're going to find for the spell?" he asked, after both moments—first charged, then slightly awkward—had passed, mind drifting back to the other problem at hand. It probably wasn't a good sign when a mysterious magic ritual seemed less insurmountable than overcoming potential romantic disaster.

"...I have an idea. But I'm hoping to think of another one." Now Pixie looked pained as well as a little disappointed, and Jude didn't ask any follow-up questions. He'd dragged enough painful admissions out of Pixie for one night. Instead, he headed for the fridge to grab the bottle of blood-infused sauce he could tell Pixie needed but, like the rest of what was bothering him, wasn't mentioning.

He couldn't kiss Pixie when he was sad, because that might make things worse. He couldn't kiss Pixie when he was happy, because it might be the wrong thing, and then Pixie might be sad. He couldn't even kiss Pixie when it was obvious—or would be to anyone else—that this was exactly what Pixie wanted. Was there anything useful Jude could do at all?

He could supply blood sauce. And he could find dirt. Maybe eventually he'd stop feeling like it, too.

ACT THREE: MisSing You/Touching me

"ARE YOU SURE we're heading in the right direction?" Jude asked, turning in a full circle and looking up at the bare, stark branches above them. "I feel like we've passed that tree before."

"Not completely sure, no," Eva said as the two of them made their way down the isolated foot path that cut through the park. Even in the middle of the day, and with most of the leaves down, it was overcast enough to make it oddly dark. "But Letizia said we should be able to find the place now. It's gotta be around here somewhere."

"It's almost noon," Jude grumbled, anxiety increasing. "What if we don't find it in time today? Do we have to come back tomorrow? Does it absolutely have to be noon dirt?"

"Listen, I know what you know, and that's not very f—freaking much." Eva caught herself just in time. She'd been trying to cut down on the swearing, she'd told him, which had gotten a lot more frequent thanks to recent undead events, and she wanted to avoid slipping where there might be consequences. Now she had her corporate-patience voice on, the one she used to deal with disgruntled mall patrons, or Jude when he was dancing on her last nerve. Jude had just resolved to keep his mouth shut when her face brightened and she batted at his arm.

"Wait," she said. "Look."

As they rounded a bend in the path that looked just like so many others, the object of their search came into view all at once, like the circle had just sprung into life from thin air. Suddenly he felt very small.

Jude leaned his head back to look up at the sky and the sharp obsidian spires like black dragon's teeth that bordered his vision. He shivered again. He'd been here before. This circle was burned into his brain, tangible as if he could touch it—and now, tentatively, he did reach out to touch the nearest black crystal spike. It was strangely warm, despite the overcast day, and he could swear it was softly vibrating.

He sucked in a breath, overwhelmed with the place, the recognition almost like a physical impact hitting him dead in the chest. He'd been plunged into the *presence* of it all, memory enveloping him like the surface of water closing over his head.

There was a definite charge in the air, like the moment before a storm—or a fire. He'd grown accustomed to the feeling in his old life, his old job—calling, more like. Once their lives' mission had been to drive directly toward fires and run inside when anyone sensible would be fleeing the opposite direction. Before every job, there was a charge like this between them, rising adrenaline, shared anticipation, fear and excitement and resolve all at once. Had something like that happened here? Was there a night like the one five years ago that would be forever seared into someone's mind, caught and preserved here at the stones like a fly in amber, or clinging to the area like a ghost?

Shaking the morbid thoughts away, Jude made himself focus on the here and now, focus on physical details to ground himself. Count the spires—one, two, three, four…

Someone had stuck some pieces of paper to the stones, duct taped to the smooth surfaces that would probably repel thumbtacks or even nails. Posters, torn and faded by the weather and time. Some of them looked like they might be for missing people, but Jude couldn't make out more than the vague shapes of photos and letters too worn to read.

Strange—hadn't Letizia said this place couldn't just be stumbled upon by random non-magical people? You had to know where it was, and presumably, what it was. Apparently they weren't the only ones, not by far.

"Looks like there was one hell of a party here," Eva said, nodding to the middle of the stones.

There stood a small tower of wood, still smoldering from what had undoubtedly been a bonfire. Beside it, a pile of three-quarters burnt clothes lay on the ground, corroded with a foul black liquid that looked like it had somehow frozen until it was almost as hard as the stones around them. The mess was half-sunk into the ground, melted and re-formed, as if the whole thing had been doused in acid.

"All that's left of Cruce, I guess," Jude said. "Good riddance."

"I don't like this," Eva muttered back. "Bad sh—stuff's gone down here, and is probably gonna go down again. Let's just grab the dirt and get out of—"

"Hey!" a voice shouted from the other side of the circle, and then someone was barreling toward them. Someone they had both seen before, quite recently, but not pleasantly.

"Oh, it's you," Jude said as the young man with the torn clothes and filthy red hair approached. Apparently they were just letting anyone find secret circles these days. "Run out of mall-goers to harass?"

"I wasn't harassing anyone," the scruffy punk retorted. Sighing inwardly, Jude reminded himself of what Milo had said—that this guy was loud but not dangerous, and actually in more danger than the rest of them, somehow. Still, that didn't make dealing with him any more pleasant. "Or stalking, or whatever else anybody's been saying about me."

"I don't know what they've been saying about you," Jude said, as calmly as possible. "Because I don't know who you are. What are you doing here?"

"None of your business!" he shot back, and Jude barely suppressed an eyeroll. All of this was starting to feel like an almost impressively huge waste of time.

But while the noisy stranger was focused on Jude with remarkable single-mindedness, Eva had slipped to one side with the trowel and glass jar, hiding behind the nearest stone spire. *Good,* Jude thought. He'd distract the 'guardian' of the circle, and she'd get what they came for. They'd always been good at staying on the same page.

"A better question is, what the hell are *you* doing here?" said guardian demanded.

"I… I was…"

Jude stopped whatever unconvincing thing he'd been about to say. Now he realized what was bothering him, besides the obvious. It was what Eva had told him just before the night his life had changed forever. That weird evening had started as a weird morning—some punk fitting this description had thrown a balled-up burger wrapper at Eva's face, apparently out of nowhere, and set off a chain of events that led to somebody else—somebody cute and fangy—crashing through his window. The rest was history.

He folded his arms and glared, nonspecific annoyance narrowing to a focused point. "You threw garbage at my friend."

"Your friend was probably garbage. Now get out of my circle." The young man glared, but still didn't manage to look threatening. He just looked like hell, filthy and starving. But, although his eyes were glassy and sunken, they were steady and clear.

"Your circle?" Jude repeated incredulously.

"That's what I said." He didn't look nearly as convinced as he was clearly attempting to sound. "These rocks are mine, and you're trespassing!"

"What's your name?" Jude blurted as Eva crept into the middle of the stone circle, and their opponent seemed about to turn just enough to catch her in the corner of his eye. The question made him turn back to Jude, who let out a furtive sigh of relief.

"Sangui—fuck you. My name's *fuck you,* and get away from me. And my rocks." He eyed Jude suspiciously, but still made no effort to move away.

"Sang-wi…" Jude rolled the syllables over his tongue.

The sounds were unusual for English, but still familiar in the same way his own name was, but from even further back. Latin was a relic from a time that sometimes seemed like someone else's life, but one that he'd still never forget. He knew this name, the way he'd known every terrifying thing the name 'Cruce' implied. Words like these were as automatic as his hand tracing the sign of the cross, ingrained, forever written on his brain the way the accompanying images forever marked the insides of his eyelids.

"Sanguine?"

It was an educated guess, and by the way the young man's eyes—bright blue with whites standing out all around—flicked up to his face and locked on his own, Jude was sure he'd guessed right. He didn't answer, but he didn't run away either.

"That's an interesting name." Jude said, taking in the knotted mess of red hair, filthy jeans, and grimy shirt with torn sleeves that wouldn't be nearly enough as the temperature dropped after sundown. "You don't hear Latin much anymore."

Sanguine didn't answer, and he didn't move. It was like he'd been frozen in place, as completely as if Jude had pulled a gun on him. Like he couldn't move even if he wanted to. The name certainly conjured up images of holiness and unholy creatures. The vampires they'd encountered so far did seem to like that aesthetic.

"Did you pick that name for yourself?" Jude asked, realizing there could be another explanation, just as familiar but far less ominous. "I, uh… I kind of know something about that. I'm Jude."

"I know," Sanguine said. Behind him, Eva had crouched down, carefully unscrewed the top of the jar, and now drove her trowel into the dirt as silently as possible.

"Really?" Jude blinked. He'd started out as just trying to distract Sanguine while Eva absconded with their treasure, but now he was genuinely curious. "How?"

"I—*I like the mall*, okay? And you're at the mall. So why is that weird, why shouldn't I know your—what?!" Sanguine yelped, jerking back out of arm's reach as Jude raised a hand. It looked very much like he expected to be struck.

"You're bleeding," Jude said quietly, pointing but not touching; Sanguine shrank back anyway, slapping one hand to his neck where a thin trickle of blood ran down from below his jutting jaw. If alarm bells hadn't been going off in Jude's head before—which they had, always—they especially were now, loud and clear and extremely urgent.

"This? This is nothing, this is fine—and once again, fuck you." Sanguine's tone was still caustic and biting, but his eyes were scared. Jude realized they'd really never been anything but.

As Sanguine reached up to his bloody neck, his filthy sleeve had slipped enough to expose his wrist and underside of his forearm, which was peppered with puncture wound scars, and some much too recent to have scarred over yet at all. Letting out a faint, strangled noise, he pulled his hand away from his neck—his fingers now slick with red—and yanked his sleeve back down, hiding the injuries from view.

"Are those fine too?" Jude asked with growing actual concern. Tension tightened his stomach, mixed anxiety and excitement. Certainty. This was confirmation. Not a good confirmation, exactly, but it was always better to know what he was dealing with. When had vampires become a preferable enemy to unknowns?

"I—it's—" Sanguine stammered, going paler, even under the layer of dirt on his face. He backed up one shaky step, then another.

Behind him, Eva must have collected as much dirt as she thought they needed, because she quietly got up and hustled to the edge of the circles again, slipping behind another stone. That was it, they were done, they could go—except no, Jude realized. No, they couldn't.

"Listen," Jude said urgently, and Sanguine's eyes fixed on him. "Listen to me. I know what I'm looking at. I know what you've been through—"

"No, you really don't!" Sanguine hissed, and now there was an edge of desperation in his voice. "You can actually run, so *run!* Do you know how lucky you are to have that chance? Not everybody has it!"

Sanguine was panting like he'd just sprinted an uncomfortable distance. Whatever color had once been in his thin cheeks disappeared. But he still wasn't bolting, so Jude tried one more time.

"If you're in some kind of trouble, you can—"

"Ha!" Sanguine scoffed, a harsh bark that sounded like it hurt his already raspy throat. It seemed to jar him back into motion, dissipating whatever strange spell had fallen over him to root him to the ground and shake him into silence. "I can *talk* to you, is that what you were gonna say? You want me to tell you all my worries? Cause cops are our friends, right, even fake cops? Fuck you."

"I'm not a—never mind." It didn't matter how much he'd hated his job, or that he'd just quit, he'd still worn the uniform and that spoke for itself. Especially to scared, obviously-homeless and abused young people who had every reason to fear anyone who wore one.

"Right, that's why I said *fake* cop," Sanguine said with a curl of his chapped lips, but his nervous eyes darted away, obviously looking for escape routes. "Now stay away from me, and stay away from this place," he said at last, but his voice held none of its previous fire, and none of its strength. Jude wasn't sure if he sounded more scared or tired. "I'm warning you. I don't want you to get—just fucking stay away. It's better that way. For everyone."

"Not for you. I know you're dealing with vampires," Jude blurted again, handling his desperation by laying everything out on the table. No sense holding back now. Sanguine was watching him carefully again, with no hostility or scorn. There was, however, light in his eyes that just barely began to resemble fragile, tentative hope. "I know you're under one's control, or something like it. I know a few, good and bad, and we helped some friends of mine escape that life. They're safe now. I think we can help you too."

"No," Sanguine said, but Jude hadn't missed his hesitation. He slowly shook his head as he stepped backwards. "No, you have no idea wh—*aaaagh!*"

Sanguine lurched backwards, scream ringing through the quiet clearing.

Eva had almost, *almost* made it silently back to Jude, but then come out from around exactly the wrong stone. Before she or Jude could react, Sanguine collided with her, jumping as if electrified, windmilling and obviously about to fall over completely.

"Gotcha," she said as she caught him with one arm, using the other one to fling the jar full of precious dirt at Jude, who just barely managed to catch it instead of letting it crash to the ground and render this entire exercise pointless.

"*Get off me!*" Sanguine snarled, immediately pulling away from her and putting his forearms between the two of them and his head, giving Jude an even better view of the unmistakable bite marks.

"You're welcome," Eva grumbled, backing off and sticking her hands in her pockets. "And Jude's telling the truth, you know. Fake cop or not, he really does want to help you… for some reason. So I guess I do too."

Sanguine stared at them, unblinking, for a few seconds. He held so still Jude wasn't sure if he was breathing. Jude watched that same light—an openness that made him look painfully young—linger in his eyes. Then, devastatingly quickly, he watched it disappear.

"You can't," Sanguine whispered.

Even as all traces of hope faded from his face, his lips curled up in a smile much different from his usual sneer. It was the kind of smiling mask you wore when you laughed to keep from crying, with eyes that had looked into the future and seen no way out, no hope left in the whole world, and nothing left to smile about at all. Brittle. Hollow. Jude thought of Milo's practiced retail smile, and Eva's patient corporate voice. He also thought it might be the saddest thing he'd ever seen.

"Believe me… there is *nothing* you can do."

This time, when he turned, Jude said nothing to stop him. Neither did Eva. Sanguine took one step, then another, and soon he was running like he was being chased by the hounds of Hell, or some other horror Jude had *known* existed, but had been so unprepared to see with his own eyes. Soon he was gone, but the blood and grievous scars on Sanguine's arm stayed horribly clear in his head the way Latin words forever lived on his tongue.

"Well, that was fun," Eva groused, once they were alone again. "At least I got the dirt. You're welcome."

"Did you see his arms? And neck?" Jude asked, still watching the trees into which Sanguine had disappeared.

"What? No, I was paying more attention to what we came here for," Eva said, still sounding cranky and flustered. "What was it, track marks?"

"Why, would that make it any better?" Jude said, unintentionally bitterly, but standing by his tone after the words were out. "Would he deserve our help less if they were?"

"No, but it'd be an explanation," she said evenly, looking him directly in the eye. "And I can't believe I'm saying this, but I like it better than the alternative, because addiction is at least a known evil, not... what we're dealing with every night, with no instruction manual. So what do you think it was?"

Jude hesitated, then spoke quietly. "Looked like bites."

Eva's eyebrows crept up toward her hairline. "Like *bite*-bites, or...?"

Jude thought for another second. Everything had happened so fast, maybe he had been mistaken. Maybe the scars and blood had a purely mundane reason. Occam's Razor said it was vampires, but really, nothing the kid had said or done couldn't be explained by simple desperation and late-stage Capitalism.

"I don't know," he said at last, thoughts still somewhere other than the stone circle. He just didn't know where—where could anyone living on the streets or under a vampire's thumb go? Did such a safe place exist? "I'd need a better look."

"I doubt he'll give you much of a chance. I know it's hard to accept, but you can't help someone who doesn't want it. Might as well try to let it go," Eva said, turning to leave, then stopping, letting out a short exclamation of surprise. "Hey! Look at this!"

"What?" Jude asked, shaking himself all the way out of his reverie and looking over to see her carefully peeling one of the pieces of paper off the stones.

"Look. Have you seen this boy?" she held out the flyer, and Jude could see now that it was a missing poster, this one with the picture and name legible.

He had indeed seen the boy in the picture, though now with the addition of gray skin, even pointier ears, and just-as-pointed teeth. Still, there was no mistaking the hair, or the happy, round-cheeked smile and laugh he could practically hear in his head. There was a phone number at the bottom, and in thick block letters: *CALL NATALIE.*

Jude took the paper from her as his head spun. He recognized the name, and he would recognize the boy in the picture anywhere, but seeing him like this was wrong, surreal. Once again, he felt as if all this was a particularly stressful dream.

"It's Pixie."

🔥

With the afternoon turning into evening and their work together done, Jude and Eva went their separate ways to continue the work apart. Sunset Towers might not be the fanciest place around, but it was a warm, bright place to escape everything that came with nightfall.

Eva was also grateful for Letizia's door opening automatically at her approach, already exhausted as she stepped over the threshold with the jar of dirt that had been so troublesome to obtain.

Inside, Letizia didn't look up, seeming completely absorbed in preparing for her spell. That preparation apparently involved reading passages from very old books then double- and triple-checking them against her own nearly-illegibly scrawled notes. Eva sank down onto a chair, set the jar on the floor, and took the opportunity to relax. Everything would start back up soon enough.

Nails and Maestra had emerged from their room, but it didn't look like they were helping much. Both girls seemed a lot more interested in looking all around Letizia's apartment, marveling over couches and the microwave that had probably never been used.

"Put those back," Letizia said finally, tearing her eyes away from the latest book and looking over at the girls, who were still busily poking through the apartment. Nails had found a shiny crystal pendulum on a gold chain, and Maestra held a brightly painted Venetian mask in front of her face. "A pair of magpies, the both of you."

"Sorry," Maestra said, returning the mask carefully to its place. "It's just that everything feels new, you know? Like I know we live here, but everything's clearer now, even normal stuff just feels so exciting!"

"That's it, exactly," Nails agreed. "It's like everything else was some kind of hazy dream-type thing, and now we're awake, and I swear colors look brighter, and stuff tastes better, everything's amazing and I can't stop messing with everything! I'm not even sorry, it's just too cool!"

"Yes, that'll last for a while most likely," Letizia said, not bothering to hide her smile anymore. "The thrill of being freed from a bad sire really is like a fog lifting. The world is new, and I don't blame you for falling in love with it. Just perhaps do that elsewhere."

"Kinda sounds like you're trying to get rid of us," Nails muttered, but didn't look bothered at the thought.

"I am trying to keep you at a safe distance while I work powerful magic, yes," Letizia confirmed. "And you need to rest. You going and having a lovely evening works out nicely for all of us."

"Okay," Maestra said, though she didn't look entirely convinced. "But we're here if you need us."

"I know. But right now, all you two need to worry about is getting reacquainted with your wild, enchanting, real lives. Remember who you are and what you want, and the things you've forgotten will come back in time. If they don't, consider them better off lost."

"You're really not gonna tell us what the spell you're casting is for?" Nails didn't bother to hide her disappointed frown. "We're not kids, you know, I know we're gonna look seventeen forever, but we're old enough to yell at whippersnappers to get off our lawns—"

"Go," Letizia said firmly, but without any real edge. She smiled a bit instead and the understated, wry expression made her look more like herself than Eva had yet seen today. "Explore, jog your memories—engage in some petty vandalism, or whatever kids are doing for fun these days. Just remember to document it! And don't go near the circle!"

"We weren't gonna," Nails said, and Eva didn't come close to believing her.

"I mean it," Letizia said. "That place is dangerous, and I know you'll want to see the place Cruce met his well-deserved end, but you have no business being there now. Go celebrate somewhere else."

The girls exchanged a look. One minute, they were looking at each other with growing smiles. The next, they were gone—and two bats flapped wildly away, disappearing in a flurry of wings.

"I'm never going to get used to that," she said, but Letizia didn't reply. When Eva looked over, she saw her friend absorbed in a new task—laying an empty mirror frame on the floor, as well as a pile of shining glass shards.

"Trying to undo seven years of bad luck?" Eva asked, moving to get a better look. She could swear that mirror hadn't been there a second ago.

"Try a hundred and fifty," Letizia answered, sounding distant, though the corner of her mouth curled up in a wry expression.

She started carefully picking up and placing the broken mirror shards into the frame, and somehow they fit together so well and closely that the cracks between them were barely visible. It was almost as if the mirror was fusing into one piece of glass as she filled in the pieces like a puzzle.

Letizia held something else in one hand, first close to her chest, then holding it up so she could look at it. Something about her face and the delicate way she balanced the object was reverent, like she was holding something sacred, a treasure beyond compare. Her lips moved rapidly, but Eva couldn't hear what she was saying, and doubted she was saying it to anyone in this room.

Eva took a cautious step closer until she could see better what it was the Witch held with so much awe. It didn't look like anything especially valuable to her; it was an oblong, straight shape, like a branch—or a bone. A small bone, maybe part of a finger, worn smooth over time and perhaps much more handling. As the strange realization hit home, Eva had another one; on the floor beside Letizia was a small pile of what could only be more bones, which, like the mirror, definitely hadn't been there before. Delicate bits like fingers, curved shapes like ribs, and a round-edged chunk that looked almost like…

"Can I ask what the bones are for?" Eva managed to keep her tone relatively conversational and free of anxiety—which didn't at all reflect how she was actually feeling. Was that part of a hip bone? A pelvis? It looked shattered, but the pieces might fit together like a puzzle, like the shards of shattered mirror. "Actually, I am asking. What are the bones for?"

"They'll help the mirror—closer to 'window' by the time I'm done—find what I seek," Letizia said, and she sounded more grounded and confident now. Maybe her presence really was helping in more ways than it seemed. "These pieces are… connected, to the stone circle, and the energy I need. A point of contact. I've been looking for them for a long time, and I've collected a lot. Except for their skull," she murmured, and it sounded more like an afterthought to herself than talking to Eva.

"Those are human bones, aren't they?" Eva asked, not sure she'd quite understood any of those words, at least not in that order.

Somehow, even being acquainted with vampires and witches, all that had seemed separate from actual death, true mortality. More brutal and realistic than a Halloween story, but not one that carried the weight of life and death. Jude had seen more of this, she thought, down in the caves under the mall, the viscerally frightening reality of their strange new world. Until now, Eva had been mostly spared.

"Yes," Letizia said, a little dreamily. "They'll act like a magnet. They and the stone circle share the same frequency; they still hold the imprint of the circle's magic. These pieces will be crucial when it comes to tapping into the circle and siphoning off the energy released. It'll stop the ritual from going as planned."

"Ritual…?" Eva said nervously, feeling a bit disoriented; the floor beneath her was no longer as steady as it had been, as solid.

"Wicked Gold is busy preparing for his own spell right now too. A race between us, I suppose, until the opportune time. The next full moon. And a sacrifice. Not yours, or anyone else's here," Letizia said quickly, but it still didn't do much to quell Eva's alarm. "And not mine."

"Then whose…?" Eva let the question hang, as if by leaving it unfinished she could somehow secure a less-terrifying answer.

"It's what he was trying to do with Cruce and failed. For several reasons, his timing only one of them," Letizia explained, blatantly sidestepping the question. She spoke matter-of-factly, like she was describing a rival employee's work habits. "He must not have had all the details before, but now, I have the feeling that he's going to take the opportunity to get rid of another of his enemies. Two birds, one stone, you know. And I'm more than happy to let *my* enemies destroy one another, which is why I'm not rushing to stop him from performing this ritual at all. But, failing that, he has no shortage of brainwashed humans at his disposal. Surely one of them will be willing."

"If he's controlling them, it doesn't sound like they have much of a choice." Eva suppressed a shiver.

"Maybe not, but that's the core of the spell. The sacrifice has to be willing, or else it means nothing. Coercion has no power here. The only power comes from consent and personal intention."

"'Wiling' sounds like an extremely relative term here," Eva said, voice hardening. "You don't need a magic spell to coerce someone into doing things they don't want. Someone sacrificing themself for this guy—even if they think they're doing it of their own free will, nah, no, it doesn't work that way."

"I've thought of that as well," Letizia said. "And I agree. The circle agrees—it would not accept anything but true, wholehearted consent."

"You know that for a fact?" Eva asked, suddenly feeling a bit lightheaded, and planting her feet more firmly on the floor to keep her brain from floating away entirely.

"I do," Letizia said quickly, then hesitated. "I know the witch who cast the initial spell to empower the stones. They would never have done otherwise."

"I still don't like this." Eva shook her head. "Even if he gets a totally willing sacrifice, that doesn't mean it's right."

"I know," Letizia said. "I've thought of that as well. And I don't know exactly how he's going to accomplish this. But that's not the biggest question, or the most important part of this. The real goal is the ritual itself, the magic. I want to save Wicked Gold's victims just as much as you do—maybe more, since I've seen so intimately what he's capable of. But I want to keep a very dangerous power out of his hands even more. It's a terrible thing, but there it is. Believe me, I would not be considering this if there were any other way."

"Does anybody else know about this?" Eva asked with a half-deadpan, half-searching look. "You definitely left this whole possibility-of-sacrifice thing out of the explanation earlier."

"No. I haven't told the others, not even Jasper. They're good people, but they can be a bit… sentimental, I think, when it comes to the harder things that must be done."

"I can't imagine them objecting to stopping an evil human sacrifice ritual," Eva pointed out. "If anything, they'd probably fight even harder to stop it and save the poor shmucks."

"That is exactly my concern," Letizia said, sounding thoughtful. "When, however awful, that isn't the bigger point. We may not be able to save everyone involved, but I still need to stop Wicked Gold's magic, and enact my own. Failing at that, even to save others, is unacceptable. Yes, I will if the chance arises, I promise. But the cost of failure here—of Wicked Gold obtaining the power he seeks—would be much too high. Which is why things like sentimentality have little place in a witch's hard decisions. You seem to understand the practical, even if it is… unpleasant. You seem to understand me." Letizia looked up at her, and now she just looked tired, and a little sad. "Which isn't always a good thing. For some things, you'd be better off far away."

"Hey," Eva said, trying to shake off her worries and slight queasiness, and project a braver front than she felt. Which wasn't that brave at all, but much more a strange combination of feeling honored and terrified. "I meant it when I said I was here for the long haul. I'm not dropping and bolting now just because it's getting real."

Letizia smiled at her, just a bit, and seemed about to say something else, but just then, another chime rang through the air—not the dreaded tones of her cell phone, but like the sound of a real tiny bell, though its source remained unseen.

"Ah," Letizia said, raising one hand into midair and mimed pinching something between her finger and thumb. "One moment, Eva."

She pulled her invisible cloth, and the air that followed in its wake shimmered, and then it was as if she'd pulled back a small curtain to reveal somebody from the chest up like a video call, just with no screen to go with it. Someone all in black, with long purple hair and artfully applied eyeliner. Eva stared at her young acquaintance with undisguised curiosity, and they gave her a friendly nod, the kind they gave her every morning when they passed by each other with coffee.

"Hello, little one," Letizia said with a genuinely fond-looking smile.

"Yes, I'm here," Milo said, looking a bit anxious, but earnest. "Do you need me to come over? I figured you may call on me to help, at some point. It's a major spell."

"Witches gotta stick together," Eva said, echoing the words that had started all this off. "I guess I shouldn't be surprised by now."

"I do kind of look the part," Milo said with a little smile.

"And you're just here because you want to help? That's all?" Eva watched as their eyes flicked momentarily down and away.

"Mostly," Milo admitted. "Although I'd be lying if I said I had no personal interest in making sure Letizia's spell is successful. But you don't have to do anything extra for me, and I won't cause any trouble. I just… needed to make sure everything goes off safely."

"If you won't take their word for it, take mine," Letizia said, giving Eva a steady look. "I'm glad they're here."

"Really, what can I do to help?" Milo asked, looking eager and anxious at the same time.

"Right now?" Letizia cast a glance back over the bones and mirror, pausing for a moment in which Eva could practically hear the gears turning in her head. "You can go find the girls."

"Oh," Milo said with a surprised-looking blink. "And bring them back to you?"

"No. Take them out to lunch. Or catching frogs, or riding skateboards indoors, or whatever your generation finds fun nowadays. I believe there was talk of some petty vandalism."

"Okay," Milo said, understanding dawning over their face. "The rumor mill said they were Cruce's thralls. If that's true, they must be feeling a bit—"

"Exactly," Letizia said with a quick nod. "They need someone to answer their questions, fill them in on things that may have fallen out of their heads, let them know they're not alone. Be their friend. I'd do it, but I'm afraid this ritual business has taken up all my attention." She sounded bitter about that, and now Milo's face showed understanding instead of confusion.

"I know what you mean," they said, nodding back. "And I'll do my best. Thank you for trusting me with them."

"Of course. I told them not to go to the stones, so that's where you'll find them. Be careful, and make sure they are too. That circle is going to be a very unstable place for the next few days."

"Yes it is," Milo said, and Eva wasn't sure if she'd imagined the look of worry that flashed across their face. "I'll make sure they stay safe." They hesitated, and now the anxiety on their face was undeniable. "But… you'll tell me, if you hear anything about…?"

"You have my word."

Letizia kept her steady gaze on the younger witch until Milo's image had faded, and the apartment was quiet.

"Anything about what?" Eva had to ask. "They seemed pretty shaken up about something."

Letizia sighed and rubbed her temples as if she had an oncoming headache. "Nothing that should pose a danger to you or any of our other friends. Believe me, you're happier not knowing. I would be too."

Although not remotely satisfied by that answer, Eva let the matter drop. For now. Between the bones, the sacrifice, and everything else going on right now, she had no trouble believing that there were some things she'd just rather not know.

🔥

"Is this the place?" Jude asked, trying and failing to keep the incredulity out of his voice. "It's… It kind of looks…"

"Like a total dump," Pixie supplied helpfully.

"You said it, not me."

"Oh, it totally is." Pixie gave the shabby-looking building a nod like the one you might give an old acquaintance after noticing them across the street. "Which isn't all that big a change, really. It was always a dump when we lived here before. I still think this is the place to find rose-tinted happiness, though. Just check the sign."

Jude eyed the faded, cracked walls and sunken-looking ceiling. Even in the dark, the nearby streetlights were enough to illuminate the shiny edges of broken windows, the weed-overgrown parking lot, and the water-stained, burnt-out sign reading *The Rose Dawn Motel.* He thought of his own apartment complex, the Sunset Towers, and wondered if the same person had named them, someone with a penchant for wistful titles but not much of a flair for architecture. In any case, he'd never felt more fortunate to live in his own mediocre but functional and clean building.

"And when you say 'we' lived here, you mean..."

"Me and Jeff," Pixie said, voice only a little tight, as he headed toward the steps leading up to the second-floor wraparound balcony. "This was the first real place we stayed that wasn't couch-hopping or crashing in an abandoned building. Which this wasn't back then, at least. It's—it was the first place that ever really felt like home. Never thought I'd miss it." He gave a short, unhappy chuckle that didn't sound like it should come from him. "Bet it didn't miss me."

"Someone misses you," Jude said, or more like blurted, as he followed Pixie.

He hadn't quite meant to say it, but from the way Pixie looked up at him in surprise, he was glad that he had. The accident might turn out to shake Pixie out of his reverie. Jude didn't like the look on Pixie's face, distant and sad and regretful. Maybe a little ashamed. It had no place on Pixie's face, and those awful, heavy feelings had no place in his heart.

"I found—actually Eva found something at the stone circle I wanted to tell you about," Jude said. "A missing person poster, with you on it. Your picture, and your name."

"What did it say, just 'Pixie?'" he asked after a hesitation Jude just barely caught. "Did it say who's looking?"

"The poster said 'Natalie,' and I remembered the name from when we talked to Milo. There was a phone number, but I haven't called it, I wanted to tell you and let you decide. I thought it might be a trap of some kind and didn't want to risk it."

"It—it did?" Pixie repeated, eyes widening as they locked onto Jude's.

"Yeah. Are you ready to tell me about her now?" Jude asked, realizing not for the first time that he really knew nothing about Pixie's old life. His first life, the one he'd actually been alive to live.

"Well, uh, you know I was in a band, right?" Pixie said after just a moment's hesitation, sounding a little faint, but the slightest smile pulled at the corner of his mouth.

"You'd mentioned it a couple times. Was she..." Jude trailed off, catching a glimpse of the stylized pink text on the black T-shirt Pixie wore under his hoodie, and the obvious pride with which Pixie wore it. He remembered Pixie's guitar and its sticker emblazoned with words in similar grungy font reading, somewhat ironically, THIS BASS KILLS FASCISTS. "Chaos Chainsaw?"

"Hell yeah!" Pixie grinned despite the atmosphere of tension and gloom. "Me and Natalie and Jeff. Her on the drums, Jeff on the bass, me on the guitar. Trying to break into the indie punk scene, playing underground shows—sometimes literally underground. Working on a demo. It was rough, but fun, and we were... happy. Until Jeff—until he was gone. Like he just vanished into thin air. Natalie and I made all these posters when he disappeared, stuck them up everywhere, but nobody ever called. Including him. So I guess she did the same thing for me, and I guess the same thing happened: nothing. I should really find her, let her know I'm okay at least. But some people I just can't... it's not like telling Milo about me. She doesn't know about vampires—I don't think. I'd probably just scare her. And I already feel bad, not telling her or anyone else I'm still here, but it's like, every day I stay gone, I feel worse about it, and that makes it harder to even think about talking to her again."

"She'd still probably like to know her friend's all right," Jude said, but noticed Pixie's hesitation. "She might be upset for a while, but I have to think she'd be a lot more relieved and happy in the long run. But it's obviously up to you. I can't make you tell anyone, but at least someone cared enough to put them up. Maybe she could even give you a new T-shirt," Jude suggested, only half-joking. "That one's falling apart."

"The rips are intentional. It's called distressed style, Jude." Pixie's little return-joke and half-smile were, like he'd been himself, short-lived. "So, anyway, we're here for rose-tinted happiness, right?"

"That's right," Jude said. "Though this seems like a strange place to find it."

Pixie stopped outside one of the motel room doors. Jude didn't see a number, and he noticed that the door was slightly ajar and hanging off its hinges, maybe from disrepair and rough weather, or being forced open and broken. Or maybe both. "Yeah, I know. But it used to be a pretty happy place, believe it or not. Now… now, not so much."

With that, Pixie pushed the door open easily and stepped inside, footsteps crunching as he stepped on broken glass from the nearby shattered window. Jude followed him, carefully stepping around the worst of the glass and debris—old leaves and some paper trash that had blown in from outside, along with some questionable stains. The room was mostly empty, even if standard motel tables and chairs had obviously once been here. There was a bed frame, but it had been stripped of everything, mattress included. Even if nobody had thought this particular room was worth crashing in, it had been thoroughly cleaned out. 'Clean' being a very relative term, Jude thought, eyeballing the most questionable stain yet.

"What are we looking for?" Jude asked grimly, with the unspoken implication that the sooner they found it, the sooner they could leave this awful place.

"This really old metal lunchbox we found with KISS on it. You know, the really old band?" Pixie said, stepping further inside the room and kicking some debris out of the way.

"Yes, I know who KISS is," Jude said, proud that he finally could say something like this with confidence and prove that, despite his name, he wasn't actually the patron saint of lost causes. KISS was—largely due to Jude's general dislike—one of the only band names he actually knew (besides the Beatles; as always, screw the Beatles), and he almost made some weak joke about Pixie, an ageless vampire making him feel old. "I don't see anything like that in here."

"Nah, you wouldn't! We had a secret hiding place. Let's see, if I'm remembering right—which I totally am, because there's no way I could forget—there was like a little secret compartment in the closet wall, like maybe one of those motel-room safe things used to be there, but there never was one when we were here," he said, heading over to the sliding doors and crouching down as he opened them. There were still hangers inside the closet, but the kind that were bolted to the bar. Pixie started to feel around inside, until he let out a triumphant "Aha! Yeah, here we go!"

As Jude watched, Pixie swiped away some dust, which looked more like an actual layer of grime, and pulled at a small hidden latch. He pulled and the inner closet wall came open, revealing a small, dark space into which Pixie reached with much more eagerness than Jude would have.

Pixie felt around inside and finally pulled something out: a metal lunchbox, color faded and starting to rust, but less dusty than Jude would have expected for being inside a wall for over two years.

"Look! Look, here it is!" Pixie practically squealed, sounding delighted, holding it up so Jude could see KISS themselves, faded and smeared with grime. Jude might as well have been looking at aliens, but they were aliens he felt an immediate fondness for, simply because they made Pixie smile like that.

He went to work at opening the lunchbox, whose lid seemed to stick a bit with age and maybe rust. Finally, the sticking point gave, and Pixie opened it eagerly. Jude knelt down to join him, peering into the lunchbox at—nothing. Only dust.

Pixie leaned back but didn't stand up, staring at the empty lunchbox with a perplexed, uncomprehending look on his face, as if there were no world in which it would make sense.

"Everything's gone," he said, sounding confused.

Jude waited, unsure what to say. Slowly, the confusion dropped off Pixie's face, replaced by—nothing, really. His face went blank. Which would have been strange enough for him and all his animated expressiveness, even without the oddly hollow look in his eyes. For the first time since Jude had known him, he looked almost... dead.

"I'm sorry," Jude said at last. He knew saying that meant nothing, it didn't help—but he didn't know what would. Helplessness was the most frustrating and strangely lonely feeling. There was nothing he could do, Pixie was dealing with too many sources of pain Jude couldn't reach or even understand, and all he felt for sure was that this raised a barrier between them, a distance he didn't know how to cross. In these moments, it was like they were in the same room, but miles apart.

"It's fine," Pixie mumbled, though it clearly wasn't. "I guess I should've known someone would find it. Nothing's really safe out here."

"What was inside?" Jude asked, peering into the small metal box as well, though it was unlikely Pixie would have missed something with his superior vampire night vision.

"It was kind of a time capsule type thing," Pixie mumbled, looking like he wanted to sink down to the floor and curl into a sad ball, but apparently this particular floor was too dirty even for him. "Jeff swore this thing had to be all vintage-collectible valuable, but we liked it too much to sell."

"It does look like it could be valuable," Jude said. "That's what's odd to me here. Why would someone find it, take the stuff inside, but leave the box?"

"I dunno," Pixie said with a shrug, staring at the empty closet and even emptier hiding spot, but not seeming to really see it. Jude's heart sank a little more with every passing moment.

"What was inside?" he asked again. Maybe if he could keep Pixie talking, he could keep him from sinking into somewhere too deep for Jude to reach.

"Flyers from our old Chaos Chainsaw shows. I think Jeff put his old harmonica in here too. And his favorite shirt, this dorky tie-die looking thing that said 'Always Summer' or 'Summer Forever' or something on it. I was gonna use that thing. Seemed perfect for the spell. I really thought this was going to be the thing that would help put Wicked Gold in his place."

He looked sadder than Jude could remember him seeing. Not scared, not anxious, just absolutely defeated and exhausted. Jude wondered how long he'd felt like this, with so much pain and weariness beneath his bright surface. Had Pixie ever not felt like this?

"Sometimes I think I'm never getting away from him."

Jude paused, not entirely sure they were on the same page, but wanting to keep up with wherever Pixie needed to go. "You're not talking about Wicked Gold, are you?"

"No," Pixie said quietly, almost a whisper. "Jeff. It always comes back to him, he's on my mind so much, and I'm sorry, I'm really sorry, that's not fair to you, but it does, I can't stop thinking about him."

"There's nothing wrong with that," Jude said, and meant it, even as he felt a little cold inside. "I know how it feels to lose someone and not be able to get them out of your head, no matter what you do."

Pixie almost smiled. "Figured you would."

"Tell me what's on your mind. If you want to."

"I do want to, it's just hard to think about, or get to make sense," Pixie said, and the confused look was back, the bafflement he'd had upon opening the lunchbox to find it empty. "But I keep going back to the night he disappeared, and—I knew he was dead a long time ago. He had to be, he'd never just shove off without at least saying goodbye. But nobody ever found a body and for a while I told myself that meant he might be alive, but not anymore. Now I'm starting to think, what if he didn't just die? What if he's out there somewhere—with fangs? Which isn't fun, sure, but he'd still be somewhere! And I can't think that, starting to hope like that is so dangerous. He's dead, I know he is. But there are a lot of ways to go, and… vampires, man. You saw what Cruce did to me, he was a fucking vicious monster." His eyes dropped to his hands, gray skin, white scars, small claws painted black. "But I guess, now so am I."

"No," Jude said forcefully. "No you're not. You might as well be from different planets. Cruce was a monster, but not you—and he's gone. He can't hurt anyone anymore, and we won't let his boss hurt anyone else either. Especially not you. He is never touching you again."

Pixie's smile looked weak and not at all convinced, but it was there. "I really hope you're right. Just… don't give up on me, okay?"

"Never," Jude said, more softly now. Had Pixie heard Felix say those words exactly? Did he know how Jude's heart had ached to hear them then, as it did now? "I know exactly how you feel. When I—when we lost Felix, it was like our entire world collapsed."

"Thanks, but… it's not exactly the same," Pixie said, smile dropping away and voice coming out dull. Dead. "You got your boy back. I didn't get mine back. And you had some answers even if they weren't the ones you wanted, you saw him die, I didn't even get that much. Just a whole lot of not knowing, and wondering, and no way to move on. We're not the same."

Jude felt like he'd been punched in the stomach. Something about that knocked every bit of wind out of him, and he stared at Pixie, mouth working but unable to make any sound come out at all. And he wasn't the only one in shock—Pixie's eyes widened, a hand going to his mouth, and a look of horror spreading across his face.

"I'm sorry," Pixie said in a shaken whisper. He stared at Jude as if he'd accidentally stabbed him, and would now do anything to take back the blade. "Jude, I'm so sorry, I didn't mean…"

Pixie cut himself off by stepping forward and reaching up to touch Jude's face, bringing him into a kiss Jude only had to lean down slightly to return, which he did without hesitation. Even here, in this desolate place full of memories he could feel like cold water, even if he couldn't guess at them, Pixie's kiss was a wonderful, welcome thing.

They hadn't done this for a long time, Jude thought as he leaned in and shut his eyes. He'd tried so hard to forget their first kiss, and the possibility of any others. But Pixie wouldn't let him, and by now Jude was sure it was on purpose—with his sweet face, his bright eyes and easy smile, his perfect, round belly, all of him made of soft curves, the only sharp thing about him his tiny little fangs. The way that, even now, he loved life in ways Jude could hardly imagine, so freely and with such unreserved joy. Pixie was so *alive* even without a heartbeat, more alive than Jude felt sometimes.

He'd chased these thoughts deliberately away, because every delight he took in Pixie's entire existence made him feel guilty. What right did Jude have, when Pixie himself was so sad and obviously hurting? Jude could never do something that would make his burden remotely worse.

But yes, oh yes, he thought, while he still remembered words, and anything else besides Pixie existed. This was what was missing, what *he'd* been missing sorely.

"Jude," Pixie said in a low, slightly throaty voice, pulling back just enough to let Jude catch his breath. Lucky vampires, he thought dizzily, they could kiss forever and not have to worry about little things like breathing. "Do you want me to touch you?"

"We are touching," Jude said, puzzled, eyebrows coming together. Pixie's hands were still cupping the sides of his face, slipping into his hair, and his own had slipped into place to mirror them automatically.

"No, Jude, no," Pixie said with a little laugh that sounded more sad than amused. Something close to a sob, but without the wet crack to it. Heavy with fatigue, as if Pixie didn't even have the energy to cry. "I've seen the way you've been looking at me lately. You want to get closer, but you're holding yourself back. You don't have to do that. I think… you're the one who wants to touch me."

Jude's brain ground to a halt. His mouth fell open, then closed, then open again; he felt like a hooked fish yanked up onto dry land, breathless and just as helpless. "Touch…?"

Pixie didn't answer in words. Instead, he took Jude's hands in both of his, and guided them to his round hips, placing one there, sliding the other down to his thigh. Jude's mouth fell open and his stomach jerked in surprise, and for just a moment, nothing existed except for the perfect, full heat that filled the palms of his hands and seemed to radiate through his entire body, a fluttering in his solar plexus.

He'd imagined this many times, what it would be like to touch Pixie like this, and other intimate places, feel his warm, fat, beautiful body move under Jude's hands, hearing him sigh and whine in a good way—but that had always seemed so abstract. So distant, an idea rather than something that could be true. Even when they'd kissed, even knowing that they had something between the two of them, and even wanting there to be nothing—space, clothing—between the two of them at all, Jude had never actually expected it to happen. There was just too much going on and too much healing to be done before he could even consider touching much of anything besides Pixie's fragile heart.

But here they were. Jude's head swam, and the warmth inside him grew until he couldn't feel the night's chill at all, his hands tightened their grip without his instruction, gently squeezing Pixie's wonderfully soft flesh and starting to move automatically, feeling, wanting to feel more, feel everything.

Then, feeling a thrill of both excitement and shock, Jude looked back up to Pixie's face, just to see, just to make sure—and found Pixie not looking back at him. He was staring at the ground again, eyes dull with the same unsettling blankness he'd had after seeing the empty box. Suddenly Jude felt just as hollow inside.

"No, wait," Jude said, yanking his hands back and taking an involuntary step away as reality crashed back onto him like a tidal wave that soaked him to the bone and doused any fire that had barely begun to spark. His heart pounded, and adrenaline surged through his veins with an almost-painful sting, but not for the reasons he'd anticipated when he'd imagined his hands on Pixie's skin. Not like this. This was all wrong. "Stop. Stop, what are you— what are we doing?"

"I'm sorry," Pixie stammered, pulling his own hands back like Jude was a hot stove, and he'd just now registered the burn.

Pixie's eyes were wide, pupils narrowed to slits, and although vampires didn't really sweat or turn pale or red the way humans did, his gray face looked waxy and drawn, somehow closer to death.

Along with everything else, that hit Jude hard. Pixie wasn't alive, not like he was, but even death hadn't been enough to free him from whatever terror coursed through him now.

"I thought—I was just trying to—I thought that's what you wanted!" Pixie stammered.

Jude's brain skipped again. Complete freeze, mind and body; static snow filling his head, he held perfectly still as if someone had hit 'pause' on the playback of his life. Still, he was sharply aware of everything around him, including the fact that he'd stopped breathing. He made himself breathe, then speak, finding both acts uncomfortably difficult.

"You thought I wanted that? Why would I—I mean, not that I don't—it's not—*why?*" His voice rose in both volume and pitch, and Jude tried frantically to get a grip on himself and his words. He was floundering as badly as Pixie, and if neither of them could form a coherent sentence, they'd never get anywhere. "But why now? Here?"

"I don't know, I'm sorry, I don't know," Pixie said, words falling out in the jumbled rapid-fire of someone waking from a bad dream, or trying to, only to find the nightmare had become reality. "It's just that you've done so much for me, and I haven't done anything for you except be a total leech, and I keep talking about Jeff, and *holy shit can I stop talking to you about my ex-boyfriend* for two seconds? It's not fair to you, it's not fair to anyone the way I've been acting like a sad-sack drain on everyone, and I just thought I should try to pay you back somehow but even *that* was the wrong thing, and I can't do anything right and I just—I don't know what to—"

"Pixie," Jude cut in, and Pixie didn't exactly gasp, as vampires didn't need to, but he did give a startled little jump, as if Jude had shouted. Jude opened his arms wide, the kind of gesture to show one was unarmed and coming in peace, and one that would hopefully remove all ambiguity of his intentions. "Can I touch you now?"

Despite his waterfall of words a second earlier, Pixie couldn't seem to speak now. Instead he nodded, stepping into Jude's arms which immediately wrapped around him.

"I'm sorry, I'm so sorry," Pixie whimpered, trembling in Jude's grasp and pressing close against his chest, but seeming grounded enough now to form words again. Each one hurt to hear, though, and Jude couldn't decide which condition he hated more, Pixie speechless with panic or Pixie crying and spilling his guts and generally falling apart with only Jude to hold him together. "I just thought I should—I have to pay you back somehow for crashing into your life and ruining everything! Please don't be mad!"

"I'm not mad at you," Jude said, tone much more level than he felt. "And you didn't ruin my life, but even if you had, that's not the way to fix it! You don't owe me anything, especially not that! Even if I wanted it, you wouldn't," he added as a quick, important afterthought. "Even if I were entirely allosexual, and had everything figured out and knew what I wanted for sure, you wouldn't owe—"

"Oh God," Pixie whispered, pulling back enough so that Jude could see an entirely new panic dawning on his face. "Oh God that's right, you're freaking ace, oh no, I just saw you and thought—looking, the way that men—when men look at me like that, it means they want—"

"Stop," Jude shushed him, a hand on Pixie's neck, which seemed to both ground and calm him at least a little. "Yes, I am, but you… weren't wrong, either. I think 'demisexual' is the word? Demi-aro. You're right, I don't want any of that, from almost anyone in the world. But I do want to kiss you, and—and I don't even know what else. Which makes all of this that much more confusing, I don't know how to handle any of this, but I know it's not the time. Not with everything that's going on, and you in the headspace you're in. Or me either. That's why I've been holding back. Anything else would be a mistake."

"Okay," Pixie said, burying his face in Jude's chest again and clutching at his shirt. It was going to wrinkle, Jude noted dimly, but that certainty was matched only by the extent to which he didn't care, not now. "I'm... I'm so…"

He trailed off, but there was no doubt about what he'd been trying to say. Jude was sorry too. Pixie's shoulders heaved with every sob, and Jude could do nothing more than hold him as he cried, chin resting on the top of Pixie's pink head. He didn't know what else there was to do. Pixie clung to him like a drowning man with the last life preserver, but Jude was struggling himself. Helpless—that most-hated of feelings—and fighting panic of his own, Jude forced himself to keep breathing steadily, take it moment by moment, and just get through until they were both back on solid ground.

"I shouldn't have come back here," Pixie whispered, after the worst of his breakdown had subsided, at least outwardly. "I'm so sorry. I know I keep saying that but I am."

"It's all right," Jude said, instead of what he wanted to. Telling Pixie to stop apologizing would be like telling himself to stop overanalyzing and obsessing over details and uncertainty. It would do nothing but make both of them feel bad when he failed. "I'm glad you told me."

"Thanks," Pixie mumbled, pulling back from Jude and wiping a forearm across his face. He'd left several damp spots on Jude's shirt, but Jude was far past worrying about that by now. "Can we go home now?"

"Yes," Jude said with a rush of relief. This, at least, he could do. "Let's go. Do you want to—?"

Before he'd finished the question, Pixie was gone, replaced by a fuzzy pink bat clinging to his hand. Jude carefully gathered the little creature up and stroked its head with one finger—somehow even its tiny bat face looked sad.

Jude tucked him into his regular inside jacket pocket, stepped around the broken glass, and headed out the door. Even if the memories weren't his own, he could feel the weight of what Pixie had left behind, hopefully lessened by the fact that this time, they were leaving together.

Sanguine looked terribly out of place, standing in the center of the opulent living room and trying not to drip blood onto the carpet.

Wicked Gold enjoyed the finer things in life and death, and Sanguine was hardly ever allowed into rooms with anything nice in them, except on special occasions, which he never tended to enjoy. Now he stood awkwardly, bruised and filthy, and clearly trying to take up as little space as possible. Both to avoid sullying the baroque-looking, creamy white sofa and rosewood coffee table that probably cost more than he'd ever seen in his life, and out of deeply-ingrained habit. It never paid to provide the vampire with a reason to strike. As if he ever needed one.

The vampire himself wasn't at home. He liked to go out after he'd had his fill with Sanguine – to do what, he didn't know or want to know. It could be nothing good.

The air was now free of screams or the tang of blood. But before Sanguine stood Owen, surveying the young man's bloodied face and torn clothes. He was impeccably dressed in a suit that looked exactly the same as the one he'd worn at the circle the previous night. He must either own multiple identical suits, or have them fastidiously cleaned on a daily basis. This, at least, he and his vampiric rival had in common.

"Yes, I can fix this," Owen said, sounding detached but certain. "If your master comes home to you still a mess, he may raise a fuss, and he's hard enough to work with as it is."

Sanguine said nothing, but his shoulders dropped a little as obvious relief overtook him. Owen reached out to move some matted hair away from his raw, not-quite-scabbed neck, and Sanguine flinched.

"Why do you make him treat you like this?" Owen asked, then swatted Sanguine's shoulder to make him hold still. Not enough to hurt an uninjured person, but from the wince it elicited, it was obvious Sanguine wasn't one. Sighing, he placed his fingertips between the spots of dried blood on

Sanguine's forehead, murmured a few arcane words under his breath, and began a simple regeneration spell. "Hold still. Your lord will quickly lose patience with a broken doll."

"I don't make him do shit," Sanguine muttered, but did as he was told. "If I could control anything, do you think I'd *make him* beat me to a pulp whenever he feels like it?"

"No, I suppose you'd just free yourself again," Owen said, tone disapproving, but healing magic steady. "You and that other little traitor never seemed to have a problem abandoning your sacred duty. Why not now?"

"You could have come with us, you know." Sanguine fixed him with an unblinking gaze. "The invitation was open. Still is, even after all the shit you've pulled—and you can thank Milo for that, not me. If it was up to me, we'd be done with you forever. But you don't really need us traitors, do you? You're a witch, so just witch yourself out."

"I serve the Lady. But even if I didn't, my only magical gift is to heal mortals," Owen said bitterly, and removed his hand from Sanguine's head. "Which is not generally… harmonious with my desires, or where I could be of best use. Speaking of, how does that feel?"

"Better," Sanguine said, sitting up straighter and tilting his head experimentally. "Thanks. But screw thinking about 'best use.' They only have one use for us in mind, and they'll use you until you beg for death."

Owen didn't answer. His face revealed nothing, but that didn't stop Sanguine from zeroing in.

"It bothers you, doesn't it?" Sanguine continued, taking one step closer to Owen's limit. He'd reach it soon, he knew, but until then he had some words. "You can't throw fireballs or turn people to stone, only healing, and healing bloodbags like me at that. Having to rely on your big bad Queen for protection, and even having to work for Wicked Gold."

"I do *not* work for—"

"Whatever. Must just eat you up inside, watching that miserable bastard, itching to set the world on fire so her Majesty will give you a second look.

Must really stick in your craw that she'll never love you the way she loved Mil—"

"Shut up," Owen said, but not in the fiery tone Sanguine had come to expect from him. He sounded more tired than anything.

"No thanks," Sanguine scoffed, pleased to feel that it didn't hurt to do so. "I don't answer to you—I answer to the guy who hates you way more than I ever could. So you can go ahead and take your little superiority complex, tie it up with a pretty, pretty bow, and blow it out your ass."

Owen withdrew his hands and his magic, leaving Sanguine healed but colder than he had been before he'd begun. He'd never particularly wanted Owen's hands on him, but it had been so long since he'd felt another human's touch, one that didn't inflict pain. Losing that small point of contact was still enough to leave him feeling bereft and empty.

"Oh, yes, you really pulled one over on me," Owen said with a roll of his eyes, but nothing more pointed. "You're living it up. I'm so envious."

Sanguine started to say something, then stopped, eyeing Owen with a sharp, keen gaze that hadn't dulled at all even after years of torture and abuse. He hit on the realization and turned it over in his mind carefully, like flexing a newly-healed limb. "You really are, aren't you?"

"I'm what?" Owen asked, though it was clear he didn't actually care about the answer. He glanced pointedly at his watch. "Your master will soon return. I trust you're sufficiently healed, and done ruminating?"

"Actually, my arm could use some attention too," Sanguine said, reaching out with a wince. "And…" he traced a finger down the scar running down the left side of his face, the one that had barely missed his eye. The one that never failed to bring a look of distaste to Wicked Gold's face, and that Sanguine could never quite hide with his stringy, matted hair. "Anything you can do about this? He hates it."

"Mm." Owen placed a hand on his once-dislocated arm. The pressure only carried a small flare of pain, and slowly Sanguine's clenched muscles began to relax. "Afraid I'm not the best at erasing old scars. And I thought your liege delighted in leaving his mark on you. Why's that one any different?"

"Because he didn't give it to me. But back to what I was saying." A smile started to spread across Sanguine's thin face. "You're totally jealous of me, the lowly bloodbag. Because at least I have his attention."

"I believe it's obvious that I have that in spades," Owen countered. "I bother him, as well I should. He knows I'm watching and reporting his activities regularly to my Lady, and he can't stand being overseen. The more he pretends to the contrary, the more I know he's worth my Lady's suspicion."

"That's not the kind of attention you want, though." Sanguine's smile grew into something bordering on scandalous. "You're in so deep, you want every vampire's approval, even his. You want him to look at you with something other than a pissed-off fuck-off. Basically, you wish you were me."

"I do not." Owen tightened his grip on Sanguine's arm a fraction, maybe simply to keep him still, maybe some kind of dominance instinct.

"Sure—just be careful what you wish for," Sanguine said, eyeing Owen with a shrewd expression. "Even thralls have it easier than me. Most of the poor fucks are so checked out they don't even know what's going on. Like good little drones serving the Queen."

"Thralls are not drones, and neither are we," Owen declared, passion rising in his voice at last, as Sanguine knew it would. There it was; something more than his lazy disgust. This came from poisonous love, twice as strong and even more dangerous. "We are believers. Servants of angels. Descendants of greatness, and disciples of even more magnificence. The greatest honor a human can receive!"

Now he squeezed too hard, and Sanguine hissed in pain, pulling his arm away. He didn't know if it was an accident or a message, and now he didn't particularly care. "It's not an honor if you don't ask for it!"

"We are meant to serve them, and by doing so, rule all else." The Queen's chosen consort spoke it like law, like stating a universal truth like gravity or death.

"*We* aren't meant to do anything," Sanguine snapped back. "And they aren't meant to rule. Nobody's meant to suffer like this, and nobody's meant to inflict that kind of pain."

"We are better than other mortals in every way," Owen spat, gray eyes flashing in fury almost as brightly as the vampires he worshipped. "Even you are better, despite your best efforts. You are one of the chosen. You are blessed. You'll never be just another piece of human garbage, no matter how you act like one."

"Oh, get off your high horse and enjoy the dumpster." Sanguine let out a throat-scratching laugh. It felt like he'd forgotten how. "I'm a piece of mortal human garbage, and so are you. Despite your best efforts."

"Not for long," Owen said. "Not if everything keeps going the way it has been. I'm so close to being rewarded for my loyalty I can taste it."

Sanguine suppressed a shudder. "Bet that's not all you wanna taste."

"Don't worry," Owen snorted. "Once I have my fangs, and once your treacherous master is brought to heel, I'll be gone from your miserable life forever. I'll seek out feasts and pleasures far finer than anything you could offer. I'll never lower myself to your company again."

Sanguine looked almost sad. He rotated his shoulder, and found that he could, fully and without pain. "Huh. And where'll that leave me?"

"Not free, of course, but the next best thing. The mercy of a quick death instead of a slow one."

Sanguine pondered that, then sighed. "I guess that is about as good as it gets."

Owen didn't answer, and this time Sanguine did not break the quiet. Unfortunately, the calm wasn't to last.

"Sanguine, I'm home!" called a jocular voice. Wicked Gold didn't always announce his presence before simply appearing from thin air, but when he did, it was usually loud and sitcom-flashy.

Sanguine held perfectly still and waited, head bowed. Owen took his hands away and took one smooth step backwards as the vampire strode into his personal kingdom, pointed smile flashing as brightly as his mirror-shine gold shoes.

"Well, someone's looking better than the last time I saw him," Wicked Gold said, casting a sharp gaze over Sanguine's newly healed skin, then over to Owen. "You've got some s'plaining to do. Have you two made friends after all?"

"I wouldn't go that far," Owen deadpanned, then took a step backwards to lean against the wall, pointedly excusing himself from further interaction.

"So," Wicked Gold said in a conversational tone, turning his undivided attention to Sanguine. "I didn't give you much time to use your mouth for talking before—you followed the Witch like I asked you to?" It sounded like a question but wasn't; obviously there was only one answer.

"Yes, Lord," Sanguine said, visibly shaking, even if his voice didn't. But even with his injuries healed, the circles under his eyes were still much too dark and deep, he was just as dangerously thin, and he kept glancing over his shoulder with the same well-founded paranoia.

Wicked Gold circled him, as he had Cruce in his last moments. "And?"

"And she went to the rocks. Like you thought. I tried to see what she was doing, but she disappeared—so I stayed there," he continued, looking away and speaking more quickly as Wicked Gold's expression hardened. "And then a couple of her friends showed up. They got some dirt. Like some actual dirt, they dug it up from the ground in the circle, I don't know why. I tried to stop them, but I—but they got away. I'm sorry!"

"That is irritating. But not a disaster. In fact, that might work out quite nicely, actually." Wicked Gold looked oddly pleased. He had many smiles, but the one that came from genuine satisfaction and pleasure was one of his worst. "What else?"

"Nothing," Sanguine said quickly, and continued speaking technical truths. "They left. Then I left."

"Nothing else happened? No more arguments, no interlopers, no complications?"

"No, Lord," Sanguine said. "Nothing more."

Wicked Gold looked at him expectantly, but he didn't continue. Sanguine wasn't allowed many methods of resistance. Silence was one of the only shreds of power he had left, and sometimes it was enough.

Then, abruptly, the vampire turned away and faced Owen instead, while Sanguine quickly scuttled over to one corner and sat down on the polished hardwood floor, knees pulled up to his chest. "I do apologize for playing such a poor host. I hope you haven't been bored."

"I was told to work with you and keep my Lady up to speed," Owen said, impassive as ever. "My entertainment isn't a concern."

"Oh, of course. Transparency and everything. I hope I've been as accommodating as you require. So far, I've adhered loyally to the agreement between your lovely Lady and myself—I crack the puzzle of the stone circle and collect the first wave of the energy they contain, and she gets all residuals after that. My 'lump sum' versus her 'royalties,' so to speak."

"Yes, we've established this," Owen said. "What is your point?"

"Point is, the moment of collection is much closer than it was last time," Wicked Gold said, voice hardening and dropping out of his charismatic default lilt. "And it's shaping up to be quite a lump sum indeed. You see, I've found a witch—the very Witch I was looking for, actually—and she's quite a doozy. Or, I should say, *he* found her." He waved a hand at Sanguine, who curled up around himself a little tighter. "Credit where credit's due."

"Good," Owen said with a noncommittal shrug. "She'll be glad to hear the plan is on schedule, finally."

"You don't sound very excited," Wicked Gold observed.

"The only reason I care about any of this is because *she* does." He spoke in a near-monotone, as if it were something he'd memorized. "It's her project. I don't care about anything you do, for any reason, so don't feel obligated to keep me posted."

"You're a rude thing, but you're loyal to a fault. You had the opportunity to escape, and you turned me down."

"I would never abandon my Lady."

"Impertinent *and* loyal, a winning combination," Wicked Gold chuckled. "I like that—but only in my own people. And only then to a point. It can easily get tiring."

Owen gave him a slow, unimpressed blink. Wicked Gold's own eyes widened at the impertinence, then narrowed in fury, and finally, he smiled, all casualness and light.

"And besides that, you're jealous," the vampire continued pleasantly. "You're jealous of the Witch for her power, for living her own life when you're tethered hereby your own envy and avarice. You're jealous of your Queen for her glory. And you're jealous of me. You always have been, and you always will be. Hell, you're even jealous of *him*—"

He pointed to Sanguine, who had yet to move. But the battered human had raised his head from his knees to watch, and now gave Owen a deadpan, very deliberate look, and tiny shrugging nod.

"I am *not*—" Owen started, frustration finally cutting through his daze, but Wicked Gold didn't seem to notice, or care if he did.

"—For having my attention. And you hate me! You really, *really* hate me. And even still, you'd rather feed my appetites than see a servant pick up the scraps. A crown prince, lusting after the place of an undeserving blood-bag. Isn't that pathetic? See, Sanguine, no matter who you are, there's always someone who has it worse. For someone who's supposed to worship and respect my kind, Owen, you've got an awfully funny way of showing it. And a dangerous one."

"I don't serve 'your kind,'" Owen sneered, even as he straightened and his heart began to pound faster and harder, surely audible to Wicked Gold's heightened senses. It was almost as if, despite his contempt for this vampire in particular, he was programmed to snap to attention whenever any of them fixed him with a displeased eye. "I serve my Lady, Ombra Dolce, she who possesses a higher grace and glory than you could ever hope to touch. She is a Queen. You are a conniving parasite. You might as well be a different species."

"You really do have some nerve, speaking to me like this," Wicked Gold observed with apparent surprise and something bordering on respect. "What if I sliced your throat open right here? Or drained you dry, or—oh, did any of the fun things I could think up if you give me half a second?"

Owen gave him another calm, slow, poker-faced blink. "Try it. See what happens when the Lady sees you've killed her favorite. It'll take you a much, much longer time to die than I."

Wicked Gold stared back at him, gleaming eyes hooded and dangerous. Then he broke into a bright grin, then a boisterous laugh, spreading his hands wide in a conciliatory gesture. "Well, all right then! What can I say? She's always had an ace in the hole, and I guess in this case, that's you. I should've known better, really."

Owen's voice was a combination of long-suffering patience and barely-concealed bile. "I'll be sure to send her your regards." Without waiting for a reply, he turned on his heel and left.

Wicked Gold waited until the door was closed and Owen's footsteps retreated. Then he sank down onto the luxurious sofa and stretched his legs out, not bothering to remove his gold-tipped shoes before resting them on the glossy-finished table. Sanguine kept an eye out for scratches, ready to ask permission to buff them away should any appear.

"Ugh, that boy is such a headache," he sighed. "Him and his Lady. Sometimes I think they're doing nothing but purposely trying to get under my skin. Sanguine?" he called.

"Yes, Lord?" The human started, scrambling to his feet and hurrying over, only to kneel again at Wicked Gold's feet, knees hitting the hard floor.

"No, no, get up here," the vampire said with a wave of his hand. "I need a drink."

"Yes, Lord." Tone no longer questioning, but appropriately deferent, Sanguine rose to his feet again and sat gingerly on the very edge of the sofa. He was painfully aware of his own grunginess in contrast to the pristine surroundings. Wicked Gold usually had him shower before feeding; he must really be in need. But sometimes, Sanguine thought, drinking from him while he was this dirty might be a kind of personal rebellion for the otherwise uncompromisingly-tidy vampire. A sinful indulgence, a naughtiness that made every drop that much sweeter.

Wicked Gold rolled up his sleeves and removed his suit jacket, partially unbuttoning his fine linen shirt and pushing the collar away from what may become a potential splash zone. He didn't enjoy blood-stained clothing, vampire or not.

Sanguine dutifully pulled his long, matted hair aside, exposing the scarred and bruised skin of his neck and shoulder.

"You really should cut this mess," Wicked Gold muttered, catching a stray tangle of dirty red and tucking it behind the human's ear.

"Yes, Lord," Sanguine said again, but with no promise behind it. It was a ritual by now, a kind of game—if he actually cut his hair, Wicked Gold would be displeased, disappointed, dangerous. Unless he himself did it personally, he just didn't like change.

Wicked Gold leaned in closer, mouth opening in a smile, fangs out. He turned his head to trace Sanguine's neck just a few inches away, and took in a long breath through flaring nostrils, slow and deep. Vampires didn't need to breathe, no, but that didn't mean they didn't enjoy their sharpened sense of smell, as useful for pleasure as detecting prey. Sanguine held perfectly still, and let himself slip away from this room, this moment, somewhere else, somewhere sunny. The vampire would still be here when he came back.

But it wasn't fangs that sank into his neck. A clawed hand closed around it, shoving Sanguine away but not letting go, instead tightening, cutting off his surprised yelp.

"You little liar," Wicked Gold snapped. "Really? *Really*, Sanguine?"

"Lord?" Sanguine gasped, eyes wide and terrified, every muscle locked and tense.

"You said you never got close enough to the Witch to touch," the vampire snarled with a gold-tinted flare of his eyes, all good nature in his face and voice gone, as if it had never been.

"I didn't!" Sanguine cried.

"*Then why do I smell her on you?!*"

"I don't know! I haven't seen her since this morning, and she didn't even touch me!"

The vampire reached out to place a single claw tip on his bony chest, the motion and pinprick pain recalling when he'd sliced through Sanguine's hoodie. The plain shirt he wore now was even thinner, even more easily shredded.

"And who did you say was at the circle doing the Witch's bidding?"

"The mall cop," Sanguine jittered out. "I think his name's Jude. And the lady who runs the place, Eva. She... caught me. Just for a second. I got away."

"So it's a human who smells of witch," Wicked Gold mused. "Is she a witch herself? No, surely not. Letizia should know better than to get close to any others, not after what I did to her last witch friend. But she's never been the most cautious of girls, and witches leave trace magic on everything they love..."

Wicked Gold gave Sanguine a flippant wave as he turned away and rose to his feet, rolling his sleeves back down and re-donning his suit jacket.

"Get yourself cleaned up. You've been filthy long enough—long enough to learn your lesson, I'm sure. I'm still very disappointed in you for your behavior at the circle. An unwilling sacrifice? I'm hurt. I expected more loyalty from my favorite."

"Yes, Lord." His eyes were downcast and tone flat as he began to obediently remove his grime-encrusted shirt. He showed no self-consciousness or hesitation to bare his skin before the vampire; that was one of the first things Wicked Gold tended to remove from any humans in his employ.

"But to get my hands on the Witch? I might actually need bait to *get* the bait I need," Wicked Gold mused as Sanguine neatly folded his ruined shirt and decided against laying it on the expensive table. "Sanguine, hold on a moment."

"Lord?"

Wicked Gold was looking at him with an awful smile on his face. Not satisfaction, but anticipation. He put both hands on Sanguine's shoulders, and from the outside it looked like an affectionate gesture—except for how hard he was pressing down.

"I changed my mind. Kneel."

He did, closing his eyes in anticipation. But instead of baring his fangs, the vampire took Sanguine's head in one hand—and in one swift movement, slammed it into the nearest wall.

ACT FOUR: it's Not Easy Being Gray

NOT EVERYONE who frequented the circle at night had fangs. Some just had a bit of magic, a quick smile, purple contacts, and just-as-purple hair.

Milo walked through the darkened park paths with ease. In their arms sat a large bouquet of flowers, picked from many different spots along their way from The Abyss, the one store in the mall where someone with all-black clothes, dark makeup, and multiple piercings wouldn't stand out in the least. They moved with a bouncy step and happy hum, completely at ease and unperturbed by the circle's overwhelming energy.

But then, not much bothered them, night or day. The young witch was a neutral party and they'd yet to be threatened with fangs or fire.

When they reached the ring of stones, they walked right into the middle, carefully side-stepping the smoldering embers and the black, corrosive puddle of doubly-dead Cruce. Still softly humming, they went up to the nearest stone and lay a few carefully-chosen flowers at its base. The young witch gave the dark crystal spike a respectful nod, and then moved onto the next. They continued around the inside, placing flowers at every stone, until they'd made a complete circle.

Flowers distributed, they stood in the center of the ring and held absolutely still, even holding their breath, until they heard it. Whispering. Just under the soft, cool breeze, under the beat of Milo's heart. It always seemed to grow a little louder after their flowery visits.

"You're welcome," Milo said quietly, smiling. "I missed you too."

Then, they realized, they were not alone. Milo hadn't actually followed anyone; they simply knew they'd find the ones they searched for here, the way they knew there was no place like this circle in the world. Two girls, both gray-skinned with catlike eyes, stood at the edge of the stones, staring at Cruce's remains.

"I think we knew the way because he knew," Milo heard the taller girl say faintly. "Or maybe just because he died here."

"Yeah," the other one breathed out, sounding awed. "Just… wow. There he is."

They stood there together for a while, staring at the corroded puddle of dead-vampire muck, all that was left of Cruce. Then both of them stood straight up as if they'd been poked with pins. Their focus on Cruce's corpse had distracted them at first, but now they'd both sensed the stranger's presence before a word had been spoken, but a moment later, that word came.

"Hi," Milo said, giving an awkward little wave, which turned into a raised hand as they both started and jumped backwards, eyes flashing and clearly about to run, or fly away, as quickly as possible. "Wait, stop! Nails, Maestra—I'm a friend!"

At the sound of their names, both vampire girls froze. They exchanged a quick glance, and as they looked at each other, the lights in their eyes faded along with their startled snarls. They turned tentatively back to Milo, though both were still prepared to fly at the first sign of danger, every muscle tensed and clawed hands at the ready.

"Who are you?" Maestra demanded, voice slightly distorted, warped far beyond what a teenage girl's should sound like. She'd stepped a bit between Milo and Nails and leveled the stranger with a gaze that was not so much predatory but promising; make a wrong move, and there could only be one outcome.

"My name's Milo," they said, speaking quickly and spreading both empty hands. A witch was never quite unarmed, but it did seem to calm the vampire girls a bit. "I guess you might say I'm a friend of a friend. Letizia sent me here to make sure you were doing all right, after... what happened."

"Really?" Maestra blinked in clear surprise. "Wait—why'd she tell you to come here? She told us *not* to come here."

Nails let out a snorting laugh. "That's totally how she knew we would! Oh my God, she played us!"

"I guess she did," Maestra grumbled, but kept looking curiously at Milo. "So what are you, another witch?"

"Yes," Milo said with an unbothered, friendly nod. "I know her, and I knew of Cruce, and that until recently you were under his... employ. Your secret's safe, and I'd like to help you get your bearings if I can."

Nails squinted at Milo's face, taking in their delicate features and smooth angles under the black eyeliner and purple shadow. "You look really familiar. Like, really. Do we know you?"

"Not personally, but I've seen you around the mall," Milo said, though they hesitated for a moment. "Aside from that, I am a friend of Letizia's—maybe that's why you recognize me?"

"Yeah. Maybe," Maestra said, but didn't look quite certain. "It's hard to say. It's hard to tell much of anything right now."

"It's got to be disorienting, suddenly having a whole world to explore, and a whole life to live. Like getting to know yourself for the first time." Milo gave them a little smile. "I know something about that."

"Yeah, it's been wild," Nails said, trying to smile back, but just looking uncharacteristically nervous. "Everything's weird and the whole world feels different, like clearer and fuzzier at the same time."

"It feels like when we first changed," Maestra added, eyes widening in realization. "How the whole world was different overnight. We woke up different people. It feels like we're different people now."

"Getting away from an abuser will do that," Milo said. "Your lives were defined by Cruce for over a century. Remembering who you really are is never easy after something like that."

"Yeah," Nails sighed. "Like impossible. Everything after we got turned feels like a weird dream, and I don't really remember being human at all."

"That's understandable," Milo sighed. "And you're not missing much. Being a human isn't very fun, most days."

"Some things do kind of… make noise in my head, though, even if I don't know why. Like you."

"And these." Maestra pointed at one of the few "missing" posters that hadn't been ripped down or scratched out—not one of Pixie, but a lanky, grungy-looking boy with unruly hair. "This guy here? He looks kind of familiar, but I don't know his name or anything, or where I've seen him before. It's like the images are still here, but the labels are gone."

"That sounds scary," Milo said with a slight hesitation as their eyes paused on the poster, but then gave a sympathetic nod that encouraged both of them to continue.

"Yeah, but it's been more like… lonely, I guess?" Nails said, serious as the other two by now. "Maybe just because we've been alive so long, but I don't think that's it. Time gets... weird. Like it passes really fast and slow at the same time. Years and weeks kind of start to feel the same, and nothing really changes with you, even if the rest of the world does. You can't talk to many people or they'll be scared of you or—or bad stuff might happen. Even if it's up to you, which sometimes... it's not up to you."

"It is now," Maestra said quietly.

"Yeah it is." Nails gave her a smile, encouraged. "But see, it's hard to explain. Like the time thing—some things you just have to live yourself before you get it."

Milo smiled. "I think I know what you mean. So what brings you here in particular? Do you remember something about it?"

"Not really, it's more like we felt kind of pulled here," Nails said, eyes lingering on the decaying clothes in the middle. "This is where it happened. Where Cruce died. But even besides that, this place feels... important."

"It is," Milo said. "It's one of my favorite places in the city. I come here to get away from—well, this place is just special, that's all. Can you feel that? It's like the air is electric. It even feels good to breathe. Usually does. It's felt kind of... off, lately."

"Well, we don't really breathe, but that's what that tingly feeling is?" Nails stretched out her arms and moved them through the space. As she did, the hairs on them stood up like they hadn't since she was alive. "Magic?"

"Mm-hmm," Milo said with a nod. "It's thick here, like... fog, almost. I bet that's what it would look like if you could see it. I can't, obviously. Can you?"

"Huh?" Maestra gave them a confused look.

"Vampire eyes are supposed to be different. You can probably see things even witches can't. Like this?"

They held out both hands, clapping them and rubbing them together. When Milo pulled their hands apart, silvery strands clung to each finger, forming a glittering cat's-cradle. Rainbows danced along each string as Milo twirled and looped them around their fingers in a continuous and hypnotic motion, quicksilver light transforming and blooming into more shining color.

"I'd wear that," Maestra said wistfully. "A whole dress made of that. You can't see it?"

"No," Milo shook their head, but smiled. "But I know it's there. It feels warm in my hands, a little bit like silk, or running water that... see, that doesn't really begin to say what it actually feels like, there aren't really words for it. I just know it's there."

"It's like I can tell you're a witch without looking," Nails said, giving a sniff in Milo's direction. "You smell the same way the circle does."

"So I smell like magic," Milo concluded with a contemplative head-tilt. "I guess that's a compliment. And I've known vampires before. They were always... friends of the family, I guess you'd say. Some of them closer than my blood family, who never really…" they trailed off, then shook their head. "But that was a long time ago, and I have a new family. Like Letizia. She taught me almost everything I know about being a witch, like how to read cards—oh!"

They brightened, looking excited instead of sympathetic-but-guarded, and suddenly much younger.

"I have an idea," Milo said. "Whenever I'm feeling lost, I turn to my tarot deck, or a friend's. Reading for myself is hard, but I love doing it for others. Letizia's the master, of course, but I can do my best, if that's something you'd like? Very simple, three cards: past, present, and future."

"Sure," Maestra said, this time not needing to confer with Nails even with a glance; she was already nodding. "I'd love to see what the cards think about… all this."

Milo stepped away from the center and nodded for them to follow. Just outside the stone circle was a smooth, flat stone that made a good table. Milo knelt down beside it, a deck of cards in their hand that neither girl had seen before. It was greatly reminiscent of Letizia's habit of pulling items out of thin air, though unlike her, Milo didn't accompany the gesture with a satisfied flourish.

"Do you have a significator?" they asked, cutting their deck and beginning to shuffle. Where Letizia's was the classic Rider-Waite deck, the backs of Milo's cards had an elegant silver and pastel blue design, the colors soft and painterly instead of starkly vivid.

"A what?" Maestra asked, catlike eyes following the motion of their hands as the both of them sat down across from Milo.

"A card that means you," Milo said. "Something that fits with your personality. I can use that to start. Sometimes it makes for a more personal reading."

"Oh. I don't have that," she said, and glanced at Nails, who shook her head as well, looking a little troubled, as if they were getting in over their heads. "Do we need to pick them out? I don't know anything about any of this."

"Don't worry," Milo said gently. "It's not a problem at all. We can find out together…" They pulled one card and held it up, showing its face to both girls without looking at it themself. "The past, behind you is… The Moon, reversed?"

"Yeah," Nails confirmed, looking impressed now. "How'd you know?"

"It's my deck," Milo said with a smile and little shrug. "We're very well-acquainted. So that's the one we'll start with. The Moon can be neutral, referring to a pattern of events or behaviors—a cycle. Repeating history. Reversed, and that history is a less-than-happy one. It means being stuck in a rut that isn't good for anyone involved. Less a tradition, and more a trap."

"Sounds about right," Nails grumbled, nodding with a rueful frown. "Like a hundred and fifty years of being trapped."

"So the present, beneath you…" Milo reached for another card, eyes looking faraway and a bit out of focus, but movements sure. Again, when Milo pulled it, they did not look at the face, instead showing it to the pair sitting opposite. "Nine of Swords, reversed?"

Again, a pair of confirming nods.

"This one can mean internal struggles, turmoil… taking on too much and internalizing it. Enduring a secret pain that nobody else sees. Feeling imprisoned, helpless, with no end in sight."

"More truth," Maestra said, looking disappointed. "This is kind of a depressing spread, huh?"

Milo tilted their head, owlishly peering at the card and all its blades. "You can read it that way. But this is one of my favorite cards, especially reversed."

"Really?" Nails asked, tilting her own head to look at the card, as if she might see what Milo did in its depths.

"Yes. It's special to me. 'Reversed' doesn't always mean bad—and here I think it means that there *is* an end in sight. In fact, it's already happened." They smiled a little. "You've already broken free. Cut away the ties binding you to something weighing you down. Sometimes you have to cut off an old life to live the one you were always meant to. Something I know a lot about."

It's not a bad card at all."

"So what comes next?" Nails asked eagerly. "Now that we're cut free?"

"The future, before you is…" They pulled one last card, showing them the picture of three dancing figures holding chalices overflowing with water; the image's curves were gentle and the gem-tone colors harmonious. "Three of Cups."

"It's pretty," Maestra said, just as Nails said, "hey, this one's right-side-up!"

"Yes it is," Milo said, and looked relieved. "And this one means friendship, happiness shared, emotional healing and relief. Blessings overflowing, specifically enjoyed with friends."

"Finally," Nails sighed. "It's about time. We could really, really use some fun times and friends—we got a lot to make up for."

"Easier said than done," Maestra said a little darkly, eyeing the card's carefree dance and bright colors as if finding them difficult to trust. "I'm glad you-know-who's gone, but… well, it's gonna take a while."

"I'm sure," Milo said with a sympathetic look at them, then back down at the card they laid beside the other two. "But ending with the Three of Cups is an encouraging sign. The first two were hard, it's been a difficult ordeal, but that's one of the happiest endings I can think of. Even if you can't see exactly how you'll get there."

Milo fell silent, staring at the three cards, and for a moment, didn't move. Then they gave a shiver, as if a chilly wind had swept through the clearing, though none had.

"And that's all I can tell. Sorry I can't give you more—like I said, this place hasn't felt right in a while." They looked around a bit anxiously, like the stones might somehow come to life and advance on them. "You two should probably steer clear of it for a few days at least, too."

"Why?" Nails asked at once. "I thought our spread had a good ending. The Three of Cups is good, right?"

"It is—but I have a feeling that this circle's destiny is bigger than one card, or you, or me, or any of us," Milo said, still looking uneasy. "Something... very important is coming. I can feel it. And none of us should be around when it comes."

Both girls looked at each other, then back at Milo. "What do you think is going to happen?" Maestra asked, very seriously.

"I don't know, exactly—and when I don't know, when something could go in any direction at all, I tend to be very careful in moving forward."

"Well, we've been doing pretty good so far," Nails said with a jerk of her head back toward Cruce's remains. "That's one monster down. Maybe we should keep a good thing going."

"No," Milo said, soft voice coming out a bit sharp. "No, you definitely shouldn't. This circle is a powerful place, but soon, I don't think it's going to be a good one. I'm just telling you what Letizia told me, and she's usually not wrong about these things—take it up with her if you have more questions, but I don't think she'll give many answers. I couldn't get much more out of her myself."

They stood up then, looking up at the sky as if expecting rain, very reasonable in this time and place, but their worried expression suggested they were actually expecting something more ominous.

"Now I think we should get going. You're welcome to come with me, I'm happy to be a sounding board while you sort out your feelings, or we can do something else—do you like movies? You've probably missed a lot of great pop culture moments. I'm mostly a rom-com and Disney kind of enby, but I'm up for anything!"

Nails and Maestra exchanged one of their pointed looks that contained an entire conversation in under two seconds, even without the semi-telepathic bond they still shared and always would.

"That sounds great," Nails said out loud as they both turned back to their new friend, who gave them a sunny smile. "I've always wanted to see an actual movie all the way through! Do you have anything about vampires?"

"But maybe funny vampires," Maestra said with a little wince in the direction of Cruce's remains. "I've kind of had enough serious and scary for a while."

"I think I know just the thing," Milo said as the three of them headed away from the circle and back to the trail leading to the human side of the world. "Do you know *What We Do In The Shadows?*"

"No, what do we do?" Nails asked, and Milo giggled.

"You're about to find out."

🔥

It was the morning before the night of the ritual, and Jude was about to crawl out of his skin.

He and Pixie hadn't talked, about what had happened or what was about to happen, and the sad, desperate moment in the motel played over and over in Jude's head, how blank and dead Pixie's usually more-alive-than-life eyes had been, the horror on his face when he realized what he'd done—Jude wanted to escape his own thoughts. But he couldn't leave his brain behind, so instead he left the apartment, feet carrying him to a door just down the hall before he quite told them to.

The door opened just a few short moments after Jude's first knock, taking him a bit by surprise. It usually took Jasper at least ten seconds to answer, maybe because he was in the back of his apartment with Felix, maybe just the fatigue Jude knew he was working through almost constantly.

"Can I talk to you?" he asked.

"I wish you would." Jasper did indeed have dark circles under his eyes and leaned heavily against the door frame, but he smiled, and the knot inside Jude's stomach loosened just a bit.

"Thanks. I don't mean to disturb you or Felix, but…"

"You're not, believe me. We can talk in here," he said, leading the way inside and down the short hall past the living area. Jude's eyes were immediately drawn toward a closed door that he hadn't seen the other side of in some time. There, he knew, was Felix. Jude didn't expect the wave of disappointment he felt at the sight of it, and realized that some part of him had been expecting, or at least hoping, to find it open.

"Felix is asleep—or his version of sleeping, rather," Jasper said, clearly noticing the object of Jude's attention and his reaction. "I'd like to keep it that way, for a few hours at least. He doesn't really have a sleep schedule yet, and lord knows it's hard enough for him to get there."

"It's hard on you too," Jude said. "You deserve a few hours' break."

"The shop's closed, and likely to remain closed for the immediate future. I'm only still paying rent on that place because moving everything out of there is out of the question. So I'm always on a break."

"You know what I mean."

For the first time in too long, Jude was able to see all of Jasper clearly and up close. He looked tired and run-down, even more so than Jude was accustomed to seeing him. In the early days of Felix's return, Jasper had reminded him of a new father with a baby up at all hours, sleep-deprived and concerned but happy all the same—but right now he looked much more tired, and much less happy than he'd been at first.

Jude could also tell this time that Jasper indeed had lost more than a bit of weight, and now he could see the full extent. Still substantially broader than Jude, but not by as much as he remembered. All of Jasper seemed diminished, but Jude's concerned eyes went quickly to the way his shirt hung more loosely, particularly around his waist. It was unlikely to have been intentional; Jasper had always seemed right at home with his round figure and size in general. Being fat was simply part of who he was, and a good part, like the quickness of his perceptive eyes or the wry tilt of his smile when he'd just thought of something sure to make even Jude laugh. This hurt to see. The physical evidence of how great a toll the last months had taken made Jude's own stomach feel tight and cold.

"Does your head hurt?" Jude asked, figuring Jasper's migraines were safer to inquire about, though just as urgent. They'd all had a lot on their minds, but Jasper maybe the most of all.

His friend gave a completely joyless chuckle. "I've forgotten the last time it didn't."

Jasper led him into the bedroom he and Felix shared, or had at one time, and lowered himself down to sit on the bed, slowly, as if his entire body ached, not just his head. Jude hesitated only momentarily before sitting down beside him. Once, Jude would have felt anxious and a wonderful kind of embarrassed to be alone with Jasper in his bedroom, even with Felix in the next room, but now it just felt sensible, natural. Intimate, yes, but their friendship always had been, and they were long past the point of getting worked up about little things like this, despite the distance the past months had put between them.

"Has Felix left your place at all?" he asked, making an effort to keep his voice down, even if it was probably pointless with vampires in the house.

"Only for the occasional flight to stretch his wings. But they're never very long, and he always goes back to the guest room afterwards."

"He doesn't sleep with you in here?" Jude asked, frowning.

"No. I've tried, of course, but he just seems more at ease in the guest room. I'm trying not to read too much into that. Sometimes it feels like he doesn't think he deserves it. He actually doesn't sleep in a bed at all, really, unless I'm in it."

"Then how…?"

"Standing up," Jasper said with an illustrative up-down wave. "Ramrod-straight, joints locked, like a… well, he'd make a wonderful coatrack. And it's not really sleep either, more like some kind of trance with his eyes half-open. I'm not sure if that's because of his permanently… morphed state, but it's just how he is. Does any of this sound familiar to you?"

"No. Pixie's definitely never done that," Jude said, suddenly very grateful for that. "I'd remember."

"Just a Felix thing, then. I thought as much. Hopefully it'll level off with time. I've taken to sleeping in there with him, but it's really not the same. I still wake up like clockwork thinking it was all a dream and he's not there."

"I've done that a few times too." Jude had actually done that quite a bit more than a few times, but he felt strange admitting that to Jasper. What right did he have to still be messed up about this? Jasper had the monopoly on Felix-related trauma, as much as Jude knew he'd say it wasn't a contest. Even if it was, there was no winning here to be had.

"So what has you so worried, Jude?"

"What?" Jude asked, brain only catching up to the words after a couple seconds. "Oh—nothing. Nothing important, anyway."

"I very much doubt that. Both that it's nothing, and that it's nothing important."

"I—no, really, I'm fine. I just wanted to be here instead of…" He shrugged. Words were getting harder to come by. Wasn't that always how it worked? The more he wanted to communicate something, the more important the words, the more elusive they became.

"You didn't come over just to ask about Felix… well, you might have, but I'm getting the impression that there's something else on your mind," Jasper said. Even if Jude lost every word in the dictionary, Jasper would still be able to read him like a book. "You and Pixie have both been through a major change. Living together is a big step. I've been meaning to ask, but…"

Jude couldn't speak and felt a painful ache creep into his tense shoulders. He didn't know when he'd started curling his fingers into fists around the comforter but forced himself to release it. He didn't need to add bed wrinkles to the list of Jasper's problems.

"Well, never mind that," Jasper said, mercifully, and Jude's shoulders dropped as he deliberately made himself relax. "How did your quest for spell ingredients go? Did you and Eva get the high-noon earth from the midnight circle?"

"Yeah," Jude said after nodding a few times. One word at a time. "Yeah, we did. She did most of the work. I just distracted the guy guarding them— that redheaded punk who likes to yell and cause trouble."

"Sanguine," Jasper said with a nod, then, in response to Jude's surprised look, "Letizia let me know about him a while ago. He hasn't caused any mayhem at my shop, as far as I know, and she said it's unlikely he would, but he's always had it out for her, for some reason or another."

"I think I know why."

"Oh?" Jasper's eyebrows raised.

"He had blood on his neck," Jude said, with an accompanying gesture along his own. "Punctures."

Jasper didn't look surprised, more resigned. "I suspected that may be the case. Did he give you much trouble?"

Jude shook his head. "He didn't throw a punch or anything. Even if he had, I doubt he'd be able to hurt anyone besides himself. He looked… bad. I'd almost feel bad for him, if he didn't have such a mouth on him."

"Yes, Jude, 'almost.'" Jasper chuckled, and Jude began to feel warm inside instead of chilled with anxiety. Sometimes it was nice to be around someone who could see right through you and all the fibs you told, even to yourself. "It seems to me he's insisting on fighting his own battle right now. But if there's a way to help him, and he wants it, you'll find it."

"I can't seem to help anyone right now," Jude muttered, and where his shoulders had once been creeping up to his ears, now they sagged, and he rested his elbows on his knees. "Not even Pixie."

"That's funny, I was also just talking about him."

Jude shut his eyes. He couldn't keep anything from Jasper, not for long. He'd known that when he came here. If he was being honest with himself, that's the reason he'd come here at all. "It's—he's—we've hit a couple bumps in the road."

"Tell me," Jasper said, and Jude felt the comforting warmth of a hand against his back. He leaned into it as Jasper continued. "Everything that you feel is yours to tell, anyway."

"Part of it's mine," Jude said, anxiety making his tone uncertain and halting. "Part of it, I'm not sure. I don't know if I even understand it all.

That's why I came to you."

"I'll do my best, even if my best is just to listen."

"Well, last night we went looking for the 'rose-tinted memories' Letizia told him to find," Jude said, focusing on the words, not the emotion behind them, not the worry still clawing at him, along with the memory of how hard Pixie had been shaking in his arms. "Pixie and I went back to where he used to live. This old motel, falling apart, nobody there now. He wanted to find a time capsule type thing that he'd made with—with his old boyfriend, I guess. So, a thing made of good memories, or at least something that looks good in hindsight—anyway. It wasn't there, and he got really upset, and…"

He paused, taking a breath, still trying to make the events make sense in his own mind. Jasper didn't prod or interrupt, just sat, waiting patiently. Jude felt another swell of gratitude; it was the best thing he or anyone could have done under the circumstances, and slowly Jude's brain fully remembered how words worked again, and he made himself speak.

"I think he got scared. Or he's been scared. Of everything, of Wicked Gold and getting hurt again, and us getting hurt, and—and me deciding I don't want him around anymore."

"I don't think there's much chance of that," Jasper said with a little smile Jude couldn't find it in himself to return.

"No, there isn't. At all. But he said he owed me, and that he wasn't doing anything in return for everything I'd given him, and…" he stopped, took another breath, and pushed the rest out. "He kissed me. But not like before, and not—not the *right way*, this was different, he was scared, and—he wanted me to touch him, but not because *he* wanted it, I don't think. It's like he thought he needed to repay me with sex. Like that was what he owed me, and he had to do it right then or I'd kick him out."

"Oh, Jude. That must have been awful. For both of you."

"It was," Jude agreed with a vehement nod, and he looked fully over at Jasper to see that he'd turned slightly toward Jude, holding one arm a bit out, open.

Jude only hesitated for a moment before scooting over, not fully into Jasper's thick (but still too thin) arms, but until their shoulders touched. He wanted more than anything to accept that embrace and the feeling of complete safety it had always offered, but something stopped him. Jasper had said part of him thought Felix believed he no longer deserved his place in his fiancé's bed. All of Jude believed the same thing of himself. It wasn't a refusal at all, but an inability, one that he now knew painfully well.

"It's not that he pushed himself on me or anything," Jude said quickly, when the unfortunate implications of his story occurred to him. "Pixie actually asked if he could touch me, I just didn't know what he meant at first. Scared out of his mind and panicking, he still asked."

"And when you said no—since I'm quite certain you did—yes, that's what I thought," Jasper said, smiling a bit in response to Jude's wide-eyed, deer-in-the-headlights look. "When you said no, what did he say?"

"Not much," Jude said with a tired shrug. "He cried for a while. I held him and told him he didn't have to do that—he definitely had to do that before. He said that's what men wanted from him. Wicked Gold, and just…"

"Worse men than you."

"I guess." Jude let his head hang down, oddly tired after expressing the thing that had been tearing up his insides all night. "I took him home, and I guess he didn't want to talk about it because he turned into a bat and crawled into one of my oven mitts. He's probably still there. I hope he's still there."

"You did the right thing," Jasper said. "Taking care of him, and telling me about it—although I do know what you mean now about not all of it being yours to tell."

"Yeah. I know he hasn't even told me the whole thing."

"Well, for what it's worth, nothing you've told me leaves this room. But it's good to know when a friend is struggling with that kind of pain. We can all keep him that much safer. I don't think I need to tell Felix to be gentle with him. They probably know more about each other's trauma than any of us could imagine."

"Yeah," Jude said again. "I just don't know what to do about it. I want to help, but I don't know what would make it better or worse, or…"

"It sounds like you've done all you can, for now at least. Sometimes there isn't much you can do at all, except to give him a safe place to heal. I'm in very much the same boat, so I do speak from some experience."

"Thanks. I knew I came to the right place."

They sat together in a silence that would have been awkward with anyone else. Jasper did like to hear himself talk, but he also knew when to let quiet lie over them like gentle, unbroken snow. He'd always done that, known exactly when not to speak or demand anything, and given Jude a safe place to collect his scattered thoughts and fit them back together.

Eventually, Jude turned his head to look up at his friend, whose face remained serene, despite the worrying gauntness in his once-round cheeks. "You don't sound worried about any of this."

"I'm not. We're not the innocents who stumbled in too far over our heads like when this began. We might be fumbling in the dark, but at least we've got a few matches this time."

"Fire's pretty easy to come by in a crucible, I guess," Jude said in a dry mutter.

"There is that. But seriously, Jude—I'd always bet on us every time on pure principle. The difference is, this time around, I'd actually feel good about our odds."

Jasper had always had a way of making him see other sides to a situation. They weren't always good sides, but it was always better than facing them alone. Jude risked a teasing smile. "'The innocents who stumbled in,' you said—you, innocent? I had no idea."

"Of course, you're right." Jasper smiled back, a bit quicker and more mischievous than before, reassuring in the familiarity. It had been too long since Jude had seen that private-joke smile, the one that was never laughing at him, only with, only warm. "I don't know what I was thinking."

"It's good to talk to you, Jasper," Jude said, and now it was relief rather than exhaustion making his limbs and head feel heavy. This was the good kind of tired, not the kind when you're sorely missing a soft bed, but the feeling of having just climbed into it at last, knowing that, tonight at least, sleep wouldn't be far behind. "I've missed you. Both of you."

"You have? Really?" Jasper blinked. He sounded genuinely surprised, and something about that made Jude sad. And almost as worried as when he'd noticed the weight Jasper had lost in Jude's absence. He'd thought giving Jasper and Felix some time and space was the right choice, but how could it possibly be, when Jude returned to find less of him? When Jasper was surprised to hear Jude had missed him at all?

"Yes, really. You're important to me. One of the most important people I have."

"That's lovely of you to say, but…" Jasper said and grimaced, as if he'd just tasted something bad. "I don't feel like it. I don't know how to help Felix, and that's the only thing in my brain, it rattles around like a marble in a tin can. Which doesn't help the headaches, let me tell you. Felix is so changed, inside and out, and I don't know how to reach him. It feels like he's a different person, and he is, in a very literal sense. And I love this new Felix, I would do anything to help him—but I don't know how. I don't know the things to say or do anymore, because I'm not saying them to the Felix I remember. And I know, believe me, that I'm not who I was anymore either. So we're two—not strangers, exactly, but we're trying to live like we're the same people as before, and we aren't. But I don't know how else to be. I feel so useless, every minute of every day and night."

"You're not," Jude said, aware of how weak and hollow the words sounded. Even if he meant them with all his heart, they weren't enough. "Far from it."

"Thank you, Jude. That does help." Jasper's words were heavy with fatigue as well, but, as always, Jude believed them. "You always do. You're helping Felix too, just by knocking on our door every morning."

"God, there's so much I want to say to him." Even if he couldn't see the guest room door from here, Jude's eyes went once again in that direction. "And ask him. I don't want to pry, but..."

"He hasn't said all that much about what happened, no," Jasper said, attuned to Jude's thoughts as always. "At least, no specifics. He was made to see, and do, terrible things. He was not himself, and not in control of his actions, though he certainly blames himself anyway. I haven't pressed him, and he seems grateful. And I catch glimpses of him being himself again, every once in a while—maybe not his old self, but he's finding the new Felix a little more every day."

"That's good," Jude said, and meant it, though his worries weren't fully assuaged. He paused, then pressed on with words that would have felt impossible only a few minutes ago, to say or to find at all. "I've… I've wanted to figure things out with you and Felix. Eventually. When he can—and when you can."

Jasper chuckled softly. "We're not the only ones in this equation, Jude."

"Fine, when I can too," Jude amended. "I want to… see where we are. I just wanted you to know I'm still thinking about that. I'm thinking about it a lot. About—what are we to each other? I mean, what am I to you? Or to Felix? Hell, what am I even to Pixie?"

"And what are we, considering that Pixie is part of our lives now?"

"We're—I mean, he's said he's totally fine with—with us being together, but me also seeing if you and Felix and me—he's good, he said polyamory is normal for him."

"And you believe him?"

"Yes," Jude said with a nod. "I can tell when he's holding something back or saying something's fine when it's not, even if I don't know what's actually bothering him. He's not doing that here. He really is okay with this."

"Well, good. At least some things can be simple."

"Sure, but nothing else is!" Jude made a frustrated noise. "Especially considering—okay. This is another wrinkle right here. Do you remember me telling you about the asexual and aromantic things?"

"I do, yes. Gray and demi, if I remember correctly."

"Yeah. I was so glad to figure that out. It helped so much, it's the word I needed, it made everything fit and make sense. Like how knowing I'm autistic explains so much, I'm not just weird, these aren't just random things I'm experiencing, it's real and it has a name. But I don't know the names for what I feel for you, or for Pixie, or if they're the same or not!" Jude was speaking faster now, as if his words couldn't wait to come out now that he'd found them. "I think they're different, but not in a bad way, just in a different way."

"Different in what way?" Jasper asked, voice patient, grounding.

Jude's shoulders sagged. "I don't even know how to express it. Maybe it's an a-spec thing, or maybe it's an autistic thing, but I don't know if I'm feeling the—the right things. I never really have. I don't know what the things I'm supposed to be feeling even *feel like!*"

"Jude, believe me, whatever you're feeling, it's not the wrong thing. I don't think there is such a thing as the wrong way to feel." He half-turned to look at Jude, expression equal parts thoughtful and wry. "But maybe you really don't feel the straightforward, sexual-romantic way you've been told is the 'right' way. So what if you don't? You love us the way *you* do, and that's the only way we want. Nothing else will satisfy."

Jude didn't have an answer for that. At least not one that held up against Jasper's logic, and faith in Jude that quieted some of the anxiety buzzing in his brain. Most of it.

"In any case, you're feeling more at once than most people feel their entire lifetimes. Being asexual, aromantic, autistic, and now navigating polyamory! Any one of those is a lot for one person to deal with, especially when they're all interrelated and overlap. But they're not bad things. They come together to make your brain the beautiful thing it is. And none of us have it all figured out. Frankly I'd be shocked if there was a single neurotypical among us. If there were, I suspect they'd be very confused."

"Well, it's really inconvenient to feel all this at once. I just wish my brain would make more sense," Jude huffed.

"Dare to dream." Jasper was quiet for a bit. When he spoke again, his voice was so soft that Jude had to lean in closer to hear him. "Sometimes I don't know if there should be a 'we.'"

"What?" Jude felt a cold little pang of shock and fear. "Why? What did I—why do you say that?"

Jasper's eyes flicked away from Jude, then down at his folded hands, and stayed there. "Anything I'm in seems to go to ruin."

Jude shook his head firmly. "That's not true."

"Well, I haven't done much to un-ruin anything, either. I haven't been able to help Felix at all. Or you, or Pixie, or even Letizia. I wish there was something I could do. For anyone. Anything."

"Just you being here helps," Jude said honestly, desperately hoping he was saying the right thing. He couldn't remember the last time Jasper had shown him this kind of vulnerability, the kind he'd do anything to protect and comfort. "That's all I want. That's all any of us want. Even if you don't do anything, just having you around is enough."

"Well, thank you, but, I mean something real." Now Jasper was the one to look in the direction of the room where Felix stayed, alone and silent. "I just hate seeing him hurt, and not being able to do anything."

"Yeah, me too," Jude said pointedly. "I hate seeing my most important people hurting."

"Well, then it's a good thing you're not!" Jasper said with a mirthless laugh.

"Yes I—I told you how important you are to me, that wasn't—"

"That's not what I mean. I'm not the wounded party in any of this. True, I feel helpless, frustrated, ineffectual—but that's because I can't help the ones who actually are in pain. I'm not the one who was killed and brought back and imprisoned and tortured. I'm not the one who's hurting."

"Yes you are," Jude said, and now he glared just a bit. "Don't do that, yes you are."

"Fine, Jude." Jasper looked back at him now, just as pointedly. "If I am, then it's just another thing we have in common."

"What's that? Hurting?"

"In a way. Both of us, very neurodivergent humans, in love with vampires, and not knowing how to help them. And not just because they're vampires. I can't begin to imagine the kind of trauma they've been through. Can you?"

Jude looked down at his own hands. "No."

"A good thing, I suppose." Jasper paused, then something else seemed to occur to him. "Circling back a bit—you said 'gray' made being asexual and aromantic less confusing, better-defined, better-managed. A succinct, easy term for complicated, sometimes-nebulous feelings that might change in unexpected ways."

"Yeah. It does."

"Then maybe we're gray. For now, at least." The corner of Jasper's mouth pulled up a bit. "I know, it's not easy being gray, but it's not such a bad way to be."

"Okay. Gray. Yeah." Jude nodded, temporarily satisfied, if still troubled.

For a few seconds, neither of them spoke. The apartment was completely still and quiet around them, so much so that it seemed impossible that there could be anyone else here, in the next room or anywhere else in the world. In a way, it was true; hardly anyone else alive would understand anything about them now, all they'd seen and survived.

It was a very lonely, isolating feeling, realizing that whether you had changed or the world, you no longer quite belonged to it the way you once had. But at least they could be alone together.

"It's not a bad thing that we're different people now," Jasper said quietly. "Any of us. We're all changed, and we'll keep changing, and maybe that's good. Recovery doesn't always mean everything goes back to the way it was before your world was shattered. Sometimes that's impossible." He let out a soft sigh. "But damn it all, if it doesn't feel like moving forward is just as impossible."

Jude didn't answer. But, this time, it wasn't that he couldn't find the words. Instead, it wasn't that he needed to speak at all, but act—and found the thought of it even more insurmountable.

If they were still the people they'd been before, this is when they would have kissed. If this was a perfect world, where none of the past five years had happened, but Jude knew then what he knew now, that Jasper—fat, safe, happy—loved him solidly and truly, and Felix—alive, well, whole—loved him with ease and without inhibition, and that with all his heart, he loved them, and always had. Any perfect world of his would have Eva in it too, secure and unburdened, and Pixie, another incredible, beautiful fat boy who Jude also sorely wanted to kiss right now—but no. Not if Jude wanted to keep him safe. And he couldn't kiss Jasper now, either. They weren't the people they'd been, they'd changed, the world wasn't perfect, it had changed too, and Jude didn't know this new grayscale landscape well enough to take a new step in it.

He couldn't do anything but lean just a little more against Jasper's too-thin shoulder, feel the warmth of him, feel him breathe, know they were by some miracle still alive, if not well, and that for now at least, gray was enough.

They sat together a bit longer, neither wanting to be the first one to rise. Finally, Jasper turned to him and spoke in a frank and level tone. "Jude, I don't know what it'll take to finally get Felix out of his room, or for Pixie to feel truly safe and sound, or to get us and Felix back to where we were heading—if we were heading anywhere together at all. And—"

"We were," Jude said quietly. Unquestioningly. He remembered two kisses, and regretted only that the number had stopped there.

"Yes, we were. And, as I was going to say, I don't know what's coming next for any of us. But if there's anyone I'd want beside us when we find out… well, you're a good man for the job."

Jude felt warm inside, and this time the good feeling stayed. He knew they were onto *something* before, something that had been put on hold, like so many other things, by Felix's death and all of their subsequent coping mechanisms, healthy or not. But it had been something strong, and real, and important—strong enough to last, and to be there when they could finally return to it with all the care and clarity it deserved. And they would. Jude knew that as well as he knew the face and hands of the man beside him, and how they'd be there when he was ready too. Then, and every moment until.

"Yeah, well..." Jude did smile now, wider and more brightly than before. It felt good. "I was going to be your best man."

Jasper smiled back, but it was the kind of tired, wistful smile on a too-gaunt face that made Jude's heart ache. "You still are."

🔥

"So I unlocked the door to the caves, that should be good to go. Is there anything else I can do?" Eva asked, trying not to sound too obviously bored. "Grab some eye of newt, find a creepy Latin book to read from, anything?"

Letizia had started to shuffle her cards again, but hadn't spread them. She'd been shuffling for several minutes on end, hands never still. It seemed to be more of a nervous habit than anything else, Eva realized. She must find the repetitive motion and feel of the cards calming—which she seemed to need, because her face was drawn with obvious anxiety.

"No, none of that," the Witch said, voice sounding weary. "I just... need you to be here. Just be with me."

"But what do I *do?*" Eva asked insistently, frustrated at the lack of direction. "That can't be it. You want me to just stand there, for what, moral support?"

"You can call it that," Letizia said. "All you have to do is be here. The more powerful the magic, the easier it is to get lost in. It's just safer to have someone there to bring you back."

"And you trust me with that?" Eva asked, frustration fading with a little smile. "That's flattering."

"I'd trust you with anything," Letizia said, looking directly into her eyes. Then she cleared her throat and looked away, setting the cards down at last, folding her hands as if to keep them from shaking. She looked up, and even for a vampire, she looked pale and drawn. "This is going to be a very powerful bit of magic. I might get caught in a riptide, swept out into the deep end. I need you to make sure that doesn't happen."

"And what does getting lost look like?" Eva asked, eyes searching Letizia's face, looking for signs of trouble right here and now.

"If I start to shake, eyes roll back in my head, anything like that, that's not a good sign," Letizia said, and now her smile took on some of its usual wryness. Familiar territory, Eva thought, slightly comforted. "Call me back. Squeeze my hands, give me a shake, or a good slap if you have to. Don't hold back."

"I won't," Eva assured her. "I'll be right here the whole time, but I hope it doesn't come to smacking you out of it. I will, though. With love." She gave a short, nervous laugh.

"I appreciate that," Letizia said. She sat down on the floor then, beside the completed mirror with its ring of bones, and motioned for Eva to do the same, across from her. When she did, Letizia held out her hands and Eva took them.

The Witch shut her eyes and seemed to slip into a deep trance. Sometimes, Eva forgot that Letizia and several of their friends weren't actually alive. They didn't always breathe, they didn't need to. But usually they weren't perfectly, unnaturally still like this, so it wasn't as noticeable. Now, she noticed. A shiver running down her spine, Eva shut her eyes too, and waited for the magic to begin.

And waited.

Nothing broke the silence, no smoke or flash or wind. Nothing happened at all, and finally, after what felt like years but had probably only been a few minutes, Eva cracked open her eyes, and peered up at Letizia, who hadn't moved a single muscle, still holding completely still, in a way no living human could. Eva's arms were beginning to ache from holding them out across the mirror, and just as she felt them starting to dip with fatigue, Letizia opened her eyes.

"There," the Witch said. "Done."

"That's it?" Eva asked in a hushed voice, feeling like they'd just stepped into a library.

"That's it." Letizia smiled. Her own voice sounded much stronger than it had before, and more focused.

"Huh. I didn't feel anything—I always expected magic to be more... ceremonial," Eva said, as Letizia gave her hands a little squeeze and then dropped them. "Particularly yours. You sure that was dramatic enough?"

"No drama this time," Letizia answered, and now she sounded a bit more at ease, smiling in a satisfied way. "Not for the really important things. Showy gets you killed; practical may actually work. If things do start to get *dramatic,* it means something's gone wrong."

"Makes sense," Eva said, though her puzzled look hadn't gone anywhere. "I just thought there'd be more to it than that. I mean, besides doing the counter-spell itself. I thought there'd be more for me to do, is all."

"You've already helped," Letizia said plainly, quickly. The words, which to Eva seemed like almost an admission of vulnerability, had the feeling of ripping off a band-aid. "When I said I didn't need you to bring anything, that wasn't quite the truth. I needed an anchor."

"An anchor?" Eva tried to smile, unable to resist a gentle tease. "Afraid I'm fresh out of those."

"Not an actual anchor. I meant—I meant you, Eva." Letizia stammered now, and if vampires could blush, Eva was sure her face would be turning red. "You've been the best friend to me I could imagine. This spell is dangerous, I don't know how it's going to go, but knowing it won't touch you will give me courage. Knowing you're safe will free me up to be daring and brave. I don't *want* to know you're safe, I…"

She stopped, leaving Eva waiting, eyebrows raised in surprised anticipation. She hadn't expected the beginning to that sentence, and badly wanted to hear its ending, but just as she'd left her question about the bones unfinished, Letizia couldn't seem to bring herself to complete this particular phrase. There were a lot of possible reasons for that, some much better than others. All of them pretty life-changing. None of them she knew how to put into words.

"I heard you. So that's really it?" Eva asked eagerly instead. They still had a job to do, and there would be time to explore implications, emotions, and possibilities later. Hopefully. "The spell is ready?"

"It's ready," Letizia said, letting out her breath in a little rush, as if she'd just sprinted a short but challenging distance. "All that's left is to get the mirror to the right place, and wait for the right time. Which in this case is midnight, and… what are you doing?"

"Texting Jude," Eva said, not looking up from her phone. "Letting him know the where and when. This is happening!"

"No, stop," Letizia said sharply and Eva looked up—but not before her thumb slipped down to hit *send*.

"What?"

"Don't tell—you just sent the message, didn't you?"

"Yeah," Eva said, giving Letizia a raised-brow stare. "Was that bad?"

The Witch shut her eyes and turned her face upwards, appealing to the ceiling or heavens beyond for help. "I wish you hadn't done that. Now they'll come and want to help."

"Well yeah, of course they will?" Eva said with a confusion-furrowed brow. "Are they not supposed to?"

"I'd rather them not, no."

"Why would—wait a minute." Eva slipped her phone back into her pocket and folded her arms. "You're the one who said you needed our help to get the spell done, and wanted me here while you did—whatever you just did. Why are you mad they're coming now?"

"I'm not mad," Letizia said in a carefully calm voice that did nothing to convince Eva this was true. "But your part of the spell is over. Now it's my turn to take over, and finish it myself. Everyone trying to come along will make everything…more difficult than it needs to be."

"What the hell does that mean?" Eva asked, incredulous voice rising a bit in both volume and pitch. "What do you mean, 'our part is over?' You're gonna do this whole ritual thing alone?"

"That was the idea, yes."

"This very dangerous counter-spell to a very dangerous ritual, you're flying this one solo?"

"Yes." Letizia nodded. "The last steps, I have to take alone."

"So what were we, your—your kitchen staff?" Eva's eyes hardened. "You need us to make the meal, but now you're gonna serve the whole feast yourself, is that right?"

"I feel like the metaphor is getting away from you a bit," Letizia said, still in that carefully level tone. "But yes. And as long as we're using it, let's say that tonight is a feast, and the dinner guests are all ravenous sharks. I'd just as soon keep my helper chefs away from their tank."

"Yeah? Well, sorry to burst your—your soufflé, or whatever, but it would've been nice to know earlier, before I—before we got all invested in this! Why didn't you say something earlier?"

Letizia picked up her cards and began to shuffle them. "Because you and the others have no business being in a dangerous—"

"No business?" An indignant line appeared between Eva's eyebrows. "Are we or are we not a part of this?"

"You are. A very important one." Letizia's shuffling grew faster, louder, the taps between a little more insistent. "But now you must see reason, instead of insisting on coming into a dangerous situation where you can do no good, and may be hurt, or worse."

"Don't you think that's our decision to make?" Eva retorted. "So instead of letting us decide like grown-ups, you're just making this—this unilateral decision, just giving us a kiss-off now that the feast is done instead of serving the thing all together like—ugh, forget it," she shook her head. "This metaphor sucks. And this whole thing sucks! I gotta say, I'm feeling a little used here."

"I'm sorry about that," Letizia said, as her hands and cards moved so fast Eva could barely follow them, the tap-shuffle speeding up to a frantic rhythm. "But there's nothing I can do. As I said, your part is over. I want you as far away as possible from the circle, and me, when the time comes."

"Really, Letizia?" Eva stared at her. "After all this, it's just 'okay, that's all, you're dismissed?'"

The aggressive shuffling stopped. Abruptly, the Witch slapped her hands together, then the cards down on the table, pile haphazard and lopsided.

"You've done enough already," she said, now holding perfectly still. She still didn't meet Eva's eyes, but her distress was obvious enough. "And now you're done. You need to stay out of this, as far away as you can get."

"Well, that's too bad," Eva said, folding her arms and gave the Witch a defiant glare. "You can't always get what you want."

Now Letizia did look up, eyes narrowing until she was glaring right back. "What makes you think you could help me with the actual spellwork itself? You're not a Witch. You're not even a vampire. You're a human, fragile, breakable, and to have you there would be begging for disaster. Leave the wielding of arcane forces to the professionals."

"I—you—" Eva sputtered, face beginning to flush. Then she stopped for the space of a breath, only to point a finger directly at Letizia's face. "I know what you're doing. You're doing the—the *Spiderman 2* thing!"

Letizia's iron-resolved face went blank, and she gave a surprised blink. "The Spider…?"

"You're trying to push me away by making me angry, so I decide that I hate you and don't get mad when you run off and do something really dumb and really dangerous, because you think your superpowered ass is the only who can save the day or some shit like that! Yes, I said shit, I'm tired of keeping my mouth shut, and I'm tired of you acting like you're the chosen one who needs to keep secrets and do everything by herself, because us puny humans could never handle the big scary magic! Give us some credit, get over yourself, and let us help!"

"...Are you finished?" Letizia asked when Eva broke off, panting.

"Yeah," she said with a jerky nod. "Yeah, I'm done."

"Yes, you are. Glad to hear we finally agree," Letizia said, and turned away, beginning to pick up the fragments of bone that ringed the mirror, and slipping them into a small velvet pouch that hadn't been there a moment ago. "Go home, Eva."

Eva opened her mouth to argue further, then shut it, throwing up her hands and turning away. "Fine. You know what, fine! Be like that. Say you need our help, and then push away the people trying to help you right after you're done with them. See if I care. Good luck with your big important magic."

With that, Eva stormed out the apartment with a full head of steam. She thought she might have heard her name, but it was hard to hear over the slammed door.

When Jude got home, the sun was nearly down. Almost nightfall, the ritual just a few hours away. But that was an anxious buzz in the back of his mind, and he had more important things to do first, like check the oven mitt where he'd left Pixie. He frowned upon finding it as quiet as Jasper's, the bedroom door closed, and Pixie presumably inside. He must still need some space, which Jude well understood and respected.

So, realizing that he couldn't do anything useful here, Jude shifted his thoughts to another important subject—the spell and its requirements. His work wasn't quite done.

It was a quick project, but he'd only just finished when Pixie came out of the bedroom, still looking chagrined, and Jude put his work aside, folding it up and sticking it into his jacket pocket.

"Hey," Pixie said, still sounding sad and tired, but at least a little less so.

"I'm sorry again, about earlier—at the motel."

"You still have nothing to apologize for," Jude said. "I know why you did it. I can tell you that you don't have to worry, but you're still going to. Just like you're still going to have feelings about Jeff, and grief, and you don't have to give that up or get over it for me to care about you and want you around. I always want you around."

"Thanks. I mean it. But I'm still sorry. I… won't let it get to that point again." Pixie gave an awkward shrug, hands in his pockets. "So, um, I kept thinking about the spell, and found something else that might work." He reached into a pocket and pulled something out that was bigger than a postcard but smaller than a poster. A sticker, reading "THIS BASS KILLS FASCISTS."

"That was his, wasn't it?" Jude asked quietly, looking over its weathered and scratched surface. It wasn't ripped, though; Pixie must have removed it as carefully as possible.

"Yeah," Pixie said. "I was gonna use his summer shirt, but… well, I figured this would work just as well. It's, uh, a memory of happiness. Rose-tinted. Not because it's pink, but because I know it's easy to look back and think everything was perfect when it wasn't, and to forget the good things you have now. And you have to know when to let that go. So I'm trying to let it go, and stop messing up—sorry. I'm gonna stop talking now."

"Don't stop," Jude said. "I want to hear what you think. Even if it's sad, or messy, or anything else. It's when you hold back that I start to worry."

"Okay. Thanks. I'll try to share my sad messiness more—that was a joke!"

"I know. But I'm serious. I'm here for a reason, I want to be part of your life like you're part of mine." He cleared his throat, and pulled the paper he'd been working on from the inside of his jacket and unfolded it. "I was thinking about my part of the spell too, and I think I figured it out. And hopefully it'll convince you that I meant everything I just said, and I'll keep meaning it."

He handed the paper to Pixie, whose eyes grew wide and round as he accepted it. It was the poster from earlier, the one with Pixie's name and picture on it—but the bolded "MISSING" had been scribbled out, and above it, one word written in red sharpie: "FOUND."

He heard Pixie make a soft, emotion-stricken noise, and his heart ached and felt warm at the same time.

"A dream of happiness, with eyes wide open," Jude explained, voice wistful. "Because I know we're not there yet, but... I want to be."

"Jude..." Pixie said softly, and Jude looked over, waiting. But no more words came. Pixie's eyes were squeezed shut, and his shoulders rose and fell as he took a deep, habitual breath. "I want that too. More than anything. You're—I don't know how I ended up here. I never thought I had that kind of luck in my life. And I guess I didn't. But even after everything, even dying, even all the stuff after that? It's okay. I'm here now. With you."

Jude thought about his own journey, how he'd died too, felt the sun and heard the ocean waves, and come back to find everything different. All the pain and loss and adjustment, everything he'd do all over again if he had the choice. "I feel the same way."

Pixie smiled at him, and Jude sucked in a breath—it was another of those moments, those kisses-in-a-perfect-world moments, but this time Jude felt a flutter of hope and excitement instead of fear, something pulling him forward instead of paralyzing him. He took a step forward, hand coming up to reach out for Pixie's face and draw him closer, when—

Ding.

It wasn't Mozart's Requiem, but the standard text noise from the phone Jude had never bothered messing with much was just as jarring. Sighing, he pulled it out of his pocket and glanced at the screen. Anyone else and he would have put it right away again, but not this time.

EVA: *L says it's time to go. Meet us at the mall at 9, same place as last time.*

"I guess everything's ready," Jude said reluctantly, and gave Pixie an apologetic look. "We should go—and I don't want to rush through this. But we're coming back to it later."

Pixie only looked disappointed for a moment, before brightening and grinning at him. "I can't wait."

🔥

The dark and empty mall was strangely peaceful, almost beautiful in its own odd, liminal-space kind of way.

"Are we really ready for this?" Jude asked as he, Pixie, Letizia, and Jasper stood before the heavy metal door that led to the mall's sub-basement and the network of tunnels beyond. The last time they'd been down here, it had been to rescue Pixie and confront a monster. This time, at least, Pixie was standing safely at Jude's side, though he looked more than a little apprehensive. Jude could relate.

"I am more than ready," Letizia said, her voice harder than usual. Oddly, she'd looked annoyed to see Jude and Pixie's approach, and now she stood unwavering and fixing the door with a level stare, as if she could see beyond it to her goal. Maybe she actually could. "The door should be open. Eva unlocked it earlier."

"Speaking of, where is Eva?" Jude asked, looking around, half-expecting her to emerge from a darkened storefront. He'd feel much better if she did. "We got her text, so I figured she'd be here before us. We can't do this without her."

"I asked her not to come," Letizia said, tone cool and steady as she was. "She would be much more helpful away from this place. As would you."

"What does that mean?" Jude asked, not liking something about the Witch's phrasing, or the hard edge to her voice.

"It means what I said. The preparation of the spell was for all of us. The casting of it is for me alone. I told Eva this, and asked her to stay far away."

"And she listened to that? That's unlike her," Jude said, a sinking feeling in his stomach. Letizia gave a slight nod, but said nothing more. "Also, what the hell do you mean, the casting is for you alone?"

"That's exactly what she said," the Witch sighed with a roll of her eyes. "And you weren't supposed to be here either. I meant to tell you all beforehand, but Eva had sent word to you before I could stop her. As I told her, I am truly grateful for all you've done, collecting the necessary ingredients, but we are working with very dangerous forces. The kind that you should not be exposed to."

"Well, you're right about one thing," Jasper cut in before Jude could, and more gently than he would have. "It would have been nice to know that earlier. But we're here now, and I believe we're all committed to seeing this through together."

"I didn't come this far to back out now," Jude said. Still, he suddenly felt much less sure of this entire business. He turned to look around, then back at Jasper, who stood nearby. "Is Felix not coming either?"

"Not tonight," Jasper confirmed in a flat voice, and Jude was disappointed again despite himself. He hadn't quite expected Felix to venture out of Jasper's apartment again, especially not this far, and would have been surprised to actually see him. Still, his heart sank a little too. Jasper himself seemed not so much calm as controlled. He didn't like this either, Jude could tell. "This place is a little too... relevant."

"No kidding," Pixie muttered, looking unusually dour. It was the first time he'd spoken since leaving Jude's apartment, and now he watched the door like it might suddenly come to life and attack them.

"You really don't have to do this," Jude said to him quietly. "Everyone would understand."

"I know I don't have to," Pixie replied, sounding determined, if not encouraged, and not bothering to whisper. "I want to. Kind of. I mean, no, I don't really *want to,* but I feel like it's important to do. Prove the place didn't kill me, if that makes sense."

"It definitely does," Jude said with a nod. "Reclaiming is important. So, are we—"

"No, 'we' are nothing," Letizia said in a raised voice. "I am ready to proceed. All that's left for you to do is give me your prepared items, so I can—"

Deee-deedle-deeee-dee.

Mozart's Requiem in D Minor was back, echoing off the shining floor and interrupting the near-sacrosanct atmosphere like disturbing a crowded movie theater.

"Aaargh!" Letizia snarled as she pulled her phone—or an identical one, since the last time Jude had seen it, it had been very much on fire—eyes flaring briefly as her arm flew out in a blur, flinging the ringing phone against the nearest wall, where it shattered into a dozen pieces.

"Was that a good idea?" Jasper asked, eyebrows raised and tone magnanimous.

"It's fine. It'll be back." As Letizia spoke, the pieces of the phone began to move, springing back together as if someone had hit 'rewind' on its destruction. Seamlessly repaired, it sprung back into her waiting hand. She sighed, shook her head, and stuck it back in her pocket, muttering irritated Italian under her breath.

"So, like I was about to ask," Jude said, watching Letizia steadily with a deadpan expression. "Are we all ready?"

"As we'll ever be, I think." Jasper nodded, and Jude stepped up to the heavy door and pushed. It opened with a whining of hinges and grinding of metal, but it did open.

"Wait," Letizia called, before Jude could continue into the dark, and he looked back to see her and Pixie still standing on the mall side of the door.

"What's wrong?" Jude asked. "I thought we were the ones who were supposed to stay here."

"You," the Witch said to Jasper, seeming to choose not to dignify Jude's barb with a response. "You I did ask here for a reason. You have to invite us in. Both of us."

"What?" he exclaimed with a bark of nervous laughter that made Jude jump a bit. "Why me?"

"This was Cruce's old lair. With him dead, ownership reverts to the next available power," Letizia explained, sounding a little exasperated, or maybe embarrassed.

"Probably the mall's parent corporation," Jasper shrugged. "Or maybe the city of Portland, if eerie catacombs aren't included?"

"On paper, perhaps," Letizia said, shifting impatiently. "But in spirit, I would call Eva the guardian of this place.

"Eva, who isn't here for some reason?" Jude asked with a narrowed gaze.

"Yes. And in her absence, the title would go to one of you."

"I don't own the mall," Jasper said, looking dubious. "And I certainly don't own miles of caves underneath it."

"No, but you own a shop here, and quite a special one at that. Magic responds to magic." She glanced around at them as if daring anyone to challenge her impeccable logic. "As the sole magician-in-residence of this place, that makes you an authority, and therefore a guardian."

"Really, now? A guardian?" Jasper said with a slowly spreading grin. Jude could see him warm to the idea, which warmed him in turn. "I must admit, that does have quite a nice ring to it. Well, then! Come inside! Welcome to my domain." He ushered them inside with an elaborate, hand-waving bow, and Letizia and Pixie stepped over the threshold without incident.

"Thank you," Letizia said to him with a gracious nod. "And now, your part is truly over."

"My dear, I believe we both know that isn't true," he said in a calm and level tone Jude recognized as the one he used when Jude was being particularly negative or stubborn. It wasn't smug or gloating, but it was the one that meant Jasper was right, he knew he was right, and the sooner everyone else caught up, the better. "As Jude said, we're all in too deep to bow out now. And if the forces at work are as dangerous as you say, then you're asking us to let a friend walk knowingly into that danger alone. Does anything about us, or our history—filled with questionable decisions as it is—suggest that's something we're about to do?"

"I could send all of you to sleep right now," Letizia said, with a quick glance around at all three of them, voice growing louder and more commanding with every word. "Do you know the witch you're dealing with? I could turn you to frogs. Or human statues. I could simply teleport there and be done with it!"

"Then why haven't you done any of that?" Jasper asked in that same, infuriatingly reasonable voice.

"Because..." Letizia let the word and its slight echo hang in the air. With her intense eyes darkening until they appeared completely black, she did indeed seem capable of wonders and horrors. Then she let out a sigh and shut her eyes, letting her head drop until her long hair formed a slight curtain in front of her face. "You're my friends, who I love. Of course I want you with me. Of course I want her with me. But it would be selfish to ask, and irresponsible to allow."

"Then it seems you've got a choice," Jasper said. "Do something unpleasant to us so we can't follow you, and risk us breaking out of whatever it is, following you down, interrupting your carefully-crafted spell and ruining everything... or letting your friends help you. Which I do actually know isn't always easy—but if I'm being honest, I'd much rather assist in a dangerous spell than be a frog."

Letizia didn't answer. Jude got the impression that she couldn't. But the corner of her mouth did turn up in a slow, crooked smile, and she headed into the tunnel before them without another word.

"Nicely done," Jude said to Jasper as he moved to follow Letizia.

"I try," he returned, a chuckle under his breath.

The door closed behind them. Together they went into the dark.

The corridor quickly turned to a stone tunnel bored directly through the earth, and it was every bit as ominous and oppressive-feeling as Jude remembered.

He had been terrified the last time they'd been down here, walking straight into God-knew-what, knowing only that somewhere down here waited a kidnapped and injured Pixie. Now, he and almost the same group made their way down—plus Pixie. It should have been plus Eva too, Jude thought, and he missed her. More than he even would have expected; she always let him breathe easier. Pixie stuck close to him, and the beam of his pocket flashlight—maybe Jude had the same effect on him. He hoped so.

It didn't take long until the dark, twisting tunnels opened up into a large central cavern that seemed nearly the size of the mall itself. Much too big for one vampire, Jude thought with a shiver. How many others had made their lairs here? But there was no question about who had used this place last. Only Cruce could be responsible for the large spatters of what was definitely dried blood on the floor, walls, and in spots of the cave, ceiling.

Pixie stopped, taking in the large cavern. It was mostly empty, as it had been—except for the crude wooden cross dominating one side. Below it lay several nails and a large hammer. Pixie stared at the implements of torture that had caused him so much pain, not moving or saying a word. Jasper tapped Letizia on the shoulder and nodded toward the side tunnel entrances, beyond Cruce's lingering accouterments. She unhesitatingly led the way toward one of them, as if she'd spent her life down here, and the two of them moved forward to give Pixie and Jude a moment together.

"Hey," Jude said in a low voice, not wanting to startle Pixie out of the reverie into which he'd obviously fallen, but needing to all the same. "You're still here. You made it out, and you'll make it out again. I'm right here."

"I know." Pixie gave him a little smile, faint but there. "And it's really okay, Jude. I'm okay. This is what I wanted to see—it's not the place where Cruce almost killed me. It's the place where you saved me."

Jude let out a soft sound that was almost a laugh, but instead of amusement he felt a stab of something close to pain. Close, but not quite. He reached out, still awkward as he always was in emotional moments, but at least knowing now that it was the right thing. Pixie leaning into him when Jude wrapped his arm around his shoulders just confirmed it. "I'm... Really glad you're still here."

Letizia moved past them, bringing him back to the present, and set something down on the ground, which Jude was sure she hadn't been holding before: a large, metal-framed mirror.

"All right. Everybody come here—let's begin."

🔥

Eva hadn't gone home. She knew she wouldn't be able to stay inside four walls with her brain buzzing with both frustration and anxiety, that it would just feel like a cage, and she needed to cool her head, both literally and figuratively. Before she said or texted anything else she might regret.

It was just cold enough outside that she could see the faint fog of her breath. She hadn't known exactly where she was headed when she started walking through the park—not to the mall, since she didn't want to see any witchy faces just now. She wasn't quite so impulsive as to burst into a dark ritual alone and unprepared, but the images of the stones burned in her head like a song she couldn't forget. They hung over her like the January chill, just as impossible to escape.

But she hadn't seen them. Or anything even nearby, she thought with some confusion. Shouldn't she be able to find them now, even without Letizia's charm, since she knew where they were? It didn't make sense.

Of course, nothing about Letizia made sense right now, she thought, with a surge of hurt instead of the anger she expected. Just when Eva had really been feeling their connection, enjoying working together, being on the same side, the same page, the Witch had ripped the rug right out from under her.

"Your work is done now, she says," Eva muttered. "Go home, Eva, she says. Thanks for your help, now get the hell out. Well, fine. I don't care. Don't blame me if you end up dead, or whatever vampires end up as when they…"

She stopped walking. For a few foggy breaths, she stood there, hands in her pockets and not moving. Then she turned on her heel and strode back the way she'd come, toward the mall, and her friends, and stubborn, stubborn witches who pushed people away instead of letting them close enough to—

She wasn't alone.

Unlike most humans, Eva knew for a fact that the shadows were rarely as empty as they seemed. She remembered reading some worrying statistic, that no matter where you went, there was always a spider within six feet of you in some direction. The same seemed to be true of vampires, or the humans who served them—because here he was. Again.

"Hello... you," she said, more grouchily than necessary maybe, but the last time she'd had a one-on-one interaction with this kid, he'd been guarding dirt and been a brat. And the time before that, he'd hurled a piece of trash at her, causing her nose to meet a coffee thermos in a very uncomfortable way. She still blamed him for the coffee-stain destruction of one of her favorite shirts.

The skinny, dirt-smeared boy with rats-nest-hair, glowering up at her with narrowed eyes and a tucked-in chin. He stood directly in her path, just out of the light cast by the nearby streetlight, hands jammed into the pockets of a not-nearly-thick-enough jacket for the cold, wet night. Ordinarily, if a man had planted himself ominously between her and the way home in the dark, Eva would already be making sure her mace was in easy reach, and lining up a kick to his sensitive regions, which would be even more unpleasant thanks to her heels.

But this guy always looked like he could be taken out by a strong gust of breeze, and she couldn't bring herself to be intimidated if she tried.

"It's Sanguine," he said grumpily.

"Gesundheit."

"Very funny. That's my name."

"And it's lovely. Now if you'll excuse me." She stepped around him, rolling her eyes.

"Yeah, you better run!" he rasped, whipping around to face her as she went, but not actually pursuing. "I'm not kidding, get outta here!"

"I'd like nothing better, believe me," she muttered, throwing a glance back at him and preparing to shoot back something like 'you still owe me for that shirt,' when she stopped dead, mid-word and mid-step.

He'd stepped into the streetlight's glow for her to see him clearly. And she didn't like what she saw at all—because the kid was bleeding. It trickled down from the top of his head, and now that she looked closer she could see that it matted his already almost-solid hair. Half his forehead—the entire left side of his face, really—was discolored, as if it were all one big bruise, so fresh it wasn't even quite formed. It would be ghoulish when it was done. His eyes were out of focus and too dark, like his pupils were over-dilated; another time she might have figured it was just because he was on something, but now…

"Listen, kid—San-gween-eh. Am I saying that right?"

"Close enough."

"You look like you've got a concussion. At least. What happened here?"

"Nothing," he spat, wavering on his feet, but backpedaling out of the puddle of light. "Like I said, keep moving, so nothing else happens. To you."

He raised one arm to wipe the blood from his face, and that's when she saw them—huge, messy, barely-healed puncture wounds on his forearm, wrist, and, when he brushed some of his hair aside, along with the blood, up the side of his neck.

"Oh, God," she whispered. "That's…"

"That's what?" he mumbled. One of the bite marks—because they could be nothing else—had reopened, sending a second trickle of blood down to pool in his too-defined collarbone. Jude had told her about them, of course, but seeing them for herself now, she found them much, much harder to ignore.

"What my friend Jude said when we saw you yesterday? We've seen… something like that before," Eva said, lowering her voice but willing him to understand with every word, to confirm or deny what she was beginning to suspect. "Exactly like that. On your neck and arms—"

"Drugs!" Sanguine blurted. "I do tons of drugs. Like just, really, shooting up all day, doesn't it look like I do all kinds of drugs?"

"Not really." Eva shook her head. Had those injuries always been there, weeks and months ago? Had she ever looked close enough to tell, or seen them and forgotten, dismissed him as just another troublemaker? "You do look like you need help. Just talk to me for a second. We know how to deal with—"

"No! Shut up! Just shut up!" Sanguine exploded, and he took another step backwards and away from Eva, so unsteady he nearly fell.

"I know where you got those scars," Eva said, and now, the sound of her voice seemed to hold Sanguine in place like quicksand. "I've seen them before. On a friend of mine. A few friends, actually. They were being hurt by a… very bad person. I know it sounds crazy to say out loud, and nobody would believe you, but we do. I do."

His thin shoulders sagged as if someone had just placed a heavy weight on his back. His knees shook, clearly around five minutes away from buckling underneath him from exhaustion and sending him crashing to the ground. "I'm telling you, get out of here."

"Not going to happen, kid."

"Oh my God, why?" his voice went up in pitch until it was half-shout, half-whine. "Why are you still bugging me like you give a fuck?"

"Because I *do* give a fuck about what happens to other people, even if they make it really hard!" Forget trying to rein in the four-letter words. Sometimes they spoke the language of her fucking heart when nothing else did. "Which most people do! Even when I probably shouldn't! But I know what did that to you, and nobody deserves it. And for whatever reason, dealing with 'em is kind of me and my friends' job now. It doesn't pay very well, but that's the gig economy for you. So drop the bull-crap and—"

Sanguine scowled. "I don't know what you're talking ab—"

"Do I look like your mom, walking in on you with a joint? Don't lie to me like I'm your mom, I know *bite marks* when I see them!"

Sanguine jerked backwards like he'd been slapped. His usually-pale face lost any bit of color it had, and his mouth hung slack, blue eyes wide and glassy, but not at all vacant or dull. Pained.

"You're trying to help me, but I'm the one trying to help you," he said at last, voice unnaturally high-pitched, dropping only after a rough clearing of his throat. "Listen, it's over for me. I'm done. You don't have to be done. I was supposed to—I was ordered to stop you here and distract you but fuck that, I've been saying you need to go, but now you need to actually listen to me and *get out of here right now,* run, before…"

He stopped, suddenly shutting his eyes, and cringing away from Eva as if she really were going to slap him, even though she hadn't moved at all.

"Before what?" she prodded, though the sinking feeling in her stomach gave her a very good idea. Sanguine didn't open his eyes or lift his head, still looking like he was bracing for a blow. Now, she very much did have the urge to just bolt into a run, sprint away from here as fast as possible and keep running. But there were things you couldn't run from, and things you needed to face head-on when it was too late to try. A chill shooting up her spine, Eva turned to look behind her.

She barely had time to register a pair of golden eyes, as cold and bright as polished coins, before the clawed hands flew toward her face.

ACT FIVE: Come Back to Me

ONCE MORE, the circle was lit by bonfires, much more brightly than at the time of its last awakening. Instead of just one fire, several burned within it, each stone spire casting long, flickering shadows that radiated out from the center like spokes of a wheel.

"They're not coming," Owen muttered to himself, checking his watch for the fourth time, after several minutes of resentful silence. "Of course n—"

"Hold the party," said Wicked Gold, appearing in front of Owen without any sound or sign. It was as if he'd stepped out from behind one of the spires or a tree, but there was nothing near enough for him to hide behind. "Can't start without the guest of honor."

In one arm he held an unconscious human: Eva, who he carried like a sack of potatoes. In the other, there was another nearly-unconscious human; Wicked Gold held the scruff of Sanguine's neck, who wavered and nearly stumbled upon being released.

A smear of red crossed Eva's forehead, but the kind of smear that had been purposely placed there, not from an injury. An intentional mark. Sanguine's less-precise bruise was turning an angry purple, blood darkening as it dried in his hair.

"You were late," the vampire said, punctuating the words with a disapproving slice of his eyes toward Owen, and away again just as quickly. He set Eva down on the ground, not quite dumping her, but none too gently either.

"I got here before you did," Owen said flatly. His eyes swept over Eva and Sanguine, taking in the blood and bruises, both ceremonial and otherwise. "And they're looking a bit worse for wear. I could take care of those injuries before we begin."

"Oh, don't bother," Wicked Gold said airily, glancing up at the moon in much the same way Owen had checked his watch. "It's almost time anyway."

"M'okay don't worry," Sanguine mumbled and shakily climbed to his feet, using the nearest spire for the assistance his master didn't offer. A concussion seemed likely.

"Oh God," Eva mumbled, stirring, eyes squeezed shut as if she were suffering the world's worst hangover on the world's brightest morning. "This place again. Why does everybody want these freaking rocks?"

"You'll find out," Wicked Gold said as Sanguine edged a bit closer to the other human.

"Sorry about this," he said quietly, though he couldn't hope to keep a vampire from overhearing. "Believe it or not, misery doesn't actually love company."

If Wicked Gold took offense, he only snorted and turned his attention to the dark woods beyond the circle as if waiting for something.

"You're fine, kid," Eva said, struggling to sit up and spitting out a bit of blood. Thankfully no teeth. "Thanks for…" Sanguine shot her a warning, alarmed look, as if aware of what she was about to say. He'd tried. He'd failed completely, but he'd tried to keep her out of here, and that was something. "Thanks for saying that."

"I'd apologize for all this," Wicked Gold said, turning back to Eva with a passingly sympathetic look. "But I didn't see any alternative. It's nothing personal—my goodness, having a personal issue with a human, can you imagine?"

Sanguine and Owen exchanged a silent glance behind the vampire's back, and Wicked Gold leaned down closer to Eva's level.

"Then what the hell do you want with me?" Eva rasped, glaring up directly into her captor's golden eyes without a flinch. "I already know how this thing works. You need a willing sacrifice, and my dude, that ain't me."

"That's absolutely right," Wicked Gold said with a nod and raise of his eyebrows that almost looked impressed. "And just confirms that I made the right decision in bringing you here. The Witch really has rubbed off on you. But you do serve a purpose here, a very important one." He raised one finger, long silver claw shining.

Eva's eyes widened as they followed the claw's sharp edge, its slow path toward her. "She'll come for me, you know," she said in a shaking whisper. "Letizia isn't going to let you do this. Even if she's stubborn and hardheaded and—and everything else, she's coming and you can't stop her!"

"You don't have to convince me," Wicked Gold said with a genial chuckle. "Or yourself. I know the Witch is coming for you—and that's exactly what I'm counting on."

Slowly, he pressed the single claw to Eva's cheek as if wiping away a tear. Then he drew it down, a teardrop of blood in its wake.

Deep underground, the magic began. It didn't look like magic yet, but everyone could feel the building electricity in the air.

Letizia laid the repaired mirror on the ground and sat down before it. She carefully picked up a bone fragment and laid it on the mirror's edge, then another, one by one, slowly forming a circle. With the other hand, she sprinkled the dirt Jude and Eva had recovered, forming a ring outside the mirror as well.

"Letizia," Jude said, eyes on the bones in her hand, suddenly feeling every single sensible reservation bubble to the surface. She turned to look up at him, still as one of the stones in the circle, expression blank. Jude did have misgivings about this, lots of them, but, he concluded ruefully, he probably should have voiced them earlier, before they were down in the caves about to cast a spell. Bones or not. "Never mind."

The Witch laid the final piece of bone and dropped the last bit of dirt. The mirror was complete and unbroken, a surface smooth as a frozen lake at night, and just as dark.

"Please present the items you've collected," she said in a voice that sounded detached, oddly professional.

"Here," Jude said, pulling out the "FOUND" poster and handing it over, as Pixie did the same with his fascist-killing sticker. "Rose-tinted memories, and the hope of a dream with eyes open."

"This is perfect," Letizia said quietly as Pixie placed the sticker on the mirror beside the poster. "You chose well."

Pixie said nothing, and Jude figured he was all out of words, an affliction Jude knew well. They'd come back; they always did.

"And here's mine," Jasper said then, reaching out to place two small objects on the glass with a metallic clink. A pair of gold rings, Jude realized, and while he hadn't seen one in a while, the other he'd seen every day until recently. "A sign of a promise given with the greatest intention."

"Jasper," Jude said quietly. "Those are…"

"Felix and my engagement rings, yes," Jasper said, and Jude could hear the rueful smile in his voice. "Don't worry. It's not as awful a sacrifice as it seems—his doesn't fit anymore, and I actually love the idea of getting new ones, and doing the thing right, when the time comes. It seems appropriate, under the circumstances."

"These are perfect," Letizia said quietly, though if Jude had to describe her expression, it would be much closer to pensive and sad. "And now for mine. An anchor in a storm of will."

She reached one finger out and touched it to the mirror's surface, tracing a shape—or maybe letters. Jude couldn't tell what they were, but there were three, and the glass seemed to ripple in the wake of her finger, as if she were touching the surface of a still pond. Letizia let the silence hang, then nodded to herself, as if confirming something, and turned back to them.

"I'm ready to begin," she said, and now her eyes were clear and present. "Think of yourselves as my ground control—stay calm, stay still, and do not break the circle, no matter what you see within the mirror. Unless…"

She paused, and Jude did not at all enjoy the silence and all the unknowns that could fill it. "Unless what?"

"Unless it looks as if I am getting lost in the working. Try to keep me on course, and to keep the circle closed. But if I fly beyond your reach—run."

"What does that mean?" Pixie asked, sounding alarmed. "If you get lost? Why should we run?"

"Working with powerful magic is like moving into deep water," the Witch said, steel beneath her words. "The forces are like currents, and it's too easy to be pulled under, especially alone. Your presence should ground me, remind me that there is a world here, that I am a real person, and I have other living beings depending on me. That said, if anything feels wrong—run. Get as far away from me as possible. I can weather the arcane storms, but you may be swept away."

"Letizia, none of us are going to leave…" Jasper started, then faltered as she fixed him with a sharp gaze. "All right. Understood."

The witch hesitated, then, wordlessly, held out both of her hands, Pixie on one side and Jasper on the other. They took her hands without hesitation, as did Jude when Jasper held one out to him. Pixie hadn't let go of Jude's either, and the circle was closed.

Letizia held perfectly still, and everyone else took her cue, watching the dark mirror. Jude realized he was holding his breath, a common anxiety response, and made himself suck in a lungful of air. Held it for the count of four. Then let it out as he counted to seven. They were safe here, she'd said. Nothing was going to come leaping out of the shadows. If it did, they'd be ready.

But it didn't. Nothing attacked or erupted. For what seemed like forever, nothing happened, or at least nothing Jude could tell. They all kept waiting in silence, and after a while, Jasper's hand in his started to feel sweaty. Pixie's didn't, likely because vampires didn't sweat. Or did they? Jude didn't actually know for sure, and trying to remember if he'd ever seen an example took up what had to be at least a minute of silence.

By the time he stopped wondering about vampires and sweat glands, he'd started to feel more than a little silly, holding hands in a circle and staring at a mirror in a cave. Waiting for the Witch with a lap full of bones he knew uncomfortably little about to cast a spell he knew even less about. He was just starting to feel less silly and more concerned when Letizia sucked in a sharp gasp.

"Are you all…" Jude started to ask, then stopped, the thought instantly jolted from his head.

The mirror wasn't dark anymore. Suddenly he realized that the papers and rings they'd placed on it were gone, only clear and unbroken glass in their place. Firelight shone from the mirror's surface, but there was no light in the cavern for it to reflect. Suddenly it looked more like a lit window on the floor or a screen playing a movie, clearer and more high-definition than any Jude had ever seen.

And stranger. Black spires like pieces of broken onyx—like the shattered glass shards the mirror had once been—thrust toward the sky. The image was silent, but if there was sound, it should have been the crackling of wood fires. The stones' smooth surfaces reflected red-orange flames framing the mirror's edges, as if the 'camera' was in the midst of the fire.

Water. Ocean waves, regular and calming. The far-off cry of sea birds.

Jude sucked in a breath of cool, moist air that smelled like water and salt instead of a stale cave, and tasted in the strangest way like a home he'd never seen. A cold chill ran through him, even as he remembered the warmth of the sand between his toes, the sun on his shoulders.

He gripped Jasper and Pixie's hands harder, filled with a painful understanding of what Letizia had meant when she'd talked about getting lost and needing them to find her again. His head filled with the crashing of waves.

But then Jasper gave his hand a quick squeeze and little shake, and Jude almost dropped his, realizing he'd been clenching it in what had to be a finger-crunching death grip. He loosened his grasp and Jasper didn't let go. Pixie never altered his steady grip, even if Jude had definitely been doing the same thing to him. Instead, he stroked the back of Jude's hand with his thumb, the way Jude had done several times with him before. Jude shuddered, but from emotion and gratitude instead of fear. Sometimes he forgot how strong the sweet little vampire was, in more than one way.

Letizia began to lean forward over the mirror, face eerily lit and cast in strange, shifting shadows from the orange fires below.

"I'm here," she whispered, and her eerie voice sent a new wave of shivers down Jude's spine. Jude could barely see something shining travel down her face. A tear, he realized, glittering in the firelight—but she was smiling more brightly than Jude had ever seen her, as if she'd only just now begun to hope. "I've always been right here, for so long. Please… come back to me."

Now she swept the bones up, pulling them into her lap and hunching over them as if protecting something priceless and fragile. Their part was apparently done, and the rest left to the mirror. Letizia's shoulders shook with every breath.

If the mirror was acting like a TV screen, its 'signal' left something to be desired. Maybe it hadn't been fully assembled and used in centuries, or maybe it was still fragile, but the image of the stone circle, clear as it had been to start with, soon warped and dissolved into something like static snow. Letizia began to mutter quietly but fervently under her breath, and images began to flash across the glass, fast and disorienting, from different angles. The circle from above, the bonfire in the center, the night sky as if the 'camera' had fallen to the ground.

Then the mirror cleared. Free of all distortion or interference, the image resolved itself into something unmistakable: a human face, gray, with bright golden eyes.

"Oh, God," Pixie whispered, and his grip tightened on Jude's hand so hard it almost hurt.

"That's him?" Jude asked, though there was no mistaking the look of stunned horror on Pixie's face. He didn't pull his hand away, squeezing back instead.

"That's him." Pixie stared at the screen, as if physically unable to look away.

Jude looked back at it, studying the face of the monster who'd inflicted so much pain on all of them in different ways. Aside from the telltale skin and teeth, Wicked Gold looked like an ordinary middle-aged white man in a nice suit, an incongruently unassuming appearance for someone capable of such brutality. Or he would have been, if he hadn't been smiling, sharp white teeth bared in a shark's grin as he regarded something off-screen, something nobody looking at the mirror could see. Jude didn't like the look of satisfaction on the vampire's face—he didn't like anything about him, really, but that was somehow the most ominous.

"I didn't think we'd actually..." Pixie said faintly. "I mean, I know we were supposed to see him, but still, actually seeing him is—"

The image shifted. A flurry of static-like distortion, and the vampire's face disappeared, replaced by two more. Undeniably human. One unfamiliar, a smart-looking but haughty young man in another nice suit. The other, seemingly restrained, and obviously furious, sweating, disheveled, face bruised and smeared with dirt—

"Eva!" Jude gasped, almost letting go of both Pixie and Jasper's hands in shock, but they barely managed to hang onto him. "Eva, she's there, they have her, she's—"

"Don't break the circle!" Letizia's voice snapped through the darkness, and Jude squeezed Pixie and Jasper's hands again. Panic rang through the cave, loud and clear as, in the mirror, a silver claw reached toward Eva's face, touched it, then drew a line of red. "Keep the spell alive! No matter what you see!"

Jude looked up to argue, shoot back that he didn't give a fuck about a spell anymore, or anything but his missing friend who wasn't so missing anymore, and don't bother arguing because he was done, done and gone—but there was no one to argue with.

Letizia was gone.

🔥

Just before midnight, someone headed through the woods toward the stones. Alone, hood up over their face, and hunched over a bit against the cold. Still, they had never been the best at stealth or hiding, and as Milo barely avoided tripping over an exposed tree root and planting face-first into the ground, their hood flew back and a wisp of purple hair caught the dim moonlight.

Milo crouched a small distance away from the stone circle and waited, eyes on the eerie light of the bonfire inside, and the pair of dark silhouettes. They'd cast every masking and stealth spell short of flat-out invisibility that they knew, like layering on sweaters made of magical camouflage. It wouldn't stop anyone searching for them specifically, but if they'd done a good enough job at laying low—always arguable, they had to admit—nobody would expect them to make an appearance tonight.

They kept their gaze locked on the pair of figures by the fires, one in particular. Owen leaned casually against one of the spires, his expression and stance haughty, as if he owned not only the place, but the magic happening therein.

"Some things never change," Milo said quietly to themself.

"What never changes?" a voice whispered from directly behind them.

Milo jumped and narrowly managed to avoid falling over again. "Wha— what are *you* two doing here?" they whispered back urgently as they recognized the two winged, gray-skinned, pointy-eared-and-fanged figures lurking just beside them. It was impossible for anyone to have crept up on them like that without making some noise—anyone human, at least.

"You said something big was going down," said Maestra in a dignified tone that said their presence were entirely reasonable and natural. "And we thought—"

"That you'd come see what it was, even though I said not to come anywhere near the place for a few days?" Milo demanded, eyes narrowed in an annoyed glare that looked out of place on their usually mild face.

"I mean, it was mostly *because* of that, yeah," Nails said with a nod, obviously unbothered by the human's ire. "Kinda played yourself there."

"That, but mostly we wanted to make sure *you* were okay!" Maestra cut in quickly. "That looks like a major magical thing, and it has to be dangerous."

"It is," Milo said, looking wary, but this time not because of them. "And I'm here to try to stop it, if possible. If it's not, there's someone I need to grab, and get as far away from here as possible."

"Who?"

"Him." Milo pointed to Owen. "He thinks he knows what he's doing but he doesn't... something that seems to be going around quite a bit lately."

"Hey, believe it or not, we do know what we're doing," Nails retorted. "We've been around for about a hundred and fifty years longer than you!"

Milo sighed and dropped their head a bit. "That's exactly what I meant. I've gotten this far, but I... well, I have no idea what I'm doing, actually."

"Well, we're here now," Maestra said levelly. "We can save him together."

"Thank you," Milo said, giving them a tired but grateful look. "You're good friends. I still wish you weren't here."

"Who is that guy anyway?" Nails asked, squinting at the young man Milo had pointed out. "He looks familiar. Like really familiar."

"Yeah," Maestra said thoughtfully, then let out a soft gasp. "I know where we've seen him before! Milo, he looks just like—hey. Where'd they...?"

They looked around, but Milo wasn't where they'd been a moment ago—then Maestra pointed to the small, hooded figure creeping at the edge of the light, hiding behind a spire and inching closer to their intended target. No human should have been able to move quietly enough to slip past a pair of vampires, but then, witches were something else.

"Oh boy," Nails murmured. "There they go."

Maestra rose to her feet and made to follow their friend. "And here we go. Again."

The mirror and its magically projected firelight cast strange shadows on the walls that did nothing to reassure Jude that they weren't all about to die in some horrible way or another. Dark shapes flickered across the glass surface, moving too quickly to catch another solid glimpse. He couldn't tell if Eva was still there, or if she was hurt, or much of anything else.

"Should we follow her? Or stay where we are?" Pixie asked, sounding obviously apprehensive about either possibility. "The spell's still going, I think. Does it need a witch to work? Or is it like, on autopilot or something? She told us to run if something went wrong, not what to do if *she* bugged out!"

"I don't know, I only saw Eva for sure," Jude said tightly. Her dirt-smeared and bruised face blazed in his mind as brightly as any bonfire. He, Jasper, and Pixie had rejoined hands, not knowing what else to do, and now both of his were thoroughly sweaty and cold.

FLASH. A brilliant light flared from the center of the mirror, shocking all of them into silence, except for a startled squeak from Pixie. Then it was gone entirely, as if the mirror were a lightbulb that had exploded, plunging them all into near-complete darkness.

"What happened?" Jude demanded. "Did we break the spell? Was it supposed to do that? Did Wicked Gold—do something?"

"I have no idea," Jasper said breathlessly, sounding like he was still holding it together, but only just. "But I don't think that's how it was meant to go, and I'd say that a wildly malfunctioning bit of magic is our cue to leave!"

"Second!" Pixie said, before promptly turning into a small pink bat that attached itself to Jude's shoulder.

The circle of hands broken, the three of them made a frantic dash for the cave exit and thankfully didn't get lost on the way, bursting back into the mall without incident, which was, equally thankfully, still dark and empty.

"Wait," Jasper panted as Jude made to sprint for the exit, coming to a stop. Jude whirled around, a frustrated retort on his lips, but stopped, seeing Jasper looking pained and more than a little scared. "Felix—I have to get home. I didn't tell him about—I have to make sure he's—"

"Go, I'll go find Eva, and hopefully Letizia too," Jude said, and Jasper headed off toward his shop, and its back exit leading toward home. "You can go home too, if you want," he said to Pixie, who'd transformed back into a human, standing so close he was almost touching Jude's elbow. "It's probably safer there. Actually it's definitely safer there."

"I don't think so," Pixie said. "After what I saw in that thing—after seeing his face—I don't want to be alone. Even if you're going to where *he* is, I don't want to—"

"Are you sure?" Jude certainly wasn't.

"Yes, Jude!" Pixie practically shouted, voice echoing in the empty mall as much as it had the caverns below. His hands clutched at the scarf he always wore, the one covering the worst of his scars, and Jude was painfully reminded of exactly whose teeth had left them on Pixie's neck. "I'm not letting Wicked Gold hurt any more of my friends!"

"Okay," Jude said, as calmly as he could, though his mind still raced through possible ways to get Pixie out of there fast should tonight go even more wrong than it already had. "Okay, let's go find them."

Eva strained at the ropes binding her wrists. It was useless, and she knew it. She could no more escape them than she could sit there and not even try.

"Don't fight it," Sanguine said quietly. "It'll just make everything harder. Believe me, I know."

"Well, you don't know me, kid," Eva returned, teeth gritted, but she stopped her struggling for a moment. If she pulled much harder she'd cut her skin, and if there was one thing she didn't want to do around a hostile vampire, it was bleed more than she had already. "And you don't know my friends. They're all over this, and they're coming for me—for us."

"I told you, that is exactly what I'm counting on," Wicked Gold said with a roll of his eyes, as if she'd just pointed out that water was wet, or that he was a bloodthirsty predator. "Are all humans this slow, or—ah!"

He exclaimed in delight and snapped his silver-clawed fingers, gesturing to the edge of the bonfire's light, where a figure appeared from the darkness. Tall in flowing black, with a wide-brimmed witch hat. At the sight of the familiar silhouette, Eva let out a startled cry that quickly turned to one of joy. "You're here!"

"Oh, good," Wicked Gold said, a bright, gold-flashing smile spreading across his pale face. "Now it's a party."

"Let her go," Letizia snarled, her voice distorted into a blood-chilling snarl no human throat could hope to replicate. "We all know it's me you want anyway. You've got one blood bag, surely you don't need another."

"You can never have too much fresh blood," the other vampire returned, picking Eva up by the collar with one hand and raising her up until her toes barely touched the ground. "And believe me, I've got exactly who I need."

At the sight of Wicked Gold's growing, terrible smile, Sanguine shrank back and slipped over to shelter by one of the stones. Owen also took notice, but he stayed where he was, straightening in clear interest for the first time.

"I'm taking Eva," Letizia said, ignoring both of them and focusing on

Wicked Gold and her friend, like they were all that existed in this place or the world. "And we're leaving. You're not hurting anyone else tonight."

"Is that what's going to happen?" Wicked Gold said, and now his voice was low and dangerous, though his rictus grin stayed perfectly in place. "I don't think it is. I think she's staying right here with me, and so are you. You're in the right place, at the right time, and not a minute too soon."

He raised his free clawed hand, which began to ignite ominous flames in the air. All around them, the circle of stones began to hum and glow faintly. But instead of the circle's usual electricity, this charge felt sharper, almost painful, as if in anticipation for the blood about to be spilled.

Letizia bolted forward just a few steps, but it was too late even for a vampire's speed: Wicked Gold's spell reached its crescendo, and sheer magical force swept down upon all of them.

As it did, something odd happened to Owen. He'd been standing at the edge of the light, and then the shadows at his back seemed to come alive, lurching forward to seize him and drag him backwards into the darkness. Wicked Gold paid no mind, but Eva's human eyes could just barely catch a glimpse of what looked like shadowed wings.

Sanguine also had been cowering in his place, half-behind one of the stones, but now he jumped backwards and scrambled away before he could be hit by the wall of magical force—and it was a wall. A barrier cutting the circle off from the rest of reality, creating a tiny snow globe-like world in which there could only be one ruler.

The two of them were gone. Only Wicked Gold, Letizia, and Eva remained in the center, and the ground stopped its shaking, the air falling eerily silent. The edges of the stones and the woods beyond looked distorted, as if the three within were looking out from inside a soap bubble, and suddenly the physical world seemed very far away. The sense of isolation was as unmistakable and undeniable as a locked door in an empty house: Letizia and Eva were alone, cut off from their friends, or any escape.

"There, that's much better." Wicked Gold broke into his usual gleaming smile and spread his hands, showing off every long, curved silver claw, some of them still stained red from Eva's blood. "I thought we should really do this privately."

"Go ahead," Eva spat. "If you're going to sacrifice me, then cut the dramatics and try it!"

"I understand—you must be feeling a little betrayed right now," Wicked Gold said in a mockery of sympathetic tones. "It's always hard to think you're about to spring a trap, only to find out you're the bait. You'd be a worthless sacrifice. But you have other uses. Like getting me closer to much more important—"

"Bastard!"

Faster than anyone but a vampire could move or even see, Letizia charged forward toward Wicked Gold—but she never connected. By the time she would have, he was gone, and Letizia ran into Eva instead, nearly slamming her off-balance but stopping just in time and using the movement's momentum to slash through the ropes binding Eva's wrists. Snarling, huge wings flaring out in a shield between Eva and her opponent, Letizia whirled around to glare at Wicked Gold who now stood, grinning, on the other side of the circle.

"There it is," Wicked Gold laughed. "I'm not usually a betting man, I don't like making wagers I haven't already won—but tonight, I'd bet everything that someone would give *their* everything—for one little human. Don't you understand? You're not the sacrifice. You never were. I wanted the Witch. I only *ever* wanted the Witch."

"Well, you've got her," Letizia snapped. "But I don't plan on sacrificing anything, her life or mine. You want me to choose? I choose to save us both!"

"And even one puny human like me isn't going to go down without a fight," Eva shouted, freed hands balled into fists. "And then your spell's screwed!"

"Oh, you're feisty," he said with a surprised-sounding chuckle. "I like that, you'd make a good vampire. But you're right, any power you have is borrowed. Rubbed off by proximity—but there's a lot of it there. You're practically saturated in it, it clings to you like a smell that just won't wash away." He grinned over at Letizia now. "You smell like Witch."

"And you're almost out of time," Letizia grinned, baring her fangs and many more sharp teeth. "If you're going to make your move, you'd better hurry—it's almost midnight, your time's almost up! And first, you'll have to get through me!"

If she was trying to provoke her opponent into a hasty and careless move, it didn't work. Wicked Gold circled them and Letizia did not move but turned along to stay facing him, never surrendering her position between him and Eva. They sized each other up less like duelists and more like feral cats, eyes burning and claws and fangs out. Both their faces warped until they barely appeared human at all, and Letizia appeared every bit as monstrous as her enemy.

Then Wicked Gold was gone—only to reappear right in front of her, claws raking at Letizia's throat. He'd moved so quickly he'd seemed to teleport, and as they grappled and snapped at each other, their outlines blurred until Eva's eyes couldn't follow them at all. It was like watching a video sped up past anything natural, uncanny-valley disturbing to the human senses because this couldn't be real, this was alien, this was *wrong*.

With an enraged shriek that sounded like a siren from Hell, Wicked Gold disappeared again, popping back into sight closer to Eva—and blocked by Letizia again. Over and over, they both vanished and reappeared, in different places and poses, one or the other seeming to have the upper hand before reality skipped again and reset.

"You're just stalling me, Witch!" Wicked Gold snapped as he and Letizia appeared atop one of the sharp-edged spires, clinging with claws that left cracks in the smooth, unbreakable-looking surface. "You can't kill me, you can't even beat me, all you can do is slow me down!"

"Of course I'm stalling!" Letizia screeched back, but her face was twisted into a terrifying smile instead of a snarl. "That's all I need to do to beat you tonight!"

Wicked Gold's only reply was another distorted shriek, a sound that made Eva's blood chill and the goosebumps that swept over her skin were actually painful—and Letizia's howls blended until they crescendoed in a riot of screams as if from the throats of a thousand demons. The sound was primally terrifying, something that set off a bone-deep instinct to run, hide, escape it at all costs, because the only thing that could make it was something that should not exist, a glitch in reality, a monster.

But one of those monsters was her friend, Eva screamed silently to her terrified human heart, willing herself to stand her ground—and so far, her friend was winning. As the stones grew brighter and brighter, Wicked Gold's movements became more erratic, desperate, as if instead of fighting to reach his prey, he were fighting for his life. The teleport-fast moves grew faster and faster, and as they did, the stone circle's glow grew so brilliant that they were like floodlights, like the kind that would beam down on a night football game—or a deathmatch between two creatures from out of a nightmare.

And then, like a candle flame in the rain, their light began to falter.

"Do you feel that, Wicked Gold?" Letizia cackled, triumph ringing in the alien sound, and now it made Eva's heart soar instead of quake. "You're too late! The moment's almost here and you're not ready—all this for nothing!"

The vampire's eyes flashed, standing out in the dark like high-beam headlights, the last thing so many unfortunate night-strollers had seen, accompanied not by a blaring horn but a blood-freezing scream. For once, Wicked Gold had no words on the tip of his tongue, only rage and the promise of death.

His hands flew up not in a slash but raised to the sky, then came sweeping down. Fire flared around him, igniting the air and sending Letizia stumbling back with a pained screech of her own, shielding herself from the magical heat. His own fire wouldn't burn him, but to her, it was like the first lethal rays of the sun.

Two could play the stalling game, and that momentary distraction, that second-long delay, was all Wicked Gold needed. Before the Witch could so much as open her eyes, she heard a strangled cry, high and terrified, and cut off brutally quickly.

"Eva!" Letizia forced her eyes open, and screamed again, this time in horror, at the sight before her.

Eva had just barely had time to gasp before the vampire's claws dug into her neck. Wicked Gold pulled her head back, exposing her neck, and baring his teeth, fangs long and glittering like those of a cobra about to strike. But he didn't bite. Instead, his silver-clawed hand came off as if to stroke the human's face—and then in one quick flick of his wrist, he drew that claw across her bare throat, a sharp red line in its wake.

Letizia's scream—which now had a very human edge of horror—sliced through the air, and Eva dropped to her knees. Wicked Gold shoved her away and the Witch rushed forward, catching her before she could drop entirely, one gray hand pressed against the lethal wound to stop Eva's life from slipping away and onto the cold ground. But it was useless, and from the terror building in her wide, staring eyes, Eva knew it as well as she did.

"No! No, no, no, I can't lose you too!" Letizia cried as more blood seeped past her fingers and the claws she struggled to keep from doing more damage, but the liquid was as impossible to hold as grains of sand through the hourglass of a human life.

Then her mouth opened wide again, and her too-long, too-extended fangs made her look like a snake unhinging its jaw, ready to devour its prey.

"I could turn you," she offered, pleaded, voice still distorted but heavy with pain and near-panic, eyes entirely black and fixed not on the blood pouring from Eva's neck, but her face. "It would save you. Forever."

Eva couldn't speak. Her mouth was filled with blood and her grasp on this mortal coil weakening—but she shut her eyes and jerked her head in one silent gesture. No.

And that was all it took. Consent had never mattered to vampires, historically, but Letizia had broken tradition her entire long life. She snapped her mouth shut on air instead of flesh, fangs retracting—but that didn't mean she was happy to do it.

"Damn it all!" Letizia's voice rose again, a wail filled with frustration and despair. "I can't lose another one to this place!"

"Then save her!" Wicked Gold snarled back, pointing his clawed hand toward the bonfire. "You know what you have to do to save her! The magic wants what it wants!"

"I—" Letizia looked frantically from Eva to the fire: the only thing present that could kill a vampire. For one second that seemed to stretch into eternity, she stared at the raging flames. In her eyes were flames, and tears, and a world of possibilities, of what would happen if she set Eva down and walked into that fire. Her second death, final and irreversible, to buy another's life.

Letizia took a step forward and began to lower her friend to the ground. Then—

"No." Eva's hand shot up and grabbed at Letizia's face, smearing a bloody handprint across her cheek but making her look down and away from the fire. She forced the words out like each one was a shard of broken glass. "Don't," she gasped. "Not that either!"

"I'm saving you," Letizia whispered. "I promised I would. I promised I'd do anything, and I'm going to keep—"

The stones came alive one last time, raging with life and heat, a supernova of magic that made even the oldest and most powerful of vampires into something small, young, and lost. The air inside the circle blazed bright as noon on a summer's day, and hot as a backdraft from a burning house.

"What—?" Letizia exclaimed as all of that power, all that energetic glory, chained for one hundred and fifty years into stones awoke and flew free—and as Eva's body in her arms began to blaze as hot as any flame.

As Letizia gasped and instinctively, unwillingly let her go, Eva's body left the ground.

The power from the stones lit her up like a halo of fire, light pouring from her eyes and mouth like Cruce in his last moments, but this was nothing so deadly. The stones weren't just glowing faintly now; they shone with a white light that lit up the circle so brightly it was like the sun had just rose from its center, like each spire was a crystal with a blazing star captured inside it, and every bit of power flowed into Eva until she lit up too.

Then, as suddenly as if a switch had flipped, the lights went out, and the humming fell silent. Eva dropped to the ground but didn't hit; Letizia had caught her again and held her close, frantically feeling at her neck and face.

"You're okay, you're fine," Letizia murmured, but sounded less certain and more like she was trying to convince herself. Then she stopped, holding very still. When she spoke again, her tone was awed. "You're okay!"

"Hell yeah," Eva mumbled, head rolling to rest on Letizia's shoulder. She smiled, lopsided but wide, and let out a woozy-sounding giggle. "That was… some good shit."

"I thought you weren't swearing anymore," Letizia said, a smile spreading across her own face, though her eyes were wet.

"Well… special occasions."

But the circle was not finished with them yet. The ground shook once more, and then the hurricane wind returned, but it seemed to come from the sky. There was a feeling of pressure, of something being torn down, and Letizia flared out her wings. She wrapped them tightly around herself and Eva, shielding both of them from the force.

Under the roar came the sound of Wicked Gold's frantic, confused curses, but they were tiny, futile sounds, nearly drowned out under the infinitely more powerful surge of magic. He was like someone standing on their roof howling into a thunderstorm and expecting to be heard and feared. Nature would always have its way, and magic was nothing more than a particularly strong and beautiful natural force.

Then, as if that storm were moving off quickly and the skies above clearing, the wind and sound died down. The air had lost its charge, and the light from the stones was extinguished. The bonfire flames were gone, leaving only faintly smoldering embers behind.

Slowly, Letizia lowered her wings, unfurling the cocoon she'd wrapped around herself and Eva. The stones were dark, the air was still, and Wicked Gold was gone. The woods did not move around them, and even to a vampire's superior senses, all signs pointed to them being the only two people around for miles.

Letizia and Eva were left standing in the center of the circle, alone.

ACT SIX: Boys of (endless) Summer

NAILS AND MAESTRA didn't do many things silently, but as they flew, skimming just over the treetops, they made no noise at all, even while carrying a body each—both Milo and Owen alive and unharmed, though Owen did seem shocked into silence. They touched down, setting their new friend and likely enemy down gently.

"Thank you," Milo said, only a little wobbly from combined adrenaline and relief. "This should be far enough away that he won't be on us immediately, but we should still—"

"Angels!" Owen exclaimed breathlessly. He hadn't said a word during the flight, but as soon as his feet hit the ground he spun around to take in both vampire girls and sucked in a shocked gasp, eyes wide and jaw dropped. He fell to his knees amid the underbrush and bent forward into a pose of worship and surrender. "Glorious divinity, immaculate creations filled with the grace of Heaven! Blessed am I to be—"

"What?" Maestra cut in, stemming the flow of his adulations. "What's happening right now? Are you talking to us?"

"Sublime angels, I am your humble servant," Owen continued, still facing the ground. "Unworthy to receive your grace, but only say the word, and I shall be blessed beyond—"

"Uh, okay, this is weird," Maestra said, and Owen immediately fell silent. "I've definitely never been called an angel before. Usually people think we're the opposite of that."

"Is this guy for real?" Nails asked, sounding caught between concern and laughter. She gingerly extended one wing to poke at Owen's bent back, and though he didn't get up, he did suck in another audible gasp.

"Unfortunately, yes," Milo said, grabbing Owen by the elbow and hauling him up to his feet. "Now come on, we don't have time for this."

"No—stop! What are you doing?" Owen cried as Milo pulled him away from the fire's glow and deeper into the dark forest-in-the-city. "You're interrupting the most important night of my—of our lives! The ritual, it's happening right now—"

"I know!" Milo shouted back, not releasing their death grip on his arm or stopping for a moment. "I know what tonight is, and I'm getting you as far away from here as I—"

"Wait—wait!" Owen shook his arm free and stumbled back.

"What?! We have to move, Owen! I'm saving you!" Milo cried.

"What? No! No, now I can finally save *you!*" Owen stared at Milo, sweaty and panting but smiling. "You're here. You've come back! You're finally going to take your place as—"

"No," Milo said flatly, fear dropping off their face, replaced by a tired, studiedly blank expression. "I'm doing no such thing. I just came to make sure you weren't about to get sacrificed or anything, and now that I've done that, I believe we're done here."

"Done, really?" Nails cut in, a disappointed groan in her voice. "That took like five seconds! Come on, there's gotta be more to it than that—we should go back and kick his ass for real!"

At the sound of her voice, Owen looked back over and seemed shocked and awed all over again at the presence of two vampires. He didn't speak this time, instead once again falling to his knees in a position of submissive supplication.

"No need, that ritual is thoroughly derailed," Milo said, sounding well convinced, and ignoring Owen's rapture. "And Wicked Gold is wise enough to know when something's a lost cause. Still, you two really shouldn't have done that," they added, looking over at their friends over Owen's huddled form.

"Done what? Saved you? Or saved him?" Nails asked, folding her arms and wings and leaning back on her heels in a satisfied kind of way, as if soaking up Owen's humbled praise came naturally. "Because I could get used to this."

"Well, I couldn't." Now Milo glanced down at Owen with obvious fatigue, but something else beneath it, a mixture of emotions as difficult to express as they were to discern. "Not if it meant either of you getting hurt in the process. Though I have to say… part of me is glad you came along when you did. I didn't know how I was going to get him out of there alone."

"You're welcome. Now what?" Nails asked, a sharp adrenaline edge still clear in her voice. "Wicked Gold is still out there, even if we messed up his special night. We should go right back and—"

"No. Now you two get as far away from here as possible," Milo said firmly. "I appreciate your help, but this time you have to listen to me. Owen and I have some… unfinished business."

Slowly, Owen raised his head to look up at them. Milo didn't want to look back, but they did. They made themself look, made themself stand up straighter, taller, and look Owen directly in the eyes. The eyes that were so very similar to their own. Same slight build and delicate features, and exactly the same age—aside from the four minutes Milo had on him, and always would. Except for his hair—slicked-back, dark brown, immaculate, tame— and his distinct lack of any sense of aesthetics whatsoever, the man's thin, pale face was identical to Milo's. They were mirror images of one another, perfect and symmetrical, despite Milo's best efforts.

"This is going to be hard enough as it is," Milo said, eyeing Owen warily. "We've needed to have it out for a long time."

"You're going to fight? Then we should stay!" Nails protested, eyes flaring briefly. Owen started, and returned to his facedown bow. "Are we friends or not? We want to help!"

"No, we're not going to fight, physically—at least not if I have anything to say about it. It's just a personal issue… a family issue." Milo gave them a tired smile. "And you've already been a big help. Now keep helping me by getting somewhere safe and staying there."

"Are you really gonna be okay?" Maestra had turned her searching gaze to Milo now. She looked dubious; between the ritual and the strange human, she seemed reluctant to leave Milo alone.

"Yes," Milo assured their friends, managing to sound convincing. "I'm fine. He's not going to hurt me. And I suspect the most exciting part of the night is over. When I see you again, I'll explain everything. And I'll make it up to you, I promise."

"Yeah?" Nails brightened. "How?"

"I'll—show you some more magic," Milo blurted as Owen raised his head, a curious look on his face as he glanced from Milo to their winged rescuers and back again.

"You mean it?" Nails grinned fangily, now oblivious to the groveling human on the ground. Maestra watched him out of the corner of her eye, but with more wary confusion than satisfaction.

"Yes," Milo promised, and they sounded more sure of it now. They actually smiled, and it immediately made them look much younger, closer to their actual age. "More magic, soon. Friendship goes two ways."

The pair exchanged a glance, then turned back to their friend and nodded as one. "Okay," Maestra said, clearly considering the matter settled. "Let's go."

"No, wait," Owen protested, abandoning his genuflecting to clamber once again to his feet. "Don't leave! Please, at least tell me your names. Have you been recognized by the Lady Ombra Dolce? If you oppose Wicked Gold, perhaps an alliance—"

"Don't answer that," Milo said quickly as Nails opened her mouth. "And

Owen, stop trying to drag these two into your political games. They have much more important things to do. Their lives are their own, and much too glorious to commit to anyone's cause but theirs."

"Yeah," Maestra said with a slow smile, obviously catching the pointedness of Milo's words. "And we're gonna have fun exploring all that and getting re-acquainted with ourselves. See you later, Milo."

No sooner had she stopped talking than the girls were gone, a pair of wildly flapping bats in their place. They shot up into the tree canopy and beyond, disappearing into the near pitch-black night sky.

"Wait!" Owen called one more time before realizing the action's futility. Face contorting into a scowl, he whirled around to face Milo. "You've ruined everything!" he snapped. "Again!"

"Ruined what? You throwing your life away for a monster's designs? Honestly, Owen, exactly how far gone are you?"

"Throwing my life away?!" Owen exclaimed, voice rising in pitch and bordering on hysteria. "What exactly did you think was happening?"

"Well, the ritual does call for a willing sacrifice," Milo said, as if patiently explaining a simple math problem to a disinterested child. "And unless I'm completely wrong, you've been a willing participant in everything else your whole life."

"Of course I wasn't being sacrificed! I'm a loyal servant—but more than that, I'm the Lady's chosen envoy, and much more valuable alive than dead. Wicked Gold wouldn't dare lay a finger on me, no matter how I annoy him."

"Glad to hear it," Milo said with palpable relief, even as they shook their head. "I just wanted to make sure you were safe. If only because I don't want your self-destruction on my conscience. Goodbye, Owe—"

"Just wait! Just hear me out, please," Owen said, usually-calm voice tight, words tumbling out. He stepped in front of Milo to block their exit, but his steps were stumbling, his movements uncoordinated. Instead of calm and controlled, his body language screamed desperation. "You don't have to say anything, just listen. I'm sorry for before—for the way we left things. I'm sorry for hounding you all these years, and I'm sorry that I—I don't understand you at all, Milo! Not the first little thing, you're right, I don't! And you don't understand me, but I want to change that. I want us to be a family, the way we were meant to be. If you come home, we can have that. Come home and everything will change. It'll be different. I'll be different!"

"You've said that ever since we were kids," Milo answered after a pause, face and voice weary, but with the faintest ghost of a smile, something fond but quickly gone. "But it's never been different. You've always wanted to serve your 'angels,' and I wanted… a different life. As long as those are both still true, how could anything ever be different?"

"Because she's going to grant us our reward now," Owen whispered, voice filled with genuine awe, wonder, and anticipation. In spite of themselves, hairs rose on the back of Milo's neck. "Once she has the power the circle holds, my pledge to her will be complete. Finally, after all this time. The vampire's kiss. Our honor. Our purpose. For both of us, not just me, but for you too. All you have to do is come home!"

"No," Milo said firmly. "I don't know if you're lying to my face or simply misguided, but at this point it doesn't matter. I can't trust a word."

"Why? How can you possibly say—someone's been poisoning you against your family haven't they?" Owen's eyes narrowed into a glare. "And I'm certain I know who. Sanguine, that wretch. It was him, wasn't it? He's never known his sacred place, his duty, and he dragged you into his mess too. That snake has been speaking lies into your ear, but he's just jealous! Jealous of everything we have, everything I'm offering you!"

"Nobody's been poisoning me against anyone," Milo sighed. "Except for you, just by showing me who you really are. Don't try this again, Owen. Don't make me disappear again."

"I'm not making you do anything! But I wish I could make you see reason," Owen lamented. "You say you want a life among the humans, but you're better than that! You're better than any other human! You're not like them! You will never be like them!"

"No," Milo insisted, and Owen made a strange, truncated movement as if he didn't know whether he wanted to throttle his sibling or crush them in a desperate hug until they saw sense and stayed with him. "I am *just like* other humans. And so are you."

Owen laughed, but it sounded strangled. When his composure slipped, he seemed much smaller. Younger, angrier, and much more impotent. None of these perceptions were acceptable, Milo knew from years of experience, and Owen would do anything to avoid admitting he experienced emotions like helplessness or despair. "It really *was* Sanguine, wasn't it? Well, who are you going to believe? The food, or me?"

"I believe that we're done here," Milo said, voice flat, words seeming to die in the cold night air. They turned their back to their twin and took a step away. "Getting involved in any of this was a mistake. One I'll be sure to never make again."

"You can't run away, Milo!" Owen practically shouted, voice filled not with triumph but what sounded like near-panic. "Not from me, and not from destiny! Underneath all that—that eyeshadow and vulgar metal you've profaned your sacred vessel with, we are still connected! Siblings, twins, counterparts, we are one! All the paint and piercings in the world can't cover that. We'll always be a matching set. We will always belong together. You know this, Milo. Your heart knows this."

"We may look the same," Milo said quietly, and now they did turn to meet his eyes steadily, without hesitation. "But that's the only thing we share. We don't match, not anymore. Maybe we never did. Goodbye, Owen."

With that, they were gone, disappeared into the dark woods without footsteps, sound, or a trace. Owen stood still, alone in the dark woods, until a single fat raindrop splatted against the top of his head. Still, he didn't move, even as the rain intensified, aside from a slow slump of his shoulders and bend of his head.

"Shit."

"Oh, God..." Eva croaked as the world spun and her stomach lurched. "Is it over?"

"It's over," Letizia said, gently lowering the both of them to the ground, supporting Eva's back to keep her upright. "For now. Now hold still. I'm not the best combat medic, but I should be able to do something about... oh. It looks like I don't have to." Blood still covered Eva's neck and shirt, some dry and some still wet, but the cuts themselves were gone. Every scratch had been completely healed by the circle's stellar light.

"What happened?" Eva croaked. "I'm alive. How am I alive?"

"Remember the power locked in the stones?" Letizia asked gently, peering into Eva's eyes and obviously checking for hidden damage.

"Vividly," Eva said, and spat out a little blood. "Did he get it?"

"No. No, it looks like the power has found a new home," Letizia said, eyes growing a bit wider as the full implications hit home. She tapped Eva's newly healed chest. "Right here."

Eva stared at her like someone about three drinks deeper than was a good idea, who was now being asked to decipher a strange bus schedule. "Is that... good?"

"I don't know," Letizia said with a borderline-bewildered shrug. "I actually have no idea what the circle's power will do in a mortal's form, but... given the nature of that power, I'm not surprised to see it healed you first. You're very lucky, and blessed."

"I'm very stupid. I shouldn't have even been out here tonight," Eva groaned, head down and eyes squeezed shut. "I know better than to be out alone at night, with sh—stuff like this going on, I should've just gone home!"

"That is what I suggested, yes," Letizia said in a way that suggested diplomacy, but still earned her a glare as Eva raised her head.

"You told me to just butt out of everything and cut me loose," Eva protested. "Expecting me to bow out just like that, after everything, like that wasn't gonna piss me off. So really, me being out here…"

"Is my fault," Letizia said with a little sigh, but no hesitation. "Yes. I'll accept that. I just wanted to keep you safe—to keep you away from all this, to keep exactly this from happening—but I could have… phrased it better."

"You think?" Eva muttered, but looked slightly mollified. "I mean, at least you came to get me."

"Of course I did," the Witch said, as if it were the most obvious thing in the world. "Wicked Gold counted on it, and he was absolutely right. There was never any question that I'd do otherwise. I was always the sacrifice he wanted, and that's the other reason I didn't want you involved. Because I knew what he'd try, and what I'd have to do."

"Wait—you knew what he was doing?" Eva pulled back a bit to look Letizia carefully in the eye. "You knew he was just using me as bait, and that he wanted you to die protecting me, and you played right into his hands? Why?"

Letizia gave her a wry, fond-looking smile. "You are such a clever, perceptive human. In most things. In others…"

"But why didn't it—do the thing, the way you said?" Eva persisted, forcing her bleary eyes into focus. "The stones lit up without anyone dying. There was no sacrifice!"

"But there was the intention," Letizia said, face becoming thoughtful, words reflective. "Which… which just makes too much sense. Of course they wouldn't ask for blood to be spilled, only for a heart's desire to protect…"

Eva gave her a confused look in reply, and opened her mouth to ask what the hell the Witch was talking about, but she didn't get that far. Her eyes widened as she caught sight of something moving in over Letizia's shoulder.

A bush rustled, shaking in a way that suggested something bigger than the usual squirrel or raccoon, and Eva sucked in a tense breath. Letizia released her from the hug and both of them turned, the Witch raising a hand in preparation, ready to fling a fireball, or something like it, when Eva's own hand shot out to stop her.

"Wait—Jude!" Eva cried, as he burst out of the increasingly wet woods and pounded into the clearing, hair mussed and tangled with leaves. Eva sat up straight, raising one arm in a careful wave, as a pink bat jumped off Jude's shoulder, becoming a boy before it hit the ground.

"Eva!" Jude yelled back, obviously out of breath and sweaty aside from the rain. "I saw what happened! Are you okay?"

"A little banged up, and there's some freaky magic shit going on inside me now, but—yeah!" She tried to give him a reassuring smile as she rose to her feet, but then that statement seemed much less certain as her knees wobbled under her.

Jude rushed forward in one last burst of energy, managing to catch and steady her before her legs gave out entirely. He pulled her close, as gently as he could, and shut his eyes. "Are you really okay?"

Eva's fingers curled around his jacket and held on tight. "I'm really... here."

"I'm so glad you still are—and Wicked Gold isn't." Jude shot Letizia a look over Eva's shoulder, which the Witch returned with an excellent pokerface. "Freaky magic shit?"

"Tell you later. Hey, it's no big deal," Eva said, squeezing him back. But her voice was shaking, along with the rest of her, and the blood on her face and neck hadn't yet dried. "You really think I'm going to let a B-movie villain and his little henchmen get me? But I guess I did have some help," she said in response to Letizia's mock-annoyed *ahem*. "Still, I totally had it covered."

"I know you did," Jude said, and held on just a little longer. Trauma like she'd been through tonight wasn't so easy to laugh away, even if he hadn't directly seen it, and she couldn't talk about it just yet. Someday she'd be able to, and he'd be waiting. "Just thought I'd make sure."

"Thanks. I appreciate it." Eva gave him a grateful nod, then, as he expected she would, changed the subject. "How's your leg?"

"Sore. Both of 'em," he said with a wry little smile, then smacked the prosthetic one he wore. Organic or not, they'd both been pushed to their limits tonight. "But yeah, this one's not meant for running. Might have to upgrade if we're gonna be doing a lot more of this action stuff."

Pixie had stayed quiet during this, giving them space for a reunion, and Letizia had moved off a bit, walking up to one of the black crystals that ringed them. She reached out one hand and placed it on the stone's shining surface, eyes shut and apparently listening intently. Then her shoulders slumped as if she were letting out a long, defeated sigh.

"Hey," Eva called, concern leaking back into her voice. "What's the matter?"

"Nothing," Letizia replied, voice flat and dead-sounding, head slightly bent. "It's… nothing." The Witch turned away from the stones, shaking her head like shaking off a bad memory, and headed back toward them. "It's safe to go home, little one," she said, turning her attention to Pixie, who'd remained on the edges of this reunion, uncharacteristically silent. He looked up, clearly a little surprised that she was talking to him. "The one who hurt you is gone. For now."

"For now?" he asked in a small voice, and she gave him a bittersweet smile.

"They always seem to come back, don't they? Come," she held out a hand to him. "I will take you. I may not be able to slay your demons, but you don't need to face them alone. If we're lucky, you won't have to face them at all, not for a long while. I'd feel him if he was anywhere nearby—and, I believe, so would you."

"Okay," Pixie said quietly, and tentatively reached out to take her hand. "Hey, Jude?"

He nodded, and for once, said nothing. Pixie obviously had no idea what he'd said, and Jude wasn't about to dismiss his real fears with any joke, however small. "I'll see you at home. Eva and I would go with you, but not all of us have wings."

"But we do have sore feet," Eva sighed, shifting uncomfortably in her mud-spattered work shoes. The power heels were dead after tonight, and good riddance. Her feet throbbed. "After all that, my blisters have blisters."

"Eva," Letizia said, giving her a deliberate, steady look that revealed little but promised much. "I'll see you tomorrow."

Both humans waved as Pixie and Letizia disappeared, replaced by one large bat and one small, who winged off together into the night. Then Jude turned back to Eva, face serious again and eyes sweeping over her in concern. "Are you really okay?"

"Honestly?" she shifted her shoulders in an experimental way, wincing a bit. "Probably not. I'm sure it'll all hit me right when I'm trying to go to sleep. But right now—I'm better than okay. For a couple different reasons." Eva actually smiled, looking exhausted but genuinely happy. Maybe it was just the lingering adrenaline from almost dying, but Jude suspected something else.

"I thought you and Letizia looked... close," Jude said, offering Eva his arm as they started slowly down the path toward smooth pavement. She leaned on him for a few steps, then sighed and bent down, slipping her shoe-shaped torture devices off. He could see her entertain the thought of hurling them into the underbrush, then think better of it. Same old Eva.

"I think we are," she said thoughtfully, still with that funny, slightly giddy smile. She moved more easily with her feet freed of their torture devices, but she didn't let go of his arm. "I really think we might have a good thing going. We'll still have to figure everything out, of course."

Jude thought of Pixie, and Jasper and Felix, wherever they were. Hopefully safe. If they weren't safe, he'd have a lot more of this strange night left ahead of him. "I know the feeling. I've got so much rattling around in my brain I don't know where to begin."

"Hey, at least you don't have to go in to work tomorrow," Eva said, voice taking on a little teasing tone. "So that's one less thing to worry about."

"You know, you could always take a day off," he said.

"I might have to," she said with a bone-weary sigh. "Or maybe a week."

"Why stop there? You could quit."

"Do you have the real Jude tied up in a basement somewhere?" Eva peered at him sideways.

"I've recently gotten into the habit of quitting jobs I hate," he said with dignity. "And I strongly recommend it."

"Mmmm—no, unlike you, I don't actually hate my job. Besides, someone has to make sure the mall doesn't explode."

"Do they? It's such an eyesore."

"You really are the absolute worst security guard ever."

Jude grinned. "Good thing I'm not one anymore. Now I can focus on what's really important."

"Start by carrying me home," Eva grumbled, leaning on him again as they walked away from the circle and back toward their lives. "When we get there, I'm burning these shoes. There's a ritual sacrifice for you."

"You know it's not a full moon anymore."

"Burning. These. Shoes."

With every second that passed, Felix got more and more worried. It had been hours since he'd last seen Jasper and even longer since he'd felt he had a good grasp on the situation, or any situation at all. Jasper had simply said he was going out to meet Jude for the evening but not elaborated, seeming perfectly calm and cheerful—unless you were his fiancé, in which case, he couldn't have been more obviously anxious and stressed if he'd had a neon sign.

Felix hadn't asked any questions. He rarely did. Jasper's business was his own, and the outside world was a strange place Felix didn't quite feel he belonged in anymore. The threshold to normalcy was one he just couldn't cross, even when invited.

But that had, indeed, been hours ago.

Before he'd felt a surge in his blood, a wave of stinging energy that swept over him like a gust of burning air. It was a strangely familiar feeling, as if it was years ago in his old fire-fighting life, and he'd opened the door on a burning building and taken the brunt of the backdraft.

And familiar in a different way as well.

"Wicked Gold…" he murmured to himself, daring to draw the blackout curtains away from the window. "What are you doing?"

And where was Jasper? Where were Jude and Eva, on this night that screamed, sang to Felix's blood that magic was vital and alive and striking like a lightning bolt? But this was not a healthy magic. The charge in the air was not wholesome, and every bit of him knew, the way he knew his sire's name, that something wicked this way was very much to come.

Felix only hesitated for a moment before sliding the window open and easing his way outside, huge wings tightly folded across his back. Then he spread them, and leaped into the air.

He soared over the city lights, high up enough to be nothing more than a nearly-invisible black spot against a clouded, starless sky. Felix liked feeling invisible. Unseen was safe; hidden was unbothered, unexposed. But even this wasn't enough to reassure him, and anxiety stung through him, even more urgent and alarming than any unsavory magic. Frantically, he searched the ground for any sign of his chosen family. Though he saw nothing, the strange magic that pounded like warm blood through his undead veins intensified as he turned toward a dark spot on the ground, a thickly wooded park with a faint orange glow in the center.

The air was tinged with the scent of wood smoke, and Felix was just about to head directly toward the source, when he saw them. A figure on the ground that caught his attention as if they were lit up by a spotlight.

Someone stood alone in a gap in the trees, a small parking area at the head of a trail, one streetlight, no cars or people. At the sight, Felix felt a spark of recognition, one that made him bank toward the ground, and fall. Felix landed surprisingly lightly on his taloned feet, folding his wings. But although his descent had been almost silent, the figure still started and turned to face him.

Sanguine wavered on his feet, pale and obviously terrified—and moving unsteadily, in a way that suggested something very wrong. Anyone seeing

Sanguine now would simply assume he was drunk or high, since the reality was so far removed from anybody's point of reference it would never enter their minds. Most abuse was, even of the non-supernatural variety.

He froze at the sight of the dark figure, but didn't run.

Then Felix moved enough for the light from a nearby streetlamp to hit his face and instead of screaming, as any rational human would have done, this one broke into a wide, relieved smile.

"Hey, buddy."

"Hello, Sanguine," Felix said, his own cheeks aching; he realized he was smiling as well. His face was still nowhere near used to that. It was a strange expression for his permanently half-transformed face, but not a frightening one, once you recognized what it meant.

"Oh man, I can't believe you're here. I thought I'd never see you again!" Sanguine cried. With his face lit up in excitement and joy, the obviously unwell young man looked much younger. Alive, instead of someone living a numb half-life in the hands of a monster. But it didn't last for long. Sanguine had barely had time to smile back before his tired face sobered again, and Felix could see tension overtake him once more. "Honestly, I kinda hoped I wouldn't. You shouldn't be here."

"I'm sorry," Felix said, heart sinking despite its stillness. "I didn't mean to scare you."

"Are you kidding?" Sanguine said with a raspy, cough-like noise Felix recognized as a laugh. "This is so much better than any other way my night could be going right now."

It had to be an understatement, Felix thought, quick medic's eyes flicking over his friend's visible injuries. But he didn't need to see the blood on Sanguine's face and in his hair. He could smell it from here. He'd been hurt like this for some time from the smell of him, and lost quite a lot of blood. Likely concussed. That might explain his unsteadiness, the glassiness in his eyes, his blanched face and dark circles.

"Are you all right?" Felix asked anxiously, foolishly; of course he wasn't.

He hadn't been for a long time. Felix knew that much, and nearly firsthand.

"I'm..." Sanguine's mouth twisted and Felix could tell he was about to retort something sardonic, but then the expression dropped off his face, leaving only exhaustion behind. "I could be worse. Not much worse, but... considering everything else that happened tonight..."

Felix stood up a bit on his clawed toes to sniff at the air and feel for any lingering magical charge, but the electricity-like feeling was fading. The storm was moving on. "What did happen? Was anyone else there? I can't find anyone. That isn't good."

"Yeah, I've seen your friends." Sanguine looked again like he wanted to smile, or do something besides struggle to exist, but just didn't have the energy. "Wicked Gold tried a big ritual thing at the stones in the park. I dunno what for, but he had Eva—wait!"

Felix froze mid-leap; at the sound of his friend's name he'd immediately made to shoot off into the air again, but he stopped, lowering his spread wings at the pleading look on Sanguine's face.

"She's okay! The Witch came and got her, they're fine!" Sanguine babbled. "They fucked up his spell, and then he noped on out of there, but they're okay, and if Jude and them weren't at the circle then they've gotta be fine too, just—just don't go yet, okay?"

"I'm glad to hear that," Felix said in a vast understatement of his own. At least now he could check their homes and actually expect to find someone. Jasper may be home by the time he got there, even. Hope bloomed in his chest instead of fear, and now he was able to turn more of his attention to the filthy, ragged young man before him.

Someone had hurt Sanguine, and Felix had a very good idea who. Many times. Not just tonight. Felix knew the look of new injuries and old scars, and this boy had too many of both. His clothes were hardly more than torn rags by this point, except for the T-shirt he wore over the rest, its clean fabric and colorful design stark and almost wrong-looking on the rest of him.

Guilt sunk its claws into Felix again, and he folded his wings into a cloak that did nothing to block out its chill. "Why are you happy to see me? I left you with that monster. I should have come back for you. I *wanted* to come back for you! I'm so sorry, I haven't—"

"No!" Sanguine cut in, raising his hands. "No, no you definitely should not have. You got away, you're gone and need to stay gone, at least until Mr. Gold fucks off to Europe again or whatever. And I told you, stop apologizing—or at least, not to me," Sanguine said, eyes dropping to the ground. "I'm not the one who needs to hear it the most. You did better than I ever expected. You…got the three of them out. The two girls, and…" he paused, licking his chapped lips and swallowing, blinking hard. "Is he okay?"

"He's doing fine," Felix said gently.

"I miss him."

"I know," Felix said again, just as softly. His voice was rougher than it had been, distorted by his half-transformed vocal cords. Sometimes he didn't even recognize it himself, but it was the one he had now, and in this moment he meant every word. "He's fine. As much as he can be, under the circumstances. But he's safe. I'll make sure he stays that way."

"Good," Sanguine said, thin shoulders dropping as he sighed. "And remember, don't say anything about—"

"I know," Felix said, watching as Sanguine wrapped his arms around his thin torso. It was a cold night, but he got the feeling that wasn't the source of the human's shivers. "That's for you to say, when you see him again."

"Sure. Right." Sanguine's voice was deadpan, completely flat and devoid of hope.

"Come with me," Felix rumbled, unable to hear that despairing voice, see those living-but-dead eyes anymore, not without at least trying to help once more. "I have friends. I'm not alone anymore. We'll keep you safe."

Sanguine hesitated, mouth hanging open. A silence stretched between the two of them, unbroken by the sounds of cars or people. The light from the bonfire was gone, the hum of the stones undetectable. Even the woods seemed to hold still, as if holding their breath so as not to interrupt this strange, desperate meeting and inevitable parting.

"No, I can't," Sanguine said then, quickly, mouth twisting into a bitter grimace, and took a step backwards.

"Please. You're hurt and it's cold. You shouldn't be out here alone. Or at all."

"He'd know. He always knows somehow," Sanguine's voice rose a bit as a note of panic crept in. "It's like he's got some kind of tracker bug on me, probably a spell, or some other vampire thing, but he almost always knows where I am, except for a few places—like that freaking circle. I'd lead him right to you. And I'm not going to do that, not ever!"

Felix couldn't argue. He knew his friend was right; he'd known it before he'd even offered, but he'd had to. He could see the clean tear streaks down Sanguine's blood-and-grime coated face now, the sharpness of his collarbones and wrists.

"There has to be something I can do."

"I told you, just keep taking care of yourself, and him."

"For *you*. There has to be something I can—"

"There really isn't. Not if you don't want Wicked Fucking Gold to be onto you in a second—and if you really want to make me happy, you'll avoid that at all costs. Fuck, I have to get out of here," Sanguine said, panic ringing in his voice like a metallic clang, stumbling backwards so fast he almost tripped. "I shouldn't have asked you to stay, he'll know I was out. He'll know I saw you—he'll smell you on me! Obviously! Fuck!"

Felix pulled back too, horrified at the idea that he might have brought down another barrage of punishment onto Sanguine's head.

"Wait," Felix tried, though even as he spoke he felt the brief connection slipping through his fingers, if he'd ever had a hold on it at all. "It doesn't have to end like this!"

"Not for you it doesn't," Sanguine said, carefully shaking his bruised and bloodied head, and taking a few steps backwards, half-stumbling. "You got away, man. You made it, so run with it, don't you fucking dare throw away that chance just because you're sad I didn't make it too. It took us too long for you to waste it now, so just go. Tell yourself it's for me if that makes it easier, just disappear. While you still can. You could never get me out alive anyway."

"Wait!" Felix cried again with a pang of desperation, as he saw the distance between them grow, Sanguine's walls coming up, hard and cold and defensive against further disappointment. "I'm still going to help you. There must be a way! I will come back for you. I will get you out of there."

"Nice of you to say that," Sanguine said, voice flat and entirely devoid of hope, plainly refusing to rise to the bait, and the hooked barb that surely waited along with it to pull him down again. "And I hope you're having a great life in the real world. Really."

"I—I still hope—"

Sanguine cough-laughed again. "Hope's a kinda dangerous thing, isn't it? No. You stay right there, and don't you dare follow me. I need to get as far away from you as I can, because fuck if you're getting caught again because of me. Nobody's getting hurt because of me anymore. Not ever. I'll make sure of that."

"Sanguine? What does that mean?" Felix asked, feeling a chill despite the fact that cold hadn't bothered him for just over five years. It never would again, but that didn't keep steely fear from gripping his heart.

"Like I said… I was never getting out of this alive."

"No," Felix said. Suddenly he felt as if he were airborne again, a mile up, looking down at the tiny figure on the ground, unable to reach or help or hope for an ending without tragedy. "There's another way out of this, there has to be. What are you going to do?"

"Don't ask questions you don't want the answer to, my dude," Sanguine said with a mirthless twist of his mouth. "And don't make promises you can't keep. I better not see you around. Now go find your friends. They need you more than I do."

Felix felt paralyzed as Sanguine stepped away, out of the light. He was right here, slipping away before Felix could save him or even reach him. Felix was failing, again, for what felt like the thousandth time, and now he was falling like a stone, wings or no wings.

"Wait! Sanguine!" Felix cried, desperation nearly making it break. But Sanguine didn't turn or stop, and Felix made one last, wild try. "*Jeff!*"

Now he stopped. The young man stood frozen for a moment, then turned, taking a step back toward Felix, just enough to cast light on his face and red hair.

For the first time, Felix noticed the design on his white T-shirt: a stylized sun, with the block-letter words *Endless Summer.*

Something about it, about seeing the sun at night, about seeing such an optimistic thing on the chest of someone with every reason to hope for nothing the rest of his life—and the spots of blood, when Sanguine had obviously tried to keep it clean—made Felix's heart ache.

"Haven't heard that name in a while," his friend said, a tired, bitter smirk on his face, the kind of thing that tried to be casual and ironic, but just came out looking exhausted and sad.

The ache in Felix's heart became a stab. He longed to rush forward and pull the ragged young man into his arms, wrap him in a protective cocoon of wings, and fly him far beyond his cruel master's reach. But shame rooted him to the sidewalk, and he could feel the precious chance of rescue passing him by, leaving him empty.

"This isn't goodbye," Felix said quietly. "I will find you again. My friends and I will keep you safe. This isn't the end, this isn't forever—you have not been abandoned. Remember that."

The slow, full, real smile the young man gave him was the most bittersweet thing he'd ever seen. The joy and despair at odds and at one within it would stay with him forever, Felix knew, even as his friend stepped back again, out of the light for good. Then he took another step away. Then, as if taking the plunge before he could change his mind, he broke into a run down the dark path through the woods, and disappeared.

Felix didn't pursue him, even if his heightened senses easily picked up the receding footfalls. Instead, he stood there alone until even he couldn't hear the human anymore. Then, shaking his head, he took a few running steps in the opposite direction and launched himself back up into the cool night air.

🔥

When Jasper closed his door behind him, he gave a sigh of relief to see Felix waiting for him, in nearly the same place as when he'd left, and this whole chaotic night began.

"Oh, thank God," he said, wearily opening his arms, into which Felix readily stepped. Jasper had begun doing that instead of actively touching Felix, making the physical offer available and waiting for him to take it. Happily, more often than not, he did. "I'm so glad to find you here—you wouldn't believe the time we've had."

"Are you all right?" Felix asked, voice tight with tension. He brought his wings up to wrap firmly around Jasper, one clawed hand going to gently cradle the back of his head. "Where were you tonight? What happened?"

"It's a long story," Jasper said, and heaved a deep sigh. "I'm just glad you're safe."

"Why wouldn't I be?" Felix asked with a confused blink, pulling back enough to look him in the eye. "I'm not the one who left without saying where I was going. I know something happened tonight. Magical. I felt it, like a storm. Was it you?"

"I... yes," Jasper said, and if he'd had any ideas of pretense or excuse, they were quickly abandoned. "I didn't... you were worried, weren't you?"

"Of course I was," Felix said, though he sounded more hurt than concerned at the question. "You were gone, Jude was gone, everything was wrong. I could feel something coming, something strange, something frightening, and I couldn't find you anywhere. Head started rushing, couldn't think—like a bad dream. Then I went out to find you, and it got worse."

"Oh," Jasper said, a look of horrible realization crossing his face. "Oh, no.

Felix, I am so, so sorry. I didn't think—no, that's not true, I did think of you, I always do. I just thought exactly the wrong thing, didn't I? But wait, you went out looking for me? What happened, worse how?"

"I want to tell you," Felix said again, but he did hesitate this time, wrapping his wings and arms tighter around his fiancé. He sounded genuinely regretful, pained. "But not now. I'm sorry. Soon. I know it's wrong of me to want you to tell me, and then not tell you, but—there's too much in my head right now. Hard to make the words fit together. Please, you first. Just tell me what happened tonight. It's the only thing that'll quiet the noise."

His wings were soft and warm as he maneuvered them down onto the couch, which seemed to sigh along with Jasper.

Slowly at first, eyes closed, he told Felix everything that had transpired that night and the nights leading up to it. The ritual, the required ingredients, the seemingly botched counter-spell, the ominous sights in the mirror. Felix listened silently, his only response to hold his fiancé a bit closer as Wicked Gold entered the narrative. When Jasper finished speaking, he didn't let go, or answer right away. After almost a full minute of silently mulling it over, he spoke in a low rumble Jasper could feel in his chest.

"You didn't have to keep all this from me."

"Yes I did," Jasper sighed. "You've got quite enough on your plate without worrying about any of this."

"No," Felix said, a little more firmly. "I wish you'd told me. I wish you'd tell me in the future, when things like this happen, or you're in trouble or need help, or worried about anything. I want to know. That's what I'm here for. I promised I would be, for better or worse, and I'm not going to break it."

"If I recall, we hadn't quite gotten to that part," Jasper said a little dryly. "But I know what you mean."

"And *I'm* not going to break either," Felix added, voice stronger still, not aggressive or angry, but clear and resolved. "You don't have to walk on eggshells or treat me like anything you say is going to make my recovery harder. It won't. My fiancé keeping things that hurt him to himself makes it harder. That hurts me too."

"I understand," Jasper said, words low and earnest. "And I'll try to never hurt you like that again. I can't promise perfection, but the best I have is yours. The best of me is always yours."

"I don't want perfection," Felix replied, and by now, this had to be the most words he'd said in a single conversation in a long, long time. "I just want you. That's perfect to me."

"What in the world did I do to deserve you?" Jasper asked, resting his chin on Felix's shoulder and breathing him in. It wasn't a scent cloying with death or decay, but the same one he remembered, a breath that made the years fall away until they were both young and unscarred and completely, beautifully alive. But then, they were still alive, he mused. Just in a different way than before.

"I ask the same thing every day." Jasper didn't see or even feel Felix smile, but he knew it was there all the same, the way he knew the sun would rise, or that the air would still be there the next time he took a breath. The tiny glint of humor amongst the serious, thoughtful words was pure Felix-ness, and Jasper breathed this in as well. "I'll tell you when I figure it out."

They lapsed into a silence that wasn't just comfortable but restorative, a quiet moment of actual rest and relaxation after too much tension and worry. Words weren't necessary, not when you'd found someone who understood you without them.

Then, Felix's arms tightened around Jasper's waist, as if suddenly frightened he may slip away. "You're thin."

"No, I'm not," Jasper laughed. "Not nearly."

"Too thin for you," Felix rasped, looking into his fiancé's face with serious, searching eyes. "You have been since I got back, but even more now. You haven't been eating, have you?"

"Clearly I have been, since I'm still among the living," Jasper said dryly. "At least, last time I checked."

"Not enough." Felix's voice grew a bit rougher, not in a growl, but as if the words were becoming more difficult to push out. "And you know what I mean. It's the first thing to go when you're troubled. I haven't been here for you. You've been so busy taking care of me, I haven't done the same."

"Darling, it's nothing—"

"It's not nothing. It's everything, you're everything."

"Like I said, you've had a few things on your mind, more than enough without worrying about me."

"And like *I* just said, I want you to tell me these things. I'm still your fiancé. It's my job to worry about you. And make sure you eat something." Felix hugged Jasper's waist again, still wide and soft but too sunken for comfort. "Besides. You're disappearing. That's always going to scare me."

"Point taken," Jasper said, and now he sounded more serious as well. "The next time you feed, I'll see about feeding myself as well. Please don't be afraid, Felix. I'm not going anywhere—not ever."

Felix buried his face against Jasper's shoulder again, and curled his wings a bit more securely around the two of them. Neither of them moved, as if the moment they did, this precious moment of peace would be lost forever.

"Love, I do have one question you might be able to answer." This time it was Jasper who broke the lull, rather confusedly. "About what you just said… but also in regards to something I heard earlier that I just can't wrap my mind around."

"Anything," Felix said, his dry-leaves voice low and soft.

"Does just… having me around help?" he said, repeating Jude's words slowly, with much less certainty than he'd heard them said before. "Even if I don't do anything?"

"More than I can say. And not just because talking is hard for me."

"Hm."

"Is it hard to believe?"

"Not for other people," Jasper said. "For you, Jude, anyone else who's a positive influence in my life, yes absolutely, simply having you around helps immeasurably. My brain simply refuses to accept that the same could be true in the reverse. The concept feels foreign. I'm not sure if it's depression, or arrogance, because I can't stop thinking 'if I were doing enough to help, nobody I love would be suffering as much as they are.'"

"You're not arrogant," Felix rumbled. "The farthest from it I know. You want to fix everything. You can't, but you keep trying, and wanting to. Part of why I needed you in my life. Both lives. But you don't need to try so hard. You wouldn't ask me to. Or anyone else."

"I know. I know it makes no sense, and that it's just more cognitive dissonance brought on by trauma or imbalanced brain chemistry, but it's like thinking day is night and up is down. My presence, alone, being not just worth something, but actively helpful in itself? Impossible."

Felix held out one clawed hand and turned it over thoughtfully, flexing his elongated fingers. "A lot of impossible things have happened."

"That's an understatement," Jasper replied. "I suppose I'll just have to keep trying to trust the impossible—even when it's inconvenient for a brain determined to find the worst in everything."

"Please do." Felix's voice dropped further, even as it turned a bit rougher. Words were leaving him; soon he would lapse into silence, entering the semiconscious state that let him recharge without quite sleeping the sleep of the undead, but close to it. "That way one of us will believe in something."

"Oh, my darling boy," Jasper murmured, turning his face up to kiss the corner of Felix's jaw. "Even when I can't believe in anything, I believe in you."

🔥

As strange as the mall had seemed at night, dark and empty, it was every bit as normal during the day. Bright, cheery, capitalistic, reassuring that everything was as it should be. Letizia sat at her usual table with coffee and cards, but this time, instead of shuffling her cards, she held a fragment of bone, running a thumb over it like a smooth stone.

"Keeping it as a reminder of last night?"

"In a way," Letizia said, giving her coffee companion a smile that only looked a little sad. The second difference: Jude was off the premises, and instead, Eva sat beside her. Nails and Maestra had offered their presence, but the Witch knew enough to be sure they'd only be bored with an old lady's coffee date, and they were likely off causing mayhem, or reconnecting with one another after a long imprisonment that had to have felt like a separation, or both at the same time. "Even if it didn't quite go as planned, it was an important night. For more than one reason."

"Yeah it was." Eva started to say more, then reached for her coffee, hiding her smile behind a long swig. "So, do we still need to worry about Wicked Gold taking over the circle?"

"No," Letizia said, and she sounded certain, but her face hardened with obvious worry. "If he'd gained the stones' power, I'd know, believe me. And, as I said, so would Pixie. He's still connected to his sire, even if I severed his control. A surge that strong would be impossible to miss."

"But you don't seem that happy about it."

"I'm not. The circle… we're not done with them. I feel it."

"Done with what?" Eva asked, not angrily but emphatically. "You still haven't told me exactly what the deal is with this whole circle thing, or what the ritual actually does, or any of it. And after last night—now that the power or whatever is *in me*—I think I deserve that much."

"You're right," Letizia said quietly, shoulders sagging. "You deserve all that, and more."

"So tell me." Eva's voice carried a challenge, but not an aggressive one. "Tell me what's in this circle that's so important. What's worth dying for?"

Letizia closed her eyes. When she spoke, she didn't open them. "It's not a what. It's a whom."

"A whom?" Eva repeated. "What does that mean? The circle is alive?"

"Not the stones themselves," Letizia said, eyes still closed. "The witch inside the stones."

"There's someone *in there*?" Eva asked, voice sharp with alarm. "A witch—

a person witch?"

"There was. A witch from another time and place. My time and place. Their spirit has been locked within that circle of power—they are the reason *why* the stones hold any power at all—and the thought of Wicked Gold getting his hands on them is—is impossible. Unbearable. I had to stop him!"

"Why didn't you say all this earlier?" Eva asked with a shake of her head. "Why not just tell everyone you're trying to help a friend? You're *our* friend, we would've helped you! And we would've done it with a lot less complaining, if we'd known it was that important."

"I..." Letizia stopped, voice nearly cracking. "It's not that I don't trust you. It's that I've kept this secret for one hundred and fifty years, and every year it gets harder. It's one of my deepest and most precious things to guard. The stones, and the one sleeping inside them. If they were lost... *I'd* be lost."

She fell silent, both hands clutching at her coffee cup as if she was trying to soak up all its warmth into her undead bones. Eva didn't push, and, slowly, Letizia's hands relaxed, along with the rest of her.

"I charged those stones myself," the Witch said in a calmer tone. "I cast the spell at the beginning, and I've been keeping them active all this time. We go way back."

"So *you* put someone—someone's spirit—in the stones?" Eva asked, in a tone firm enough to require an answer, but gentle enough not to shake Letizia out of her reverie. "And... if I got circle-blessed or whatever—they're *inside me* now?"

"No, not themself," Letizia said with a shake of her head. "I would feel that, and I don't. I have no idea what that would even look like."

"I'd rather not guess."

"Indeed. No, you just received the benefit of a witch's power, and their unbreakable intent to heal and protect." Letizia smiled, but it carried melancholy a century in the making. "I don't know exactly what effect the magic will have on you, but I promise you won't be alone to figure it out."

"Then help me figure everything else out," Eva said. "Why was there a witch in the stones? Why any of this?"

"It..." Letizia hesitated again, looking away. Her hands faltered and she paused, not putting the bone down, as if holding it was one of the only things keeping her centered. "I did it as a last resort. Wicked Gold... did something terrible, to someone I loved very much. They were—they are—one of his most powerful enemies, and he tried to destroy them. I was able to save them, by putting them into a kind of... magical sleep, inside those stones."

"Who exactly was—is your friend?" Eva asked. "What was their name?"

Letizia was quiet for a few seconds, eyes faraway. When she spoke, so was her voice, soft and wistful. "Zadkiel."

"Pretty name," Eva said. If she was surprised by the unconventionality, she didn't show it.

"They'd appreciate that. It was self-chosen, like everything else about them. Like their destiny. Except for the last part, when me sealing them inside a stone circle was the only way to save their life." Her tone grew even quieter, face more thoughtful, and regretful. "Zadkiel always treasured independence, choice. The ability to walk their own path. Trapping them in those stones... it felt like taking all choice away from them. What right did I have?"

"Sounds like you didn't have much of one at all," Eva observed. "A choice, I mean. You or them. I would've done the same thing."

"I know," Letizia said, and now she smiled briefly. But it was indeed brief, and her face hardened again. "And the stones' power began to fade, and Wicked Gold threatened it. It was all that kept Zadkiel alive! And if they never woke up, or if Wicked Gold captured them at last—that wouldn't be their choice either. They would die without ever... I would never know if I did the right thing."

"That's what your spell was really about," Eva realized. "Keeping Zadkiel safe from Wicked Gold. Because that's what *he* wants, not just some vague power, and not even you—though he was totally trying to kill two birds with one stone back there, taking you out too. He wanted Zadkiel, specifically."

"Yes!" Letizia said, giving the table a little slap. "And I had to use the energy he gathered to break the spell on the stones instead, and wake my friend up. But it didn't work. Why?!"

Letizia let out a frustrated noise, then seemed to collect herself, smiling just a bit, in an ironic, bemused kind of way.

"You asked me before, why did the stones come to life without an actual sacrifice, without blood being spilled? Because even though I cast the spell that protected the witch inside them, it was a collaborative effort. Zadkiel was—*is*—a remarkable person. They would never ask for blood—and I've been a fool all these years to believe otherwise. Wicked Gold could never imagine anyone suffering what Zadkiel did, and not becoming bloodthirsty and vengeful, but I should have known better. Of course they'd stayed kind."

Letizia was silent for a moment, and Eva held perfectly still, as if moving may spook the Witch like a deer, and bring all her defenses back in force.

"Of course all the ritual would require is the intention to save someone else, the desire to give anything to see them safe, even one's own life. It was my wish that powered the spell that saved their life."

She locked her eyes directly onto Eva's and held her gaze.

"No, the circle's power will not harm you. It was made from selfless love. Magic itself is wild and neutral, but a witch's will is not. The raw energy could be directed to do evil, but on its own... no, it would only heal." She chewed her lip with all the care fangs demanded. "The past century and a half has been a poor way to repay a friend's sacrifice."

"That makes sense to me," Eva said quietly. "Zadkiel sounds like someone I'd like to know."

"And I'd love for them to know you," Letizia said, face falling. "But it didn't work, it wasn't enough, they're still asleep, if—they're even still alive at all," she stammered a bit, voice hitching. "The stones are silent, it's like they're just gone—again! Nothing is where it should be, because this shouldn't have happened. It should have worked! Why? I did everything right! They should be here!"

"Sometimes that's the way it is," Eva said in her unique combination of realistic and sympathetic. "It happens all the time. Your work is perfect, you do everything right, but it still comes out wrong. It's a hard pill to swallow, but some things are simply outside our control."

"Not mine," Letizia said bitterly. "I'm a witch, this is my world, and it's mine to change as I wish. This is what I do, harnessing and understanding magic, navigating its currents to change things for the better, stopping those who would misuse it—it's what I've given my life to, ever since I was as human as you are. And for what? It failed—I failed."

"But Wicked Gold doesn't have the circle's magic, or Zadkiel," Eva said. "That's what you were trying to prevent, right? It sounds like that worked."

Letizia paused, then slowly looked up. Gingerly, she removed the dark shades she always wore, revealing her unearthly-looking eyes with their catlike vertical pupils. "You're right. I did save one person I care about. Very much."

"Yeah, you did," Eva said with a satisfied nod. But then her confident expression wavered. "And I'm... I'm really glad. I was sweating it pretty bad last night. And you didn't have to. I mean, given the choice between saving me and taking down the big, scary bad guy, any sensible person would..."

"Oh dear. Have I given you the false impression that I'm a sensible person?" Letizia said, black lips curling up into a smile.

"At least not a boring one," Eva said, a laugh on the edge of her voice. "But seriously. I'm glad you came for me."

"Of course," the Witch said without hesitation. "I would do anything for you."

"You really would, wouldn't you?" Eva stared back at her, eyes wide and wondering.

"Yes. Is that not... I mean... I have had the feeling sometimes, that you would also for me." Letizia's voice dropped, and with no sunglasses, and no frenetically-shuffled cards, she seemed much less witch and much more mortal, soft, vulnerable. If it weren't for her gray skin and inhuman eyes, she may have seemed ordinary, Eva thought. "You have helped me more than any other person, when I needed it the most."

"What, with the spell?" Eva gave a crooked smile back. "Anyone could get a jar of dirt."

"That isn't what I mean."

"I know."

"You would help me even if you did nothing, for the rest of your life. Just having you here does more than—well, more than all the dirt in the world."

"Thank you so much!" Now Eva did laugh. "The feeling's mutual, I promise. At least I think it is." She sobered a bit, still looking hopeful, but with the smallest hesitation now. "You know I'm aro-ace, right?"

"We had discussed this, yes."

"Okay. Just making sure," Eva said, relief clear. "Just 'cause… I'm loving everything you're saying, but it is definitely sounding pretty, uh. Gay."

"As everything coming from me should," Letizia said, voice deadpan but lips smiling wider, revealing a pair of thin, elongated, very sharp-looking fangs. "But no, I assure you. I know how you feel, and I ask nothing you do not want to give. The gift of your company alone is enough. You need offer nothing more than what we already share. Just know that between vanquishing my enemies, or achieving magical power, I would choose you, every time."

"I'm… same," Eva said, cleared her throat, and took another pull of coffee in the place of any flustered words threatening to fall out. When she set it down, her face was still burning, and not because of the steam. "Have you ever heard of being queerplatonic?"

"I know the two words, but not together," the Witch said with a curious tilt of her head. She really looked more like a cat than a bat, Eva thought. Usually Cheshire, but elegant and independent even without her smile. "Tell me m—*damn!*"

Once again, the moment was spoiled by Mozart's Requiem in D Minor. Letizia pulled out her phone, which looked whole and unscratched as always, despite her best efforts, and looked as if she wanted to snap it right in half. Eva was fairly certain she could do it.

"I take it getting your number unlisted wouldn't help, huh?" Eva asked, resting her chin on her fist.

"If only," Letizia said, snarling at her phone, and just barely remembering to replace her sunglasses to hide the white flash of her eyes. "None of my magic can touch it. Do you know how frustrating it is, to be brought low, hobbled by such a little thing?"

Eva rubbed at the blisters on her heels. She hadn't had time to change, and the power click brought her no joy anymore. "I've got an idea."

"I should really take this," Letizia said, snarl fading, fatigue in its place. "He must really want to get ahold of me. I'm… I very, very much want to talk more about what you just said. But this could be…"

"Take it," Eva said. She went to take another sip of coffee, but found it empty. She frowned, then grinned when the Witch slid her own cup over. "I'm happy right here."

"Yes? What? What, in God's name, could be so urgent you have to hound me day and night?" Letizia didn't get up or so much as turn away as she spoke into the phone, only lowering her voice to a sharp-edged whisper. "Yes, I'm alone. What sort of fool do you take me for? …Because I'm still perfecting my English, that's why. If you'd kindly do the same?"

Eva raised her eyebrows in a clear question—*English practice, really? Sounds fine to me.*

Letizia actually winked in reply, tilting her head toward Eva. *I'm saying this for you. Listen up.*

Feeling a bit warm inside already, Eva sampled the Witch's coffee as she listened. She started with a tiny first sip, in case of any extra ingredients. To her surprise, she tasted nothing out of the ordinary, though it was much, much sweeter than she would have preferred, or expected.

"The circle stands," Letizia said, voice much more serious now, less hostile, bordering on grave. "He has not attained its power—and neither has the Lady. Sadly, neither have I. I told you I'd report if there was anything to say, and there isn't. We remain at a stalemate. Something's going to give, but not yet."

She paused, mouth open. After a few seconds, she shut it, mouth a straight black line as she listened to what sounded like quite the monologue on the other line.

"Understood. But remember," she said at last. "My business here is mine. If you attempt to make it yours, I will be forced to respond in kind. We are not friends. Right now we simply happen to be heading in the same direction."

With that, she hung up, fingers flicking in a way that reminded Eva of shooing away a fly.

"Well, that didn't sound very fun," Eva said.

"It isn't. But I can tell you that the man I made a deal with… you're in no danger from him. He's only ever had eyes for me." With that she clenched her phone in her clawed hand. "Now, infernal device, that's the last time you'll bother me, spell or no spell," she said, giving it a murderous look and pulling her arm back as if to hurl it to the ground—but a hand suddenly appeared on her shoulder. Fine-boned and long-fingered, with gleaming black nails.

"May I?" Milo asked, and Letizia tossed the phone—which had begun to ring again—at them as if it were a hot potato right from the oven. Milo caught it in one hand and covered it with the other, hands cupped like holding a tiny bird.

"How long have you been there, child?" the Witch asked, still grumbling from her off-putting phone call.

"I was just walking by," they said, both hands still pressed over the phone. "I should have thought of this a while ago. It's just your magic that the communication spell resists, isn't it?"

The melody's volume started to decrease, not from the muffling of their hands, but like the phone was getting further and further away, falling down a mineshaft until it was quiet. When Milo handed it back, the screen was dark, even though they obviously hadn't tapped the screen or pushed a button. "There. That should dampen the connecting spell for a while at least. It's too powerful to dissolve entirely, but it'll at least give you a break."

"Bless you, darling witchling," Letizia said with a relieved half-groan, half-sigh. "When this is done, I have some fine herb with your name on it."

"Magic herbs?" Milo asked, looking most curious.

Letizia snorted, and this did reverberate a bit. "In a sense."

"Oh. I don't smoke," they said with a short answering laugh.

"Coffee, then," she replied, and this time Milo didn't object, although they didn't seem quite as excited about this prospect.

"It's good coffee," Eva said, sliding the cup toward them. "Just a little sweet."

Letizia caught her eye and smiled. For the first time, with the phone silenced and trouble over for the moment, she looked fully relaxed and thoroughly happy. Eva rested her chin back on her fist, elbow on the table, as the Witch's face regained its Cheshire smile, and felt that, like the mall in daytime, the world was back in order, the planets re-aligned.

"Yes," said the Witch, whose eyes never left Eva's face. "And how sweet it is."

🔥

Outside, the sun shone on an uncommonly bright and clear day. Inside, in Jude's room kept dark and safe by the blackout shades and layers of duct tape, Pixie nestled closer against Jude's side and rested his head on his chest. It was more intimacy than Jude was accustomed to, and not just because his prosthetic leg was leaning against the wall instead of fitted below his knee. That should have left him feeling naked, he thought. Too exposed, too vulnerable, but it didn't. Not with Pixie. It simply never entered his mind to worry, and in Jude's experience, that was very new.

All of this was new, and wonderful, and the way it should be. Everything was the way it should be. At least everything inside this room.

"So how's it feel to sleep in for once?" Pixie asked eventually, voice low. He radiated warmth like an electric blanket, chasing away the wintery chill and all of Jude's stress; how had he ever thought vampires were cold, lifeless things?

Jude let out a little chuckle. "It's a big shift in my routine, and that was really one of the only parts me and my autistic brain liked about that job. No changes."

"Really, you don't like change? I'm shocked." Pixie's tone was teasing but his eyes were nervous, and Jude smiled.

"But I like this one," he said with certainty. "And I'll get used to it. How are you doing?"

"I'm... I think I started to say this before," Pixie answered a little hesitantly. "But it's different, knowing Wicked Gold's out there somewhere, and seeing his actual face. It's like he's real now. He's right here."

"Yeah, I bet," Jude said, keeping his voice down too, despite the fact that they were alone in his own apartment—this was the first moment of peace they'd gotten in days, and it would have felt wrong to risk breaking it. His thumb stroked Pixie's arm softly, back and forth. "But he's not here. He is never getting his hands on you again, not if I can help it."

"That's what worries me," Pixie said in a low voice. "I don't know if you can help it. I don't know if anyone can."

Jude felt hollow inside. He wanted to promise Pixie that he was safe here, forever, no matter what, but he couldn't. He was determined to never lie to Pixie, and damn Wicked Gold, damn all of them, Jude had no way of knowing if such a promise was a lie or not. "At the very least, he's never getting in here—he'll never be invited."

"Thanks. But I still just—God, I hate seeing him smile like that." Jude felt more than saw Pixie's face twist into a scowl. "I hate seeing him happy. Why does he get to be happy about anything? After everything he's done?"

"He might be out there," Jude said carefully, hardly daring to tread on this ground that felt fragile and sacred all at once. He was also painfully aware of the fact that no matter how he wanted to, he couldn't ever really relate to anything Pixie felt here. All he could do was offer sympathy without real understanding, and hope that was enough. "But you're still here too. You looked at his face, but he didn't see yours. You saw him even if he didn't know it. Something about that seems like a victory to me. Like you're looking at him on your own terms, not his, and walking away."

"Yeah," Pixie said quietly, and some of the tension and frustration in his voice faded away.

He turned his head to look up at Jude with something that might have been a smile if it wasn't so tired. Still, his eyes were completely unguarded, vulnerable, the trust in them real, even with such a history of bruises. Pixie's bubbly personality and breezy laughs weren't fake, not by a long shot, but they weren't the whole story either. Jude felt a little awed, and humbled, to see all of him. Pixie didn't say anything else, but slipped his hand into Jude's free one, where it belonged.

"Hey, I've been thinking about something," he said then, giving Jude a searching look. "The night you died. When you saw the stones and the person in the water and everything?"

"Yeah," Jude said quietly. "I think about it a lot too. Why?"

"I mean, the sea and person didn't happen, but the stones were definitely real, so that part came true," Pixie said, sounding thoughtful and more open to the idea than Jude may have been in his place. "And that just kinda seems like a good sign to me."

"How do you figure that?" Jude asked, unable to keep his misgivings from coloring his voice with anxiety. "If anything, it seems like a dream-come-true gone wrong, or like the version that happened last night is from a bad timeline. Why would the stones be there but nothing else? It was even daytime when I saw it before, and there was definitely no blood ritual happening. Was I supposed to stop Wicked Gold from finding it at all? I still don't know what any of it meant. Or who the person I saw there was—they asked me, 'is he all right?' And I don't know who they meant either. I don't know anything at all. Maybe it really was just a dream. At least then I wouldn't have messed everything up and not even know how."

209

"I don't think you messed anything up," Pixie said without hesitation. "And I don't think it was just a dream either—but hey, even it was, I probably know more than most people that sometimes dreams aren't just dreams."

"All right then, what do you think it meant?" Jude looked down at him, eyebrows raised.

"Well, definitely not nothing," Pixie said, brow furrowing, tone still uncharacteristically measured, and wheels obviously turning in his head. It was adorable, and appreciated. "Because a magic stone circle made of black crystal claw-things is just way too specific. And it's real, it's right here, and you found your way to it, which doesn't seem like it should be possible. So that's two impossible things right there. And when impossible stuff starts piling up... I dunno, it just seems like maybe you're exactly where you need to be."

"Hmm," Jude grunted, unwilling to extend too much hope just yet, but not wanting to be the one to shake Pixie's optimism and unworried faith. After everything he'd endured, it was a minor miracle he had any left.

Pixie raised his head enough to bump it gently against the corner of Jude's jaw and give it a nuzzle. "Just keep your eyes open, okay? I will too."

"Good." Jude found it in him to smile, and the arm he'd slung over Pixie pulled him closer. "At the very least... you're still here. So this must be where I'm supposed to be."

"Oh my God, Jude," Pixie said with a mock gasp. "That was smooth as hell. I didn't know you could be smooth! You've been holding out on me!"

Jude's laugh snuck up on him. He couldn't remember the last time he'd really laughed, or when he'd last heard Pixie sound so happy as he joined in.

"See, there you go," Pixie said, grinning at him through his giggles. "Feels good, huh? You should do it more often."

"Maybe I will," he said. "And you're right. I'll try to assume we're on the right course, not the wrong one. Everything else, all of us, where we're going from here... we'll figure it out."

"You don't just mean about the circle dream, do you?"

"No," Jude said with a sigh, smile fading, and shut his eyes. "I mean we'll figure out what we all are to each other. You and me—and Jasper and Felix, because we did have something, and we still might have something, but I just don't know what it is, or if they still want it, but this isn't sustainable, this weird, nebulous…"

"Why not?"

"Why not what?"

"Why isn't this sustainable?" Pixie had propped himself up on one elbow, and was looking directly into his face now. His thoughtful, serious expression was at odds with the way Jude was used to seeing his face, round-cheeked and bright-eyed. It wasn't a bad look, just a very focused and earnest one. Like Pixie's previous vulnerability, Jude couldn't imagine him showing this to anyone he didn't trust. "Why do you have to figure everything out right now?"

"I…" Jude stopped, frowning. He thought for a moment, folding his arms across his chest as a shiver of anxiety went through him, collecting like cold water in his stomach. "I don't like uncertainty. I've never known what to do with it, with a change in routine, not knowing exactly where I stand or what's coming next. Jasper said it's all right for things to be gray, and he's right—I am a gray, demi aro-ace, that's right for me, there's no doubt there. But it's different when there's so many other people and unknowns—I'm so jealous of Eva and Letizia. Not *of them,* I mean, I'm so happy for them, but how sure about each other they are. They're…"

"Queerplatonic girlfriends," Pixie supplied happily. "That's what Eva said, anyway. It's great seeing her so happy! I'm totally gonna get them a card or something. Or maybe make one. I don't think greeting cards have quite caught up yet—but go on."

"They know who they are and who they are to each other," Jude said, pushing the words out before he could change his mind. "And I want that. About where we all stand. With attractions, sexualities, dynamics, everything. Not having that kind of certainty, not knowing what comes next—it makes me feel unstable, like I'm walking on ground that might crumble at any moment. Like if I don't put a name to it, everything will disappear and it'll be like... like it was five years ago."

"I hear you," Pixie said gently. "Like I really, really do. But even if we're not totally one-hundred-percent on everything else, we know we love you. In whatever way you need. I'm pretty sure you're stuck with us while we figure it out."

"I just wish we could figure it out now," Jude almost whined. "So I could stop worrying. I know that won't make any of us safer or better, but..."

"But brains are weird and sometimes really bad at existing," Pixie finished sagely.

"Especially very autistic, PTSD-having brains," Jude muttered.

"Eh, I still think yours is really cool. I'm sorry I can't make everything go faster. But here's one thing I know for certain."

"Wh—" Jude didn't have time to get the word out before Pixie kissed him, warm and soft and with only a vague sharpness from careful fangs.

Jude leaned into the kiss and gave back as good as he got, letting all his accumulated tension fade in a soft sigh as he wrapped his arms around Pixie's chubby waist and the small of his back, hugging him close and letting everything else disappear except for the sweet boy in his arms, all of him wonderfully warm and soft in a cold, sharp-edged world—and his vaguely spicy, sauce-flavored kiss.

"I don't know what comes next," Pixie said quietly when they parted, but left their foreheads gently resting together. "But I know that I wanna figure it out with you."

"Now who's smooth?" Jude said, and now he found it very easy to smile indeed. "I think I'm okay with not knowing, as long as you're here. That's what makes it an adventure, right?"

"Well, look at you, with all the personal growth," Pixie giggled, and his large ears gave a big, happy twitch. "I'm so proud, I really am."

"Thank you. Oh, by the way," Jude said, studiedly casually, and reached over to his nightstand drawer. Pixie's eyes followed, a mischievous smile on his face—which quickly turned to surprise when Jude revealed what he held in his hand.

"These are..." Pixie whispered, reaching out to take the shiny things with careful fingertips. A pair of tiny, cartoon-looking metal bats dangled upside-down, their pink stone eyes seeming even brighter than usual in the low light.

"I saw you looking at them," Jude said, losing the fight to keep from smiling back. "But then everything happened and kept happening... and I figured you should still have them. Thank Milo too, they wanted to give them to me for free."

"You went into the Abyss..." Pixie stared at him in wide-eyed awe. "For me?"

"Isn't that what you do for people you love?" Jude cleared his throat, and his philosophical tone turned a little dry. "It's not like that's the first time we've done that. And I'm sure it won't be the last."

Pixie didn't comment, instead taking out some of his plainer earrings to replace them with his new, fancy friends. He let out a happy squeak that reminded Jude of the feeling of a soft pink bat snuggled in the palm of his hand, turning his head to show them off from all angles.

"I love them!" he cried, flinging his arms around Jude and squeezing. "And you. I really love you, too."

"You heard that, huh?" Jude said, faux-chagrined and genuinely happy.

"Jude, come on." Pixie's ears, new decorations sparkling, twitched again. "These things pick up *everything*. They look good on me, right?"

"Yeah," he said, seriously and honestly. "Like they always belonged there."

"Like little bats finally finding a good home? I know the feeling." Pixie's eyes lit up again. "Ooh, ooh, now that you're a free man, maybe we can go back again, and get *you* a real cool makeover this time! Some tasteful piercings, hair gel, maybe some eyeliner, you'd *really* rock the eyeliner, Jude—"

"One step at a time." Jude said, but laughed, and pulled Pixie in for another kiss before either of them could say anything more.

Epilogue

TWO NIGHTS after the half-botched ritual, Sanguine sat on the damp ground, face aching, hood up, and back pressed against one of the stones in the circle that had seen so much drama, and enjoyed the relative quiet. The fire had burned down to embers, but somehow not gone out entirely, hissing in response to a few scattered raindrops, but remaining.

Sanguine—sweet as it had been to hear Felix say the name "Jeff," he could still never think of himself as anything but this, as if his own name was worthy of being spoken by a friend, but not himself—felt a very rare feeling: safety, or at least the passable illusion of it.

He was well used to Wicked Gold appearing from nowhere to drag him back into pain of some kind or another, but he'd never been able to find Sanguine here. Hurt him once they were both here, yes. But maybe something insulated this place from his sight as well as the rest of the world's. Magic aside, it was unlikely Wicked Gold would deign to come anywhere near the place of his recent, unacceptably humiliating defeat.

It wasn't his first night on the streets, and probably wouldn't be his last. He'd carefully tucked his summer-memento shirt into a plastic bag, replacing it with one he'd dug out of a dumpster that didn't look too horrible. The precious sun and text remained faded but mostly clean. But that was about the only upside here.

He knew what he'd implied to Felix—'nobody else is getting hurt because of me, I'll make sure of that.' The ideation under those words was obvious, and Sanguine felt the urge wholeheartedly, so deeply and purely that by this point it was almost like being in love. Infatuated with the possibility of oblivion. Head-over-ass for the thought that all this could be over, his pain and that of anyone connected to him. Every time he'd told Felix to disappear, he'd been telling himself, too. Remove a possible vector for more suffering and death, not necessarily in that order. Shuffle off the mortal coil to keep anyone else, mortal or not, from getting hurt in the crossfire.

But some things were easier said than done. And some other, better things, like eternal summers and stubborn, boneheaded hope, and now Sanguine himself, refused to die, even when maybe they should.

"Fuck. Fuck. Fuck."

The word, one of the only self-expressive indulgences left to him, tasted metallic; a healed cut on his lip reopened and started to bleed. He would need to leave the circle sometime. And once he did, Wicked Gold would find him. The vampire always found him when he tried to run. No matter where Sanguine went, his master always, always found him. If he was smart, he'd run back right now, apologize, beg for mercy, and swear to never disobey ever again.

"Fuck me."

Sanguine weighed the risks in his mind, measured death against a continued existence like this, in the service and hands of a monster. Added up the pros and cons of staying alive, and like always, came up in the negative, but something kept him from dropping all the way into a decision he could never take back.

It was what he'd said before on a cold, damp night like this one, at this circle. Wicked Gold had asked if he still had something to live for, and he'd said yes. Sanguine had meant it then. He still meant it with all his heart. His life might be made of winter now, but he lived for the hope of summer, and if he wanted to live, first he had to survive.

"Fuck it. And fuck *him*."

With a grim, resigned, but determined smile on his thin face, Sanguine got up and started walking, every step taking him farther away from a painful past, a hopeless future, and Wicked Gold. Maybe now, with the monster distracted by his own embarrassment, Sanguine could try to survive again. Maybe this time things would be different. They rarely were, but hope sprang eternal, even in a heart as battered as his. Hope, or at least, one last defiance.

Sanguine allowed himself one crooked smile. "Fuck yeah."

Then he stopped, freezing mid-step, shivers rushing up and down his back. Electricity filled the air again, sweeping over Sanguine like an ocean wave, every hair on his body standing on end until every inch of skin seemed to vibrate.

A silvery keening filled the air, like the high hum of an old television, and Sanguine slowly turned around to see the circle come alive once more, each spire glowing with a strange, unearthly light that came from the stones themselves—

And there was someone inside that light.

Paralyzed with fear and confusion—*what the fuck?*—Sanguine could just make out a silhouette. Thin, long-limbed, somehow listlessly graceful, they hung suspended in the air, and he thought, near-panicked, of stories and iconic 90s TV shows about alien abductions, terrifying accounts of people being raised high into beams of light, paralyzed and helpless, until they disappeared. This seemed like witnessing an alien abduction in reverse, but just as strange and terrifying.

Sanguine stared, feeling as if he was caught in the light as well; he could no more run than he could vanish into thin air, or turn into a bat and fly away. The light was so bright it should have hurt his aching, battered head, but it didn't. That almost made everything more strange, more unearthly. Part of him wanted to run very much—a sensible part that knew this was something nobody else on Earth had ever seen, maybe something he wasn't supposed to.

But a bigger, louder part of his brain, the one that hadn't yet been ground down into the dirt under Wicked Gold's boot, told him that this was exactly *why* he should stay. He *should* see this. He should be right here, and nowhere else. So he stayed, and waited, until the light went out entirely.

It didn't fade, instead simply turning off like someone had flipped a switch. For a disorienting moment, Sanguine couldn't see a thing, until his eyes re-adjusted to the darkness.

Now he could see the person from the light again. They lay on the ground, having been dropped unceremoniously several feet, and now struggled to push themself up to all fours. Sanguine carefully stepped closer, not at all sure he was moving in the right direction. But they didn't seem dangerous, more weak and confused—and hurt. He could hear the soft gasps from here.

"Hey... are you okay?"

The stranger didn't answer. But, slowly, they raised their head to look at him, long black hair streaked with white falling around their shoulders. Their face was thin and pale but bruised, smudged with ash and sweat, features long and angular in a way that reminded him of a Tolkien elf. They might have been considered elegant if pain and terror hadn't been so clear in their fever-bright black eyes.

They wore what looked like a simple, rough-hewn white dress, but the edges were jagged and torn as if by claws, blackened and scorched like they'd endured a run through fire. Maybe they had, as awful, painful-looking burns stretched across large swaths of their skin. But that wasn't what hit Sanguine hardest and gave his blood a chill, not the strange injuries, but the familiar ones. All down their exposed arms and legs, their throat, collarbone and shoulders, were bite marks. Fresh as the ones on his own neck.

Finally, Sanguine said the only thing that came to mind. It really was such a versatile word.

"...*Holy fuck.*"

The stranger—escapee?—sucked in a ragged breath that sounded painful. When they spoke, their voice was faint and shaking. It was also in a language

Sanguine didn't understand. Maybe it really was aliens, he thought wildly, bordering on a hysteria he worked hard to push down.

"I'm sorry," he managed to say relatively calmly, which he considered a huge accomplishment given the circumstances. "I don't know what you just said—but I want to. Do you speak English?"

The person on the ground shut their eyes, face tensed into an expression of exhaustion and pain. Clearly gathering their thoughts and strength, they took in another slow breath that made their thin shoulders rise and fall.

"Where is he?" they asked, with an accent Sanguine's rattled brain couldn't immediately place. Spanish? Italian? Their voice was a bit stronger, but still unsteady as the rest of them. Still, they stubbornly pushed the words out, each one seeming to take a monumental effort. "Is he all right?"

"I... I, uh..." Sanguine tried to answer, tried to say he didn't know—who 'he' was, why he wouldn't be all right, who this person was, where they'd come from, what any of this was at all. But he was all out of words; they'd been driven out of his head by confusion, concussion, and lingering vampire-induced anemia. All he could do was stare, and that was apparently all the stranger could do as well, until the silence bordered on awkward. No matter what kind of first contact this was, they weren't doing a very good job of it. "I don't know. But I'm gonna help you if I can. My name's—"

He stopped. Came so close to saying what he wanted to say, burned to say it when faced with a blank slate, a fresh chance—but, as in so many things, backed out at the last second.

"I'm Sanguine," he said at last, words heavy and bitter but right-feeling on his tongue. Solid, like words written in stone, a contract signed in blood.

Yes, he was. He hadn't chosen it, but he couldn't go back now. The boy he'd once been was dead. And he had to stay dead, if Sanguine and the people he loved were to stay alive.

"How about I get you inside—somewhere?" he said. "Then we can figure out what we're doing."

He was so wrapped up in the complexities of names, identities, and survival that he didn't notice his own mental shift until the words were out and too late to take back. *We*. They were a *we* now. He'd had no idea what to do on his own, completely lost no matter where he looked, but now at least he had a direction: take care of someone else. It was something.

The stranger nodded wearily and let Sanguine take them by the arm and gently raise them to their feet. They were much taller than he was, and he was still weary, but he put all his determination into letting them lean on him.

"Thank you, Sanguine," they said, words soft and floating atop a sigh of clear exhaustion. Their smile was weak, but clearly in a way that came half from trauma, half from relief. It was less from their mouth and more a crinkling of their dark eyes, and something about it made Sanguine think that maybe this wasn't such a terrible idea after all. Probably, but that wasn't the only possibility.

"So what do I call you?" he asked.

"Zadkiel," they said, then watched him for a moment, eyes lingering on the awful bruise that still covered half of his face. "Are you all right?"

"Fine," he murmured automatically, but he knew it was a lie. He wasn't even surprised when his knees finally buckled beneath him, or when he fell, or seemed to keep falling even though he'd felt his knees hit the cold ground, was dimly aware of the pain, but that seemed so far away. Everything did.

Even the hands on his shoulders that kept him from falling completely; warm, much warmer than he'd expected, and steady, one of them going without hesitation to his face despite the blood.

Miles became light-years, centuries, that's how far away the hands felt, and their voice sounded. The stranger named Zadkiel was talking to him, saying… he couldn't understand the words, if they were even in English.

Sanguine was done here. Wasn't he? Hadn't he done everything he was supposed to? Surely he'd done enough. He'd tried so hard…

He was almost gone when he felt it.

Warmth and relief like slipping into a hot bath. Sun streaming in through an open window. The memory of sweat and chlorine and someone calling his name, his true, secret name; a laugh, a drumbeat, a power chord, a song he knew by heart.

Every single reason to stay hit him all at once. All of them still real, even now.

And himself, still here.

Sanguine took a breath and it felt like the first one he'd had in years, since cold water had closed over his head. Now his lungs felt filled with light as vital, charged, rejuvenating magic and *life* flowed into him, taking away the pain and the cold both. Winter lost its hold on him. For one sweet, beautiful moment, the space between one heartbeat and the next that meant he was still here—it was summer.

"Thanks," he said just as quietly as before, but now his voice was stronger, his eyes clearer, and he no longer felt himself slipping away. He felt more himself now than he could remember being. No matter what he was called by others. He knew who he was. He'd been reminded.

"I believe I should be thanking you," Zadkiel said, slowly, as if they were feeling out each word not because they were unfamiliar with the language, but with speaking, with using a tongue and lips at all. They turned a bit, glancing back at the stones. He saw no surprise on their face, more a dazed confusion, a sleepwalker shaken and finding themself in a strange room.

"I have… questions," they said at last, and Sanguine thought he detected a note of deadpan irony. He liked it.

"Same. I dunno if I have all the answers," he said. Then he smiled. He liked that too. "But I got nowhere to be. Come on. Let's get somewhere warm."

Sanguine was alive. He forgot everything else.

All his attention was on his new maybe-friend-maybe-mistake, wondering how long it would take Wicked Gold to find them the second they eventually left the protective circle, what they would do then.

So he didn't notice the last, subtle, vital change.

Silence had fallen, uninterrupted by normal forest noises, or the ever-present energetic hum that had once permeated the air in this place, the continuous background noise between its powerful, ancient surges.

The low energetic buzz that had once saturated the circle was gone. The air was still, the sounds of the city muffled, like the circle was on its own isolated island under a dome of glass.

As the two of them slowly, carefully left together, Sanguine—unlike Zadkiel—had no way of knowing, but for the first time in a century and a half, the stone circle was truly, entirely at rest. The stones themselves almost seemed relieved. As if, after far too long, the old and magical place had wearily set down a burden, sighed a long sigh, and fallen asleep as Zadkiel had opened their eyes.

The sleeping witch had awakened, their sacrifice eased. And now the circle could rest, dormant until the next storm.

For now, if not forever, the work was done. The spell was complete.

Acknowledgments

Thank you, as always, beyond words to my parents, for feeding and loving me while I wrote this weird-ass book. These things are very important, and I appreciate them greatly. It also means I can keep making weird-ass books. <3

Eri, for the amazing story edits and yelling, without which this book would not exist or at least not nearly as good, and the people in it would not be who they are.

Julian, for always understanding what I was going for even when I didn't quite know. You Get It (™) and that matters more than words.

Lynn for the cheerleading and reassurance that I'm not doing everything wrong. You make me feel like I am in fact doing many things right!

Lyssa for the amazing formatting and interior graphic design. Look at this pretty thing. *Look at it.*

Claudie and Emery for being the actual best, through every struggle. I wish you 100% less discourse and nonsense, and 100% more rest and creative fulfillment. Also naps.

My awesome Patreon supporters, who saw most of this first, and liked it even in all its initial messy glory. And my also-awesome beta readers and newsletter friends, for wanting to know what weird-ass thing I did next.

Everyone in the word-making community who's been united by pain and grief and the desire to still, still, *still* put beautiful things out into the world. I hope we can always remain Friends of Corey.

About the Author

RoAnna Sylver writes unusually hopeful dystopian/vampire/space opera stories about marginalized heroes actually surviving, triumphing, and rocking really hard. RoAnna is also a singer, blogger, and artist who lives with family near Portland, OR, and probably spends too much time playing videogames. The next adventure RoAnna would like is a nap in a pile of bunnies.

Visit RoAnna online at roannasylver.com, or support on Patreon at patreon.com/roannasylver.

Also by the Author

THE CHAMELEON MOON SERIES

Chameleon Moon
The Lifeline Signal
Life Within Parole, Vols. 1 and 2

MODULATING FREQUENCIES

Stake Sauce, Arc 1: The Secret Ingredient is Love. No, Really.

INTERACTIVE STORIES

Dawnfall
The Three-Body Problem

STAND-ALONE FICTION

Moon-Bright Tides

Printed in Great Britain
by Amazon